ALSO BY HUGH AARON

Essays
Business Not As Usual – Volume 1
Business Not As Usual – Volume 2

Novels
When Wars Were Won
Driven: Notes of a Neurotic Entrepreneur

A Short Story Collection
It's All Chaos

A Letter Collection
Letters from the Good War

A Collection of Novellas
Quintet

A Travel Memoir
Go West Old Man

A Child's Story
Suzy, Fair Suzy

11/10

*For my good friend
Chet,
All the best
Hugh Aaron*

A BRIEF BIO

Hugh Aaron, born and raised in Worcester, Massachusetts, was a Seabee in the South Pacific during World War II. After the war he graduated from the University of Chicago where his professors encouraged him to pursue a literary career. However, he made his living as CEO of his own manufacturing business, all the while continuing to write. Only after he retired were his writings published. *The Wall Street Journal* published eighteen of his articles on business management and one on World War II. Currently writing plays, he resides by the sea in mid-coast Maine with his artist wife.

STORIES FROM A LIFETIME

by Hugh Aaron

STONES POINT PRESS
Cushing, Maine 04563

www.StonesPointBooks.com

FIRST EDITION

Aaron, Hugh
Stories from a Lifetime
Library of Congress Catalog Card Number: 2010905306
ISBN: 1882521129
ISBN-13: 9781882521128

$15.00 Softcover
Printed in the United States of America

For

my

Annie

CONTENTS

PREFACE

I wrote these stories over the past thirty years, and one I wrote sixty-six years ago while serving overseas in the Southwest Pacific during WWII. Most of them were forgotten until recently when I discovered my original typewritten manuscripts stashed away in a file folder. They cover a wide range of subjects and locales, including several very short stories which, although written from a child's point of view, contain adult themes. Some of the war stories, each concerning a different issue, and written at a different phase of my life, have identical settings.

Since the stories were written over so many years, you will find considerable variation in the writing style. A person in his or her twenties certainly has a different view of life than, say, one in his or her fifties or even eighties, which determines not only the concerns of the author, but also the way the words are combined in the telling of a story. It often takes many years for the

1

meaning of an event to become significant enough to merit a written story. But no matter how remote a story seems to be from the actual experience, be assured the author's life is revealed in some hidden way. So in a sense one could say that this story collection is a disguised autobiography spanning eight decades of my life.

HUGH AARON
Midcoast Maine 2010

AN UNUSUAL DAY IN THE LIFE
OF GEORGE AMEN

George Amen awoke at his usual hour of 7:00 a.m.; had his usual breakfast of scrambled eggs, toast, and coffee; smoked his usual first cigarette of the day; kissed his children and wife good-bye; scanned the state of his lawn as he backed his car out of the garage; and joined the usual morning traffic on his way to work. But George Amen never arrived at his office.

In accordance per his usual habit, he drove to the factory in which he had his office, and at 8:25 a.m. approached the driveway to the parking lot. At 8:26 a.m. he passed the driveway to the parking lot, then passed the entrance to the factory itself, and, without so much as a glance, continued into the countryside. This would not be—it suddenly became clear to George Amen—a usual day.

George Amen had not been aware of his intention either at 7:00 a.m. when he awoke or at 8:25 a.m., one minute before he normally would have turned into the parking lot. He was not in a trance; he was not ill. He knew what he was doing the instant he broke his routine. Although he was not aware why, he knew he had to continue driving into the countryside. He had no destination in mind; he simply had to head out on the open road.

At 10:30 a.m. he returned to his home. The children were at school. His wife had washed the breakfast dishes, made the beds, and had planned to spend the afternoon downtown with a neighbor; she was just preparing to sit down with a cup of coffee and a home decorating magazine when she saw George's car enter the garage. She did not complete filling her cup, but instead put down the pot of hot coffee on the wooden kitchen table and rushed to the back door.

Accustomed to George's routine of being away from 8:00 a.m. until 5:30 p.m., she shouted to him in panic as he came up the walk.

"What's wrong, George?"

George grinned and waved her back inside. "Nothing's wrong."

"Are you ill?" she asked as she examined his expression, which seemed quite normal.

"No, I'm fine. Nothing's wrong, absolutely nothing."

"Then you haven't been fired or…"

"Don't be silly. They wouldn't be that generous."

George Amen paused for a moment. He stood motionless in the center of the kitchen. His eyes widened and his forehead wrinkled upward. He felt a sensation of surprise.

"So that's it," he said.

"What do you mean?" his wife asked.

"I'm not sure."

George Amen thought nothing was wrong, yet he sensed that everything was wrong. He assured his wife that he felt well, that his spirits were high. Perhaps a little too high, he thought to himself. He was aware of an inexplicable elation.

None of this was satisfactory to his wife, yet he insisted that she accept it. Outwardly she did, while waiting for the truth to emerge. She poured a cup of coffee for him, and bemoaned the scorched circle left by the hot coffeepot on the tabletop. Unlike his typical reaction, he said nothing about the damage and drank his coffee in silence.

At 11:00 a.m. the phone rang. His wife answered, and immediately covered the receiver with her hand: "It's your boss, George. He wants to know where you are. What should I tell him?"

George sat motionless.

"He's ill, Mr. Cartwright. No, no, he can't come to the phone. He's sleeping now. Well, he has a fever. Yes, I'll tell him. I don't think it's really serious. I mean he ought to be at work tomorrow. Yes, thank you. Good-bye."

George continued to drink his coffee without changing his position. His back was to his wife.

"Mr. Cartwright hopes you'll get well soon, but he wants you to take all the time you need. He said not to worry about your work. He'll take care of it."

Except for sipping his coffee, George remained motionless.

At noon the children came home for lunch. They kissed him.

"Why are you home for lunch, Daddy?"

"Your daddy isn't feeling well, children. Don't trouble him."

George Amen hugged his children and asked them about school, about what they did there that morning.

After they ate, the children went out to play for the rest of the day with their neighborhood friends.

George's wife made sandwiches for the two of them, and they ate in silence.

"I don't understand," she said finally.

"I think...," he began. "Oh, I'd rather talk later."

"Certainly, dear."

George went into the living room and chose a CD. He sat and listened to *La Boheme* in its entirety. From time to time Puccini's music brought tears to his eyes.

That night George helped his wife tuck the children into bed. He told them a story about traveling around the world on a flying carpet. Ah, how marvelous it would be to fly on a carpet. What freedom.

At 10:00 p.m. he and his wife went to bed. As they lay side by side, hand in hand, George Amen spoke of his unusual day.

"It was the first time I've felt free in years." She squeezed his hand. "I did everything I wanted to do, not what someone else wanted me to do."

"You can do what you want any Sunday, can't you?"

"It's not the same."

His job wasn't the worst job. His boss wasn't the worst boss. There's the house with the mortgage, the new car with its payments, the wife and children he loves. Yes, tomorrow at 8:26 a.m. George Amen will enter the driveway to the factory parking lot and park his car in its usual spot, and at 8:30 a.m. he will sit down at his desk and start doing what someone else wants him to do. But at least for this one day, he knew what it felt like to call the shots.

THE SHORT, SHORT VISIT

The Army truck roared off with a raucous shifting of gears, leaving me standing beside the hot, white, shimmering highway in the middle of the Pampanga plain. The dark dirt path leading to Lubao tunneled into the thick tropical growth. I plunged into the cool dampness, a worn duffle bag slung over my left shoulder.

The path had been worn smooth by generations of bare feet plodding over it. Here and there muddy brown puddles formed in its undulating surface. Ordinarily the muffled noises of the village could be heard through the growth: the mingling of pigs' squeals, clucking chickens, cries from children playing, and women's shouts. The faint smell of smoke from burning wood and oil blended with the sweetness of the damp, rotting earth.

The children came running toward me, their naked copper bodies smooth and cool. "Hi Americano, hi Americano!" they yelled in a discordant chorus. They circled around me excited, laughing and yelping like puppies. They tugged at my bag. "Chewing gum, chewing gum!" I nodded, reached in and threw a dozen packets on the path ahead of me. They ran for them in a frenzy, falling flat against the dirt onto them. They stuffed five sticks at once into their small mouths, pressing their jaws hard against the dry mass until it softened, grinning with pleasure as their drool dripped from their crooked chins. Now they were quiet, concentrating solely on their serious task of mastication.

As I strode through the cavernous growth, the prancing village youth continued to surround me. Towering stalks of banana trees drooped from the heft of their green fruit. Mango trees bore large orange spheres, and from nearby branches papayas hung like bells. Quickening my gait at the end of the tunnel, I was blinded by a white blaze of sun. I had reached the open clearing of the village.

My friends would ordinarily be there waiting, standing in the clearing in a happy huddle to greet their Americano. The women, old and wrinkled, and their daughters in crisp white dresses, would be leaning out the glassless windows waving, their teeth shining white against their olive skin. Perhaps I would hear a guitar out in the rice fields, its distant melody drifting through the hut-lined dirt streets. Maybe a girl would be there with a string of sampeguita flowers forming a ring of fragrance to be encircled gently around my neck.

But today none of this was so.

I stepped into the dazzling brightness, found it deserted, quiet except for my youthful entourage.

"Hando, Lucio, Reverend Sangco, Anybody?"

I waited and heard only the flapping of a bird's wings as it took off, startled by my shout.

Then a sharp voice cracked the silence. "Go home Americano, go home."

Smoke rose in narrow blue streaks from three of the huts.

"Why? What's wrong?" I called out.

At first silence, then the Reverend's deep, measured voice boomed from the dark interior of his hut. "You'd better go, my friend. I'm sorry."

"What have I done? I must know why."

"You, nothing."

A high pitched screeching voice crammed with hate, with anger and misery, lashed out at me. "My daughter is raped. Get out Americano. Get out!"

A wave of nausea rippled through me as I raised my hand, palm toward the swimming light of the sun. I could say nothing in return.

I turned back into the dark path, this time alone. Even the children had disappeared. I trudged slowly, bowed, the weight of my duffle bag bending my body to one side. I felt more alone than I ever imagined I could be.

THE MENTOR

If I learned nothing else in business, I learned never to hire friends and relatives. But I did anyway—twice. The first time...well, no need to go into that. It was the second time that shook me to the bone.

We had invited my wife's "successful" cousin, and his wife and their son and daughter-in-law to join us for a fine summer Sunday at our cottage on Pleasant Lake. During the twenty years that Jan and I had been married, we'd seen these people only at weddings and bar mitzvahs and funerals, where we had exchanged small talk and promised to get together. But until that Sunday, we never had.

Starting as an engineer with an expanding plastics materials company, Cousin Russell had moved up the ladder to become second in command and owner of a minority share of the business. When the owner died a few years later, Russell bought the remaining shares at a favorable price from the grieving widow.

Though Russell and I had business interests in common, I couldn't relate to him. His success, plus his background as a marine captain in World War II, inflated his ego too much for me.

"It's all luck," he'd say about his success, grinning proudly, his chest expanding, which I took as a hint that he didn't believe his own words. "A matter of being in the right place at the right time, that's all."

Before I was on my own in business, I had been moving from job to job trying to make a living. In fact, when I'd meet people I hadn't seen in a while, their typical greeting was, "Well, what are you doing *now?*" It was embarrassing. Too independent minded to work for anybody for long, I was deemed a "failure." Successful men like Cousin Russell didn't mingle with losers like me.

To make a long story short, eventually I started my own business making plastic toys. After a rough ten-year period and, as Russell would say, some luck, I became quite successful. Now that I was a "winner," Russell seemed ready to accept my hospitality. By then he had become a bigger deal still. Within a year of acquiring his company's stock, he sold it to a large conglomerate for an enormous price, securing himself a position near the top.

"Don't say anything to anybody, Joel," he said as we sat on the pine-shaded deck overlooking the sparkling lake that afternoon, "but the company is grooming me for the presidency."

"You don't say," I commented.

"But don't say anything to anybody."

"Not a chance."

Then he revealed the real reason why I was so fortunate to have the opportunity to sip highballs with him.

"Y'know, I took Nathan into the business after he quit college." A troubled look crossed his paunchy face as he stared across the lake.

"Yeah, I heard," I said, also having learned that his son was no longer there. Until his father hired him,

Nathan had moved around a lot; he had a reputation for being "unstable." Shades of my earlier days.

"He's a bright kid, y'know, and he did a great job for me, but sometimes it's a mistake having your son aboard, especially when you're in a political situation like mine and you could be accused of nepotism. I mean, he was earning a big salary, and some people were making remarks. Know what I mean?"

"I sure do," I said. "Why, when I had to let my nephew go…"

"As I said, Nathan's a good boy—bright, hardworking. I did all I could for him. So if you can find a place in your company where he'd fit in, I'd appreciate it. All the kid needs is a chance to show what he can do, a spot where he can find himself."

"Sure, sure, Russell. It just so happens we're looking for a salesman."

To this day I'm not sure why I was so hasty. Maybe I had empathy for the kid whose job experience sounded much like my own in the early days. But Nathan was no kid; he was thirty-two and newly married.

"Look, talk to him," said Russell. "If you don't think he's for you, it's okay. No favors, see?"

Before I had a chance to confer with Nathan that afternoon, his mother cornered me while I was lighting the charcoal grill.

"All Nathan needs is a chance to find himself," she said with a distant look. "Y'know, Joel, of the four kids, he's my favorite. I can't explain it; he's the one I love the most."

"I'll talk to him, Rachel."

"You won't be sorry you hired him, I promise you."

Later, while I was treading water during my afternoon swim, Nathan's wife, Cynthia, popped up beside me.

"Thanks for taking Nathan in, Joel."

"Huh?" I said, shocked. When did she hear that?

"You won't be sorry. All he needs is a place to find himself."

"Not so fast, Cyn. He's got to go through the procedure—the interview and tests, that sort of thing."

"Oh, I understand. But isn't that mostly routine?"

"Sure, just routine. I'm sure he'll work out."

Finally I got to talk to the man himself. We were in the outdoor shower. Nothing like interviewing someone when they're nude; no trappings to hide under. Though shorter and rounder than his father, Nathan was solid and barrel-chested like Russell. I noticed he had a big scar at his left hip.

"Ski injury," he explained. "It's worth a cool thousand a month for the rest of my life."

"How's that?"

"I sued. Dad's company had an ace lawyer."

"Look, Nathan, we've got this sales job available..."

"Anything, Joel. I'll do anything. I'm not fussy."

"I was going to say, it's not up to me. You'll have to come in like anybody else and be interviewed by our sales manager. Of course, I'll put in a word for you, but it's not my decision."

"That's okay, Joel. I'm not asking for any favors, just an even chance. I'm looking for a spot where I can make a career—y'know, a spot where I can find myself."

The next morning, Nathan called Ken, our sales manager, and made an appointment for that afternoon. I was impressed with his swift action.

Ken came to see me in my office after Nathan had left.

"We hired him, Joel."

"You did?"

Surprised by the fast decision, I didn't know whether to feel relieved or wary.

"I hope you're not letting his connection with me influence you."

"Not in the least. He's certainly bright, highly motivated, very personable. After six months' training, I think he'll make a good man for the New York metropolitan area."

"You told him that?"

"Of course."

"And he went for it? He'll move?"

"Of course."

"That's a tough market. Those New Yorkers will haggle for a half cent. Are you sure he'll be okay?"

"The way I size him up, Joel, underneath he's a real sharpie. He can out-haggle 'em all, mark my words."

"Okay, you're the boss of sales. If he's your choice..."

So began a mentorship that I had never anticipated. During Nathan's training period, in which he served as an ordinary worker in the plant, then as a draftsman in the design department, and finally handling phone sales in the front office, he seemed consistently interested, dedicated, and high-spirited, displaying a humorous side that delighted his coworkers. In each department he quickly became one of the crew and won their favor.

As I strode through the facility every morning, passing by his station, Nathan would greet me with a smile.

"How's it going?" I would ask.

"Great," he'd say.

"I hear good reports."

"I love it here," he'd reply.

Yes, the reports were glowing. He caught on fast to every assigned task. He seemed to be a natural. I began relaxing about having a relative aboard. Maybe he was an asset after all.

"He's smart, Joel, smarter than any of the others," Ken enthused.

From favorable comments like this, and from my own observations, emerged the first glimmerings of Nathan's greater potential. Being in my late fifties, I wanted to ease off and enjoy the fruits of my success, but that meant finding someone to take my place, someone trained in my ways, familiar with my style of doing business. When nothing negative developed during Nathan's short tenure, I came to see him as a possible successor—after a few years of careful grooming, that is.

When his stint in the main factory was completed, Nathan was assigned to train under our other salesmen in nearby territories. To a man, they found him congenial, quick on the uptake, bound to be a "sure winner." Ken, impatient to send him to New York, cut short his sales training period.

"The kid's a natural, Joel. There's nothing more our men can teach him."

"I hope you're right," I said. "You're sending him into a lion's den, y'know."

After only a few months on his own, Nathan racked up sales at an unprecedented rate. In the tough New York market where buyers are known to have no mercy, his success was all the more remarkable. Just as he had captivated his coworkers during training, he now captivated his customers.

Nathan had been staying in motels during the week, returning to his home in Boston on weekends. Although he had agreed to relocate to the New York area within six months, he hadn't yet moved, claiming that he and Cynthia couldn't find a house that pleased them. He asked for more time.

One Monday morning when he should have been in New York calling on the trade, he appeared in my office.

"I'm sorry to bother you, Joel," he said, "but I think it's time we had a heart-to-heart talk."

This was the sort of thing I dreaded. If Nathan had something to say, he should say it to Ken, not me. That's what I would have said if he weren't the son of my wife's cousin. Instead I said, "Something troubling you?" I motioned him to a chair beside my desk.

"Actually, yes."

He paused as if thinking how to begin. "I'm not earning enough, Joel. I need more money."

Our salesmen's earning arrangements had always been satisfactory to everyone, so this was a surprise.

"You should ask your boss, Nathan, not me."

"I did."

"And?"

"He gave me the usual line—you know, I'm working under the same salary and commission as the other salesmen and he can't make an exception."

"Well, he's right; it would cause problems. I'm sure you can see that."

"I understand. That's why I'm here."

"I don't get you."

"I'd hoped that you'd make an exception in my case. No one else has to know."

"I'd rather not do that," I said stiffly.

"I see."

"Look, Nathan, under our compensation plan, when you sell more, you earn more. You've been at it only seven months. Give it a year, eighteen months, maybe two years and you'll be right up there. Just be patient. It'll come."

"The trouble is, I'm used to earning a hell of a lot more. I was making five times as much with my father."

"Not when we hired you, you weren't."

"Well, that's true."

"As I say, Nathan, be patient. It'll pay off in a bigger way than you realize. Anything worthwhile takes time."

"Actually, to tell the truth, it wasn't my idea to see you. Russell suggested it. He was shocked when he found out how little I was making."

That angered me. What right did Russell have poking his nose into his son's business, into *my* business?

"Let me ask you this, Nathan: were you happy working for your father?"

"I hated it. I was bored. I had nothing to do—I just drew a weekly paycheck."

"Do you like what you're doing now?"

"I love it. Absolutely."

"In this job you can hold your head high. You're accomplishing something; you have a goal to work toward. Don't you agree?"

"Yes."

"Then what's money got to do with it? You're earning enough now to get by, right?"

"Well, we can't exactly afford to eat out every night."

"Who can when they're starting out? For the first three years I was in business, we ate only hamburg. Something's worthwhile only when you work for it. I think you found that out at your father's place."

His moon-shaped face broke into an easy smile. He seemed relieved.

"You're right, Joel. I really appreciate your taking the time..."

"Anytime, Nathan, anytime. Now you get out there and show those New Yorkers what real selling is."

I should have told Nathan that his father was the problem and not the job. I realized that Russell could also be my problem. How could I expect to win over his son's allegiance when Russell had so much influence with him. Because of his father, Nathan's talents had been wasted until he joined our firm. Now I would see what Nathan was really made of.

I said nothing to Ken about the episode, in case he'd resent Nathan's going over his head. A few weeks later, Nathan asked that I meet him for lunch at his father's club.

"What's on your mind?" I asked when he called. I wanted to beg off, but Nathan was, after all, the son of my wife's cousin.

"It's the same old problem," said Nathan.

"You mean..."

"My parents are pressuring me, Joel. They keep telling me I'm worth a lot more than you're paying me."

The club, an old mansion with oak-paneled rooms and a broad veranda running along its brick face, was strictly for men. The only women present were the waitresses. Russell had suggested I join the club, and even offered to sponsor me. "You should start rubbing elbows with these kinds of men," he said. "Nothing important happens without them." Of course, joining such a club was not my style. I didn't need "these kinds of men." What's important to me is what I make happen.

When I arrived, Nathan, in a dark blue suit, was waiting in the lobby, which was carpeted with an enormous Chinese rug. At the rear of the hall, a broad oak staircase rose from the center of the room, then separated both right and left to the floor above. A brass chandelier, suspended from the ceiling of the second floor, hung above the staircase.

I followed Nathan into a brightly lit dining room that looked onto the veranda. The maitre d' greeted Nathan by name, then led us to a table covered with a white linen cloth. We took our seats before two settings of fine china and elegant dark blue napkins. Several club members seated at the other tables said hello to Nathan. He seemed quite at home in his father's circle.

"Does Ken know you're not in New York?" I asked.

"Not yet. But I mean to tell him. Cynthia's pregnant, y'know," he said in a grave tone.

"I see. Congratulations."

"She wants me around. It's not going easily for her."

"You mean there are complications?"

"No, no, she's fine. She just needs my support."

"Of course."

"And after we have a child, there'll be additional expenses."

"Not while they're infants. Wait till they get to high school and go to college."

"Joel, I really need more income."

"It'll come. Don't worry. I told you before, our system guarantees it: the more you sell, the more you make. That's the way it operates, and no one's ever complained." Why doesn't he get the message? I wondered.

"But Dad says, even my mother…"

"Look, Nathan, what they think is their business. But all that matters is what you think. You knew about our compensation system when you were hired. You thought it was fair then. It's still fair."

His eyes shifted from mine to the tablecloth and back before he replied.

"Yes, it's fair."

"Then be your own man. Tell them that how you run your life is your business. You'll feel much better about yourself if you work for what you earn. When you worked for your father, you were paid well, but you hated it. Do you want another free ride?"

"Hell, no, Joel. I'm not looking for favors."

"Good, because you won't get a handout from me. We're a team; everybody gets paid for what he contributes. No more, no less. That's the way it is. Take it or leave it."

Although I had put aside—at least for a while—my mission to groom Nathan as my successor, I still took a fatherly interest in his development. Having been coddled by his parents all his life, he had never learned the value of accomplishing something on his own. Because Nathan had modeled himself after his father, he could never hold down a job. He expected to be paid for who he was and not for what he did. He had to learn that self-sufficiency and reward for achievement generated self-respect. I believed I could, with patience, transform this intelligent, talented young man into a responsible person, for his sake as well as mine.

A few weeks later, Nathan phoned from the road.

"Russell would like you and me to join him for dinner at the club."

"I'm not sure that's a good idea," I said.

There was a pause.

"It's not about me," Nathan said. "I took your advice and told him to stay out of my business."

"Atta boy, Nathan. I'm proud of you."

"So how about it?"

"What's on his mind?"

"Let him tell you, Joel—a proposition."

At the club you'd think Russell was some kind of emperor. The waitress hovered over him, keeping his glass filled with wine. A steady flow of fellow members came to our table to confer with him. All of them knew Nathan.

"Meet my Cousin Joel," Russell said to each one. "Owns the biggest toy company in the East."

This falsehood embarrassed me.

It was obvious that Russell was in high spirits. After each man left our table, Russell explained who he was: a judge, a senator, the president of the city's largest bank, a local newspaper columnist. "That's what counts in this world, Joel—contacts." His eyes swept across the faces in the room. "Do you realize that this country is run by just a few hundred people? They're the makers and the breakers; the rest don't matter. Know the important people and you can get anything done."

I smiled tightly. "What's on your mind, Russell?"

He looked a bit startled at my directness.

"Okay, okay. Joel, I want an honest answer. Have you thought of retirement?"

"Retirement? Someday maybe, but not yet. I'm still going strong."

"How old are you? Fifty-seven, sixty? I don't mean retire now; I mean three years, maybe five years down the line."

"I suppose someday I'd like to take it easy."

"Right, but before you can retire you'll need someone to take your place, someone to run the show as competently as you do."

"That's right."

"Nathan would qualify, don't you think?"

"He could be a possibility," I said, glancing at Nathan, who had been intently following his father's words.

"Here's another possibility. How would you like to cash in?"

"Cash in?"

"Yeah, sell the business. Become a free man, spend winters in Florida and summers up here at the lake."

"As I said, Russell, I'm not ready."

"Who's talking about retirement now? I'm suggesting that you sell the business with the stipulation that you'll stay on as CEO. Bring Nathan back into the office, teach him the ropes, and when you're ready to take it easy in a couple, maybe three years, everything will be in place."

"And you're the buyer."

Russell grinned.

"Who else? I'd give you a good deal. It's worth a lot to me to see my son's future secure. He tells me he likes the business and he likes you. With young blood at the helm and you and me guiding him, the business is bound to take off like never before. Now, how about an after-dinner drink?"

"No, no thanks," I said, still struck by the absurdity of his proposal. Although I knew someday I would ease off, and had considered Nathan as a candidate to take over, I figured that when I eventually did sell the company, it would be to the employees.

"No need to give me an answer now," said Russell. "Think it over and get back to me. Okay?"

"Sure. I'll get back to you."

Weeks passed and I delayed, wishing that Russell's proposal would go away. Moreover, I feared crossing him and causing a rift with my wife's family.

One day Nathan mentioned casually, "Russell's wondering when he might hear from you, Joel."

"How *is* your father doing these days?"

"Great. His company's board is meeting next week. He's slated to be chosen as their next CEO. It's in the bag."

"Fantastic," I said, thinking that maybe that would distract him from trying to negotiate a deal with me.

The evening after the board meeting, Russell phoned me at home.

"Where've you been, Joel?" he demanded. "I expected to hear from you."

"Well…"

"It looks like I didn't make CEO."

"Gosh, I'm sorry, Russell."

"It's that goddamned widow."

"What widow?"

"My deceased partner's widow. She screwed me royally—claimed I cheated her when I acquired her husband's stock. She sued me and the corporation."

"That's awful."

"Yeah, it's been tough. Because I was shrewd enough to find a willing buyer and negotiate a favorable deal for the stock, she brands me a crook."

"Well, she's got to prove it, doesn't she?"

"Not with the judge we've got. He's an old friend of her husband's, so of course he decided in her favor."

"I suppose you could appeal."

"The corporation doesn't want any more litigation. They're going to pay her off. I've had enough. I turned in my resignation this morning."

When Russell had offered to buy me out, he must have anticipated today's unfavorable verdict and the termination of his career at the corporation. Acquiring my company would not only help his son, it would also provide him with a way to re-channel his own future.

"What are you going to do?" I asked, not that I gave a damn.

"Well, we could do some business…"

"I've been thinking it over, Russell. I'm not ready to sell."

"What?"

"I don't want…"

"You don't even know what I'm offering."

"Money isn't an issue. It's not what I want, that's all."

"I see. Well, if it's final…"

"It is."

He expended a breath of disgust.

"Which brings me to another matter," Russell continued. "Why won't you do better for Nathan?"

"I don't think that's your concern."

"Hell it isn't. He's my son."

"But he's our employee. It's not our policy to deal with our employees' parents."

"You're a son-of-a-bitch, Joel."

"Russell, I'm hanging up."

"You goddamned son-of-a-bitch."

Click. He beat me to it.

A family rift was now in place. I wondered whether Nathan's tenure with our company was also over. I didn't have to wait long to find out. The next morning Ken tossed a stack of phone bills on my desk.

"Take a look at these, Joel—Nathan's credit card calls for the past four months."

The bills listed scores of phone calls made from Nathan's home throughout the day. Other calls originated in cities far from his assigned territory. Most were made to Florida and Hawaii, some to England. We conducted no business in any of these places.

"It must be a mistake," I said. "Did you check with the phone company?"

"I did. The calls are real."

"Why would he do this? I can't believe he's been faking his itinerary," I said.

"You'd better believe it. Just compare the times and locations of the phone calls with what he wrote down in his daily sales call reports. They don't jibe. I phoned a few customers mentioned in his reports. They haven't seen him in months. The bastard hasn't been working, Joel. I know it's touchy, with him being your relative, but I want him out." I winced. "But dammit," said Ken, "he had so much promise. Everything about him seemed right. I never dreamed he'd be like this."

"I thought he had seen the light," I said.

"What do you mean?"

"When you didn't give him more money, he came to me. I've been mentoring him...trying to teach him some values. I thought he understood. Look, Ken, I'll handle him."

"It's my responsibility, Joel. I hired him."

"No, the family will blame me no matter who does it. I'm responsible. I let you hire him."

When Nathan phoned in that day, I asked him, "Where are you?"

"New York," he said.

"Are you sure?" I questioned.

"What?"

"Never mind. I want you to drop everything and get back here. Come see me in the morning."

"Maybe you didn't hear me. I said I was in New York."

"I heard you. Did you hear *me*?"

"What's up, Joel?"

"We've got to talk."

"About what?"

"Look, Nathan, just do as I ask. Be here."

"I'll be driving all night."

"I suppose so," I said icily.

At 11:30 the next morning he walked into my office.

"Good morning, Joel," he said. Taking a seat beside my desk, he couldn't help but notice the monthly phone bills stacked on my blotter.

"It's a lousy morning," I said.

He laughed nervously. "Why do you say that?"

"When did you first become disenchanted, Nathan?" I said, meeting his eyes directly.

Without a second's hesitation, he replied, "A year ago maybe."

"That long ago? You mean you've been putting on an act all this time?"

"You don't know how to run a business, Joel. Russell could make something of this company. You know what's wrong with you? You're a small-time thinker."

"You may be right on all counts. But how I run this business is no business of yours, or Russell's."

"Sure it is. My future depends on it."

"No, it doesn't, and it hasn't for a long time. By your own admission, you haven't worked in our interest for a year. Apparently you never got my message. You could have been something with us. You've been leading me on. Well, now you're done."

"You can't fire me, Joel. I resign."

All this happened five years ago, but even now as I write about it I tremble with anger and despair. To believe in someone, to look out for their interests, and then to realize that the feelings weren't mutual—that in fact I was despised—is the ultimate betrayal.

What happened next that day with Nathan revealed the extent of my outrage.

As he headed for the door, I said, "Just a minute. The car keys."

"How do I get home?"

"I'll have someone drive you."

"I need the car."

"The car's not yours. Give me the keys."

He shook his head. In a surge of anger I struck his chest with my full fist, taking his breath away.

I was terrified at what I had done, but I didn't back down. "Now give me the goddamn keys."

"You're gonna have to deal with my lawyer for this."

"Give me the keys," I screamed, "then get the hell out of here."

He bolted into the outer office.

"If you take that car," I yelled after him, "I'll call the police and have you hauled in for theft."

He threw the keys on the receptionist's desk on his way out.

I never saw Nathan again, nor his father, nor, for that matter, anyone else on that side of my wife's family.

THE SALESMAN

A salesman visited our house yesterday and cleaned our whole living room rug for free. He was a very nice man. He smiled a lot, spoke very politely to my Ma, and said he would clean anything she wished with his extra-special canister vacuum cleaner.

The salesman showed Ma how good his vacuum cleaner was by putting a piece of tissue paper over the opening of the bag that collects the dirt. All he did was pass the vacuum cleaner over the rug a few times then looked at the paper over the bag opening. Boy, you should've seen the dirt on that paper. You never saw so much in your life, and you never saw a better vacuum cleaner. My mother's face turned red because she was ashamed. She is always cleaning around the house, and she told the salesman she cleaned the rug every day so he shouldn't think she wasn't a good housekeeper. Well, he said that the dirt wasn't her fault because she had a very inefficient vacuum and ought to buy his. It cost a lot of money, but even I could see it was worth it. Ma told him she'd have to speak to my Pa.

When Pa came home Ma told him what happened. She said that the salesman was a very nice man and that we ought to buy his vacuum cleaner for sanitary reasons. Pa told her to wait a minute while he brought out our old vacuum. He placed a paper napkin over the cover of the bag opening and did exactly what the salesman did. Then he opened the vacuum and looked at the napkin. Dirt! You never saw so much dirt in your life. Why, our old vacuum cleaner was as good as the salesman's. Ma was shocked. Pa told Ma that she just had to see the whole picture.

I couldn't believe that the nice salesman tried to fool us. Well, Pa said that he *did* try, that he knew our vacuum was probably as good as his because he could demonstrate the same thing for almost any vacuum cleaner made.

If you can't tell a truly nice man from a man who only seems nice, it's an awful problem, isn't it? My Pa said there is only one way to tell: A truly nice person is honest to goodness nice when he doesn't have to be.

After thinking it over, I guess this salesman won't be so nice when he gets to meet my Pa.

HE WHO WOULD BE KING OF THE MOUNTAIN

The receptionist asked me to wait in the lobby until Stan was free. She said he wouldn't be long.

I took a seat in one of the straight-back chairs and gazed around the room. On the opposite wall were four photos of Stan's former partner, Chris; in one, he was receiving an award for employing the handicapped, in another for busing in employees from the slums of a nearby city, in another for quality excellence from his trade association. The last photo showed Chris and Stan breaking ground for the building in which I now sat.

As I studied the photos, my eyes welled up. I had to drop my gaze. Why were these pictures still displayed so prominently? Chris had been gone for nearly three months, and the parting had been bitter.

I had passed through this lobby four times a year for the past decade to do the company's quarterly books. Back then there had been no need to be announced. I simply nodded at the receptionist, then dropped by Chris's office to promise—facetiously—that I would present him with a great bottom line before the day was over. "Guaranteed," I would say.

"I'm holding you to it," he would say. It was our routine.

Sometimes Chris wrote the bottom-line figure on a piece of paper and sealed it in an envelope before I even opened the books. Then I'd head to my borrowed office to work. At the end of the day, after I presented him with my results, we'd open the envelope together. Usually he wouldn't be off by more than a percent. And the bottom-line figure was consistently in the black.

One day three months ago, our routine changed. Instead of "holding me to it," that day he said, "We'll see." He must have had an inkling of what the figure would be. Every two hours or so, he dropped by my office and asked anxiously how things looked.

"Relax," I said. "As soon as I know, you'll know."

Long before the day's end, I knew how the figures were coming out. But I didn't want to tell him until I had the final results. At five o'clock, after the staff had departed and the building was quiet, I walked into Chris's office. I found him staring out the window into the white August heat. I could tell by the look on his face that he knew what he was about to hear.

I handed him a sheet of paper. "It's not so bad, Chris. You're in the red, but only slightly."

"Sure thing," he said, forcing a grin as he glanced at the figures. Then he pushed the paper aside. "It's only a quarter, anyway. Right?"

"Absolutely," I said. "A quarter doesn't make a year."

But it was the company's first quarterly loss since Chris had bought out Stan, his former partner, and had turned things around. During rough times four years earlier, Stan had been drawing an enormous salary and virtually raping the company with his exorbitant—

should I say illegal?—expenses: a company-purchased Jaguar for his wife and a ninety-foot yacht for himself. The company was hemorrhaging cash.

"Why don't you go home, Frank," said Chris after I had given him the figure. He was looking past me and staring out the window again.

I didn't want to leave just yet. "How about a drink down at Jimmy's?" I said, hoping that liquor might loosen him up and I could get him to talk about his strategy for the future. That probably wouldn't happen though. In the early days when things went badly, Chris simply became tight-lipped and turned his worry inward. He acted as though he could handle any difficulty and come out a winner—even in a recession and even though a major customer might have just defected. To watch Chris you'd think he was king of the mountain.

"I've got some work to finish up here," Chris said, gesturing at the clutter on his desk.

"Can't it wait? C'mon, I'll treat."

He looked at me. "Oh, why not?" he said, and he got up from his desk and grabbed his jacket. Then he locked up and we headed to his car.

When we got to the restaurant, I excused myself to use my cell phone. "I'd better call my wife to tell her I'll be home late."

While I talked on the phone, the hostess led Chris to a quiet corner booth. Evidently he felt no need to call his own wife. He rarely made it home for dinner; in fact, he usually dragged in at ten or eleven at night. His wife often complained about the "inhuman hours" he worked.

Chris had already ordered a glass of wine by the time I returned to the table, so I got right down to business.

I wanted him to talk. If he wouldn't, I would. I'd yank the truth out of him. I could see what he was doing to himself.

"Let me tell you, Chris, whether you realize it or not, you are under stress."

"You think so?" he said evenly. "Look at me." He held out his arm. "I'm calm and steady. I've got everything under control. No, sir, I'm okay."

I stopped talking and simply watched him. I realized that his face had become gaunt since I had last seen him three months ago. His drawn expression revealed the truth despite his typically cheerful demeanor.

"Do you deny you are scared?" I asked.

"Sure I'm scared. So what?"

"So *what?* You've got to deal with it."

Chris fumbled for words, but none came. He downed the rest of his wine.

"Chris, I'm no psychologist. I'm not even good at judging people. But I know when a man is scared. And you've been scared for a long time, my friend."

He chuckled and ordered another glass of wine.

"Frank, you're wrong if you think I'm worried about today's bad news. Remember what you said: 'A bad quarter doesn't make a year.'"

"I'm not talking about that. As a whole, the year wouldn't shape up badly if times were normal."

Chris stared into the distance, then said softly, "What I'm scared of..." Then he stopped, and the expression on his face hardened. "Look, if I let myself get depressed, I won't pull out of it." Then he looked right at me. "You mean the big balloon payment that's due Stan? Is that what you mean, Frank?"

I barely nodded, wanting him to say it and to confirm that he grasped its implications. He went on.

"It's true. I'm in a corner, Frank. And I don't know what to do. The cash flow isn't there."

"Have you told the bank?"

"They're the last people to tell. You know that."

"But you can bet they'll know soon enough. My advice is to level with them. It's in their interest to help you."

"How can they help me?" He seemed about to cry. "They already own me lock, stock, and barrel. You know how every asset has been pledged—the equipment, the inventory, even our receivables. Business couldn't have slowed at a worse time. And those goddamn interest rates—they're killing me."

I agreed. He was trapped between a commitment he had made four years earlier and a downturn in the economy, so he couldn't generate the income he had anticipated to meet the note that was coming due. He had believed in the future, and it was betraying him.

"Y'know, these past four years, I've worked my butt off. I turned the company around, brought us out of the red. I've cut expenses, cut staff, increased sales. But it's not good enough. What in hell have I done wrong, Frank? Tell me."

What could I tell him, this client who had become my friend? Did I know? Certainly, I knew. I had seen it time after time. A man risks everything, believing that he can surmount any adversity. He has blind faith in himself, his single greatest strength, but it's misplaced because he has no control over the random turns in the economy, of the marketplace, that seem arrayed against him.

Should I tell Chris that business is nothing more than an elaborate crapshoot? Should I remind him that he paid too much for his ex-partner's share of the company? Back then, I recall, to him any price was worth it, for as he said, at fifty-two he wasn't about to start over. Should I tell him that his sales projections were, in hindsight, overly optimistic? Or that there was no way he could have anticipated key people leaving, stealing his proprietary processes and methods—and some key customers—to set up their own business in competition with his? Didn't he know all these things? Didn't he know the answer to his question "What have I done wrong?" He did nothing wrong. He merely rolled the dice.

"What did you do wrong, Chris?" I said. "You're not asking the right question. Whatever you did made the most sense at the time. Don't condemn yourself for not having the power to see into the future. You're not God."

"I can't help feeling responsible. A man does his best for his family, for his company, for himself—yes, for the country—and it's just not good enough."

He shook his head and stared at the middle of the table as if seeing the word "failure" emblazoned in the surface.

"Go to the bank," I said. "What have you got to lose?"

"Nothing, I suppose," he replied. "Not if it's already lost."

Chris leveled with the bank vice president. He told him that he was about to default on his ex-partner's note, in which case the ex-partner would take over the business. The bank asked Chris to submit a statement of personal net worth, which Chris asked me to help prepare.

"But I really don't see the point of it, Frank," Chris said. "I told them I have no liquid assets. Everything is assigned, my house, my car; and I've signed the company's notes as president and personally. All I've got left is my blood."

"The last thing the bank wants is for Stan to take over," I reminded him. "They know he's irresponsible and a spendthrift."

As we prepared the statement of Chris's net worth, we scoured his list of assets. In every case, the amount was either miniscule by comparison to what was needed or was heavily pledged as collateral. Then we got to the factory building, which Chris owned personally and entirely after he bought Stan's half for a pittance during the breakup.

"Nothing there," he said. "It's mortgaged."

"Yes, I know, but the building was acquired more than ten years ago. Today it's worth substantially more. Chris, it's a sleeping asset."

"My god," he exclaimed. "I'll remortgage it and pay off the bastard. This will save me…I never dreamed…" He shook my hand vigorously.

Chris submitted his net worth statement to the bank, which quickly recognized the possible additional collateral that the factory building afforded. They had the building appraised, and the very next day offered to take a substantial new mortgage on it.

But the mortgage was for only half the amount that Chris needed to pay Stan. After a glimmer of hope, Chris seemed beaten again—but only momentarily.

He suddenly assumed a fighting stance. There was now a wildness about him, a strange abandon, so much so that I felt that, were he to go down, he'd take everything with him.

"I'm going to him, Frank. I'm going to offer Stan half. That's all I've got. If he doesn't go for it, I'll make a grand exit. I swear he'll never get my company."

I took his words to mean that he would leave only a shell for Stan to take over if he refused Chris's offer. But I was wrong, and unforgivably dense in not seeing another interpretation.

Chris asked me to be present as a third party during the negotiation with Stan so there would be no misunderstanding of what was said. Despite the antagonism between the ex-partners, I had been able to remain on good terms with both of them and had retained their trust.

The negotiation took place in Chris's small, unpretentious office. He sat behind his old oak desk. Stan, soft faced, jowly, pot bellied, and thick-thighed, sat across from him on a couch. I lounged in a deep chair in a corner of the room, physically removing myself from the action.

My prognosis for a successful negotiation was not good. Each man's face was taut, their eyes hard. Their demeanors read "no compromise."

"I take it you've seen the recent P&L," Chris said.

"Yup," Stan responded.

"And for the previous three quarters, you've seen that profits have been steadily declining."

"Yup. And I'm not surprised, considering the way you run things."

"For God's sake, you know damn well we're in a recession," Chris shouted, rising in his seat.

For a while both men sparred angrily over strategy. I decided to cut in. "Look, fellas, don't you think this is all beside the point?"

Chris simmered down. "You're right," he said. "Okay, Stan, I'll get to the point. You know as well as I do that the company hasn't accumulated enough cash to pay off the note that's due you next month."

"Of course. I sure do," Stan said, grinning.

"And you also know we're heading into yet harder times," Chris continued.

"So what are you getting at?"

"Here's a check for half the note," Chris said, waving it in the air, "and let's call it even."

Stan flushed scarlet. "You've got to be kidding. You're expecting me to forgive half the note? I don't believe what I'm hearing."

"The company's in trouble. Don't you see?" Chris said. His tone was suddenly pleading. "If I default and you take over, you'll inherit a bundle of problems. The whole thing will go down; you'll lose it all. Admit it, Stan, you're a great salesman but a lousy manager. I know you think otherwise, but dammit, face up to your limitations. Take the check; it's all I have."

"I don't see that there's anything more to talk about," Stan said in a huff, and he rose to leave.

"I'll tell you this," said Chris, also rising. He was losing control, his eyes bulging, his right arm punching the air. "If you take over, I'll strip this company of every asset. I'll sell the equipment, the inventory, anything I can move. I built this business while you played and lived off its fat. And I'm not going to let you have it. Never! Never! Do you understand, you son-of-a-bitch?"

Chris sounded convincing, but he knew that his threat was hollow. The bank would never allow any of the company's assets to be sold.

Stan spun on his heel at Chris's harangue and headed out the door, slamming it behind him.

I looked over at Chris. "I think we both knew it was a long shot," I said.

"He doesn't want money," Chris said hoarsely, almost in a whisper. "He really wants the business. Just before we split up, he begged me not to force him out. He even cried. It broke my heart, but I knew we'd never make it together. He would still be himself, and I would be myself."

That day in the office was the last time I saw Chris.

After I had waited about fifteen minutes to see Stan, the receptionist, a woman new to me, led the way to his office, the very one that had been Chris's barely three months earlier. It had been enlarged, freshly paneled, and newly carpeted. A massive teak desk had replaced Chris's old-fashioned oak one. Stan sat behind the desk, leaning back in a large leather chair, his hands locked behind his head, his elbows spread eagle. Quickly he rose from the chair to shake my hand.

"Ready to go to work?" he asked.

"Ready," I said. "What desk should I use?"

"The one you always used in the spare office." He handed me an envelope. "When you have the bottom line, let's open this and compare figures. Okay?"

"That should be interesting," I said, turning to go.

"About Chris, his family," Stan said warily, "how are they doing?"

"He had a lot of insurance. They're okay."

"Because, you know, I'd be willing to help out."

"You could ask them," I said.

"She won't talk to me."

"I see."

He was seated now, fidgeting in his chair. His lips parted hesitantly. Then he blurted, "Was it an accident or...? What do you think?"

"Who knows?"

"That's a dangerous curve as you come onto the causeway by the lake."

"Very dangerous."

"It's not likely he would have deliberately driven his car into the lake, is it?" I shrugged and remained silent. "Maybe he had a heart attack," said Stan.

"More likely an anxiety attack," I said. "Anyway, the autopsy found nothing wrong with him. If you'll excuse me, Stan, I'd better get to work."

By late afternoon my computation of the bottom line was complete. It showed a deepening loss. Statement in hand, I went to see Stan, but his office was empty. The receptionist said he had gone for the day. Curious, I opened the envelope containing his estimate. The figure was absurd.

A TOP-NOTCH MAN

Phil was seated behind his desk signing papers when the phone rang. He picked up the receiver and listened. "I told you I didn't want to talk to him. You mean he's here? Ingersoll's here?" Phil paused, collecting his thoughts. "Didn't you tell him I'm in a meeting? Oh, hell, then send him in."

Phil's office, on the thirty-ninth floor of one of Chicago's newest skyscrapers, was opulently furnished. Papers were stacked neatly on one corner of his immaculate desk. On the other corner stood a framed photograph of his wife and children. Behind him was a massive window overlooking the lower buildings of the Loop. He could see twenty miles on a clear day. Along one wall was a long leather couch. Two comfortable visitor chairs faced the desk.

As Calvin Ingersoll breezed in, Phil rose to shake his hand. "Calvin, what a surprise," Phil exclaimed. "Good to see you again."

"Same here, my friend, my old friend," said Cal, smiling broadly and taking Phil's hand.

"Please sit. Sit down by all means," said Phil, directing him to one of the visitor chairs. "Tell me, Cal, how long would you say it's been?"

"You mean…"

"I mean since we've actually seen each other. Of course, we've talked on the phone. That little business matter, you know, and…

"I'd say perhaps ten years, more or less," offered Cal.

"Oh, all of that. Ten years at least. It was at Fauntleroy's Tavern, wasn't it?" said Phil, settling back in his velour upholstered chair.

"Ah, yes. Excellent cuisine, I must say," said Cal, grinning.

"You were coming out of the bar, as I recall."

"Sober, I presume," said Cal with a laugh.

"Glowing is more like it. You were exceptionally cordial."

"My glow had to be genuine. Yes, I was delighted to see you after…how long had it been then?"

"A good twenty-five years. As of now, we've seen each other only twice in thirty-five years. I'd hardly call it a close friendship, would you, Cal?"

"Of course, in between there've been Christmas cards, and you're often in my thoughts, my friend," Cal said in defense.

"Sure. Well, how is it going at the college?" said Phil, offering a reprieve.

"I'm professor emeritus now."

"Finally retired, eh?"

"Not quite. I must teach, you know, so they allow me an English Lit course now and then. A mere bone, a way of easing me out rather painlessly."

"You certainly seem to be aging well, Cal."

"Actually, I'm quite fit for seventy," said Cal, crossing one knee over the other. "Be advised, my friend, that alcohol is a poor preservative for human protoplasm. I'm quite off the sauce nowadays."

"Glad to hear it."

"Hardly as much fun. Sobriety's really a bore, you know," Cal said, laughing. But he stopped when he saw that Phil, showing a hint of impatience, didn't join in.

"You were saying over the phone…"

"I hope I'm not intruding. I had to talk to you personally, Phil."

"You mean about money again?" said Phil, picking up and fingering a gold pen.

"In point of fact, Phil, this time it's not for myself. My roommate…"

"Your roommate?" said Phil, eyebrows raised. "In the old days, I remember, when I suggested we share an apartment, you insisted on living alone."

"Times have changed, Phil. If not my roommate, you might say my lover, then. That's the long and short of it. I see no point in pretending."

"I see. And she's in trouble, is that it?"

"Trouble, yes," said Cal, hesitating as he formulated his next statement. "*He's* a drug addict. Very, very unfortunate. But now, realizing how futile his habit is, he's ready to submit to detoxification. However, as you know, it's quite expensive, or perhaps you didn't know. And as it happens, I'm still somewhat short myself. Rest assured, Phil, I'll pay you back. I insist that it be only a loan."

"Just a minute," said Phil, sitting upright from a slouch. "What happened to the five-hundred-dollar check I sent you last week after our phone conversation?"

"As I explained, or I thought I had explained, that was for my car insurance."

"Yes, that's what you said, but now…"

"It's not for me this time, Phil. Five hundred dollars more, that's all. As I said, it would be merely a loan. I would repay it in due time, I assure you…in due time. Of course, I'd consider no other terms. When I receive my social security payment on the first of the month, I should be able to…"

"You were never very good at managing money, were you, Cal?"

"So what's new?" said Cal, throwing his hands up in futility. "I assume you're referring to my inheritance that I so nobly frittered away. I confess I simply can't handle money."

"You were fixed for life, but you gave it away to any lost soul," said Phil caustically.

"Ah, well. I can't bear seeing others have less than I do. But what can one do?"

Phil had to admit that Cal's innocence and helplessness were appealing. As if castigating a child, Phil said, "If you don't care about number one, who will, Cal?"

"A point well made," admitted Cal.

"I'll bet you've been taken to the cleaners more than a few times."

"I suppose I have. But I have no regrets."

"And now you're doing it again. Giving it away," criticized Phil.

"We must help those we love, Phil. Would you do otherwise?" Cal went on even though he saw Phil glaring at him, momentarily speechless. "It's obvious you're doing eminently well," Cal continued. "Of course, I had heard of your enormous success, but this," Cal gestured across the office, "this confirms it."

Cal rose, walked over to the couch, and sat facing Phil. He rested an arm across the back of the couch.

"It hasn't been an easy road, Cal."

"For neither of us, my friend."

There was a brief silence as Phil considered how to best phrase his next question.

"I've often wondered, we used to be so close when I was young; you were my mentor. Why did we drift apart? What happened?"

"Well, you married, began a family."

"But that was no reason," said Phil, glancing at the photograph on his desk.

"Your concerns simply changed, Phil, and under the circumstances I had no role in your life."

"That's ridiculous," said Phil, leaning across his desk toward Cal. "My wife always welcomed you into our home. Our friendship was never an issue."

"You made your choice. If you must know, I was hurt," said Cal.

"What on earth are you talking about?"

"Your preference was clear," said Cal firmly.

"It wasn't an either-or situation. Friends are friends."

"One of your faults persists, I see. Indeed, Phil, there are times when you're quite dense."

Phil flinched, suddenly catching on. "Are you saying..."

"Yes, I loved you. Didn't you know?"

"It was mutual, of course, Cal."

"Not in the same way, I suspect."

"True, true. I was unaware..."

"They were frustrating times," said Cal softly. "People of my ilk had to confine themselves to the closet. We loved from afar. Beset with self-hate and shame, we were emotional basket cases."

"But that's over for you. Times have changed. Now it's easier," said Phil.

"Love is never easy, my friend," proclaimed Cal.

"So after ten years, you call me out of the blue, ask for a few bucks—which, for old times' sake, I send you— and a week later you waltz in here expecting more. I have a feeling I'm being used. I'd say one donation is enough."

"I beg your pardon, Phil. It's strictly a loan, certainly not a donation."

"To tell the truth, I don't give a goddamn about your lover."

"Of course you don't," agreed Cal. "I don't expect you to. You'd be doing it for me."

"I hear there are free clinics, detoxification units, that can take care of cases like your friend's. I'm sure if you inquired…"

"You don't understand, Phil."

"I understand you're putting the touch on me," said Phil angrily. "I understand for ten years you didn't give a damn whether I was alive or dead."

"You're forgetting the Christmas cards, Phil. My notes expressing concern, always wishing you the very best."

"Big deal. No, it won't fly, not again, not this time. I won't help your friend. He means nothing to me," said Phil with finality.

He got up from his desk and stood looking out the window at the city stretching into the distance.

"True love is indestructible. In my deepest heart, our friendship—my love for you—never waned. As I explained, you'd be doing it for me, Phil."

Phil turned. "I fail to see the connection. Look, I must get back to work." He walked over to Cal and extended his hand, but Cal ignored it and remained seated.

"Yes," said Cal, "I've taken too much of your time already. But there's one more thing. I'd like to think I've made a certain contribution to your success, even if it was a long time ago."

"To my success?" said Phil, astonished. "This is all mine, Cal." He spread his arms out. "I've done it all single-handedly. I don't owe a thing to a soul."

"But you do, Phil," asserted Cal. "Like the rest of us, you're in debt from the day you're born. Have you forgotten my letter on your behalf to the dean of admissions at Harvard?"

"What letter?" said Phil, drawing a blank.

"By coincidence, while going through old files, I came upon—quite serendipitously, mind you—a copy of the letter." Cal withdrew two crumbling pieces of yellowed paper from the inside pocket of his jacket and held them up for Phil to see. "Do you recall it now?"

"Well, vaguely," Phil admitted warily as he glanced at the pages. "It was a long time ago."

"Yes, a very long time ago. Since these pages are in such a fragile state, would you mind if I read them to you to jog your memory?"

"Well…"

"You may remember that at the time you were in a quandary. You were having emotional difficulties, failing in your studies at Tech. Of course, this was typical of so many just back from the war."

Phil nodded reluctantly and returned to his chair as Cal began reading. *"Gentlemen of the Department of Admissions: Phil Solitaire has asked me to write a letter recommending his admittance to Harvard University."*

"Is it coming back to you, Phil?" said Cal. "You had asked that I write this letter." Phil remained impassive, his expression stolid. "Well, let me continue," said Cal.

"I don't know whether or not my colleagues at Harvard have passed on to you my urgent telephone recommendations regarding this man. If they have, I fear that you might consider my writing this letter to be pushing the issue a little too hard."

Cal interrupted his reading. "In hindsight perhaps I *was* pushing a bit too hard. But for a friend, one knows no limits, wouldn't you agree, Phil? To continue . . ."

"However if they have not, my letter might be of interest and use to you, so I find myself forced to write this in spite of its possible redundancy."

"Do you recall, Phil, that you had applied to the University but received no response after several months?"

"Again, my recollection is rather vague," said Phil, "especially as to the details."

"May I go on?"

"What's the point?" said Phil, becoming annoyed.

"I insist, if you don't mind. It's quite brief, really."

"First, to establish myself as a reference, a bit of personal history. I was in contact with students at Harvard as a graduate student, teaching fellow, and tutor in Eliot, Dunster, and Lowell Houses for more than five years. I believe I have as good a picture of the caliber and kind of students at Harvard as only few persons in Cambridge today."

Cal raised his eyes to monitor Phil's reaction. "They were first-quality men at that time, Phil, all of them, and many went on to become our nation's finest."

"That's true," agreed Phil.

"One of them, in fact, became our president. Now, listen to this."

"Phil Solitaire, whom I have come to know quite well in the last year, is, in my best judgment, a truly outstanding person, easily the equal of the upper fifteen to twenty percent of the students now enrolled at Harvard."

"I appreciate what you wrote, Cal, believe me. But I don't see the point," said Phil, having had enough.

There's not much more. Let me finish, all right?" said Cal with controlled hostile insistence.

"He has a high level of intelligence combined with a combative, thoughtful originality of mind that makes, in my opinion, for the kind of educable person who could benefit most fully from the program offered at Harvard."

"Very complimentary, very nice, Cal, but..."

Ignoring Phil's comment, Cal went on. *"Complimentary to these mental qualifications is his enormous stock of vitality and drive, which combined with his ambitious nature should make him an outstanding success in college and in whatever life work he undertakes."*

"It appears I called it quite accurately, wouldn't you say, Phil? Quite accurately." Phil nodded, feeling helpless. "To continue."

"There is, however, one aspect of Phil's situation that I think deserves special attention."

"Now to the heart of the problem, Phil. To the very heart of it."

"Look, I see no point in dredging up the past. It's over and done," said Phil, rising from his seat.

"Ah, but the present is the summation of all that's gone before. The present is forged by the past. At any given moment, the past is all we have. How else can we understand the present? You, more than most, should recognize that. May I?"

"*At the present time Phil is enrolled in a technical college of good reputation. But he finds the training given there not the education he so vitally wants and needs; as a consequence he is producing below his standards and is dissatisfied with himself.*"

"That was putting it mildly, wasn't it?" said Cal. "It was much more than just your failing grades. You were entertaining suicide, isn't that so?"

Phil sat down again, defeated. "I was a confused young man."

"As were so many veterans right after the war."

"I've heard enough," Phil said adamantly.

"But, I'm almost finished."

"*This is a serious strain on his personality, and I fear that if he is forced to remain in this unhealthy environment he will be unable to take proper advantage of what educational opportunities he has there. Hence, coming to Harvard would have special significance for Phil.*"

"And you said, at the time, that their acceptance saved your life. Do you recall saying that?"

"Is that what I said?"

"You did at the time," said Cal.

"I wouldn't know. I mean…"

"How strange that you've forgotten such important details. You have a memory of convenience, it seems," said Cal. "But don't we all. Only a short paragraph remains, all right, Phil?"

"*In closing, let me thank you for your interest in this case. Let me also sum up my impressions of Phil by saying that I think he is a top-notch man who, tempered, broadened, and disciplined by the Harvard experience, would be a product of which the University could be very proud. Yours sincerely, G. Calvin Ingersoll."*

Cal handed the crumbling pages to Phil. "Take them. They're yours. Destroy them. Do whatever you want."

Phil folded them and placed them before him on his desk.

"It's true, I was young, foundering, having a hard time," confessed Phil. "It's a difficult period in a man's life."

"I tried to give you guidance, and I'd say I succeeded. Look at what you've accomplished. Harvard proved to be good for you, I must say."

"Yes, it was. It gave me direction. I seemed to be back on track."

"Just as I predicted," said Cal with self-satisfaction. "And when you graduated magna cum laude, I felt proud."

"Is that so?" said Phil, surprised.

"And somehow responsible."

"That's quite a letter, I suppose," admitted Phil.

"I gave you my best," Cal said warmly.

"I must thank you."

"Have you forgotten? You thanked me often," reminded Cal.

"Then thank-you again," said Phil contritely.

"You're quite welcome, my friend."

"Now I must get back to work," said Phil, rising from his chair.

"Of course," said Cal, rising also.

"Nice to have seen you, Cal."

"Very nice here as well." Cal walked to the door, paused, then turned back to Phil. "Would it make any difference were I to tell you that I'm the one who needs the detoxification?"

"You?" said Phil in disbelief.

"Yes. You see, I can't enter a public unit. It would be generally known, reflect on the university, that sort of thing."

"Christ, how in hell could you . . . I mean, you're an intelligent guy, a genius, an IQ of one eighty as I remember."

"Let me inform you that one's intelligence has no bearing one way or the other on one's propensity for addiction."

"Look, Cal, just have the hospital send the bills to me, to the company. I'll take care of them," said Phil, willing to settle the old debt.

Cal broke into a sudden sweat. "It would be much simpler to provide me the money, don't you think?" he said nervously.

"How do you know how long it will take, how much it will cost? No, I'd rather pick up the tab directly as we go along. It will save you from having to come back for more."

"I'm afraid you don't understand."

"What's to understand? It's all very simple," said Phil, thinking he had proposed the most rational solution.

"I mean I'm not exactly ready to go to the hospital. Not quite yet."

"Then let's wait until…"

Losing control, Cal screamed, pounding his fists on the door. "For God's sake, Phil, I need it now. I need a fix now. Why are you so goddamned dense?"

Silently Phil returned to his desk, withdrew a checkbook from a drawer, and wrote out a check. He handed it to Cal. "Here's five hundred dollars."

"Many thanks, my friend. I assure you, it will be repaid. I consider this a loan, nothing more," repeated Cal, his eyes moist.

"Forget it. I owe it to you, don't I? You called in my debt."

"Certainly not. You don't owe me a thing. A friend is a friend."

"Sure, sure." Phil fastened his gaze onto Cal's jowly, creased face. "You know, Cal, you were loved. Your students loved you. I'm damned disappointed."

"So am I," said Cal, hanging his head. "What can one do? Few of us are what we seem to be."

"I'd like to get back to work, okay?"

"How's the family, the girls, Claudia?"

"They're okay, I suppose."

"You suppose?"

"Claudia and I..." Phil hesitated. "Well, we're separated."

"I see. So you live in a house of glass, after all."

"What in hell do you mean by that?"

"I mean, total success is a rare thing, Phil. I'm sorry."

"Get out of my sight. Just leave," said Phil, seething.

"I'm sorry I've offended you. I didn't intend...I see I hit a nerve. We're all victims one way or another, Phil. That's all I mean."

"Look, I have nothing more to say."

"Yes, and I suppose neither have I," said Cal. "I've said too much already." He extended his hand, but Phil refused to take it. "Well...I see. So that's how it is."

Turning his back on Cal, Phil stared out the window.

"Good-bye, Phil. I'll be in touch."

"Get the hell out," Phil shouted.

Cal, trembling, walked through the doorway into the outer office.

Phil picked up his phone. "Listen," he said, "if Ingersoll, the man who just left my office, ever shows his face around here again, or if he calls, I'm at a meeting. Tell him I'm in Bora-Bora, anyplace but here." He listened briefly. "What do you mean he's sitting in the foyer sobbing? Dammit, ignore him."

He slammed down the receiver. "Shit!" He lapsed into thought for a few moments, then picked up the receiver. "Listen, tell him to come back in. Yeah, tell him I want to see him. Okay?"

AN OPPORTUNITY NOT TO BE MISSED

It isn't often that the man who fired you from your job calls three months later to invite you to dinner at an upscale restaurant.

Forbes Fowler, my old boss, sure has guts thought Kenny, as he drove his aging car along the highway from Worcester where he lived with his wife, who was pregnant again, and their two kids. At least this time his trip was on a mild autumn day and the gentle hills were ablaze with orange and yellow, bringing Kenny some needed cheer. The past three months of unemployment had given him little cause for celebration.

Nine months earlier, in a swirling snowstorm, Kenny had made the same trip for his first interview with Forbes. It had led to his being hired at the Lord Corporation as a…well, his exact role was never made clear. He recalled Forbes's words: "We've got a bad situation at the Chicago plant. It's been running at a loss every month for the past six months. I need somebody to size things up there and report back here with recommendations."

Forbes always spoke directly and concisely. There was never a question about what he meant. But what would Kenny's title be? "We'll leave that open for now. Call yourself a consultant, I suppose, an in-house consultant." More like an in-house spy, Kenny speculated, but he accepted the job because Forbes had offered 25 percent more money than he was earning with his then-current employer.

Furthermore, the Lord Corporation was the most prestigious company in the field. It owned the gleaming glass and steel skyscraper that housed the corporate offices. Forbes himself was lodged in a choice twenty-fifth story corner retreat overlooking the harbor, which had appeared as a blurred gray expanse through the falling snow.

Kenny should have recognized signs that he was heading into the morass of a troubled company. That the Chicago plant was losing money didn't disturb him. But that it had no one on its staff to solve its problems, and had to hire someone from outside, was foreboding. But how flattering it was to be wanted for one's expertise and reputation, with the promise of being handsomely rewarded for it.

"I understand you've done a good job where you are," Forbes said, rising to retrieve a carton of milk from a small office refrigerator beside his desk. "Frankly, I didn't expect to find you so young." Kenny, frail in appearance and intense, looked and behaved younger than his thirty years.

"We've never had a loss month where I am, I can truthfully say, sir," Kenny said with pride.

Forbes poured the milk into his glass, gulped it down, and belched. "Pardon me," he said, grimacing. "Ulcers."

If only Forbes smiled, he'd be a good-looking middle aged man. There was a patrician air about him. Harvard, no doubt. In truth, it was Vanderbilt. Poor man. He seemed harassed. But he couldn't be, not at his level.

"Well, young or not, we'd like you to show us the way."

"I can't guarantee anything, sir."

"Call me Forbes, Kenny. Let's not be so formal."

"But I'll sure as hell do my best...Forbes."

"Formally you'll report to the manager at the plant. Informally, I'm your boss. Do you understand? If they suspect that you're responsible to me, you'll lose your effectiveness." Forbes belched again. "Damn, this has been a hellish day. I'll be glad when it's over."

"One question, sir...er, Forbes. Since, in effect, I'll have two bosses, what do I do if I receive conflicting instructions?"

"At such times, follow the manager's directives, but keep me informed," said Forbes gravely. "As vice president, I'm responsible for the Chicago plant and five others. If the manager causes you a problem, I'll handle it, so don't worry. Remember, I'm hiring you, and I'm the only one who can fire you." A faint smile crossed his creased face. "You're my man. I take care of my men."

Despite Forbes's reassurance, the setup made Kenny uncomfortable. His new position would be too equivocal. And his task, simply to make recommendations, worried him. What if they didn't go for his ideas? Could he trust Forbes Fowler, a man seemingly under pressure and having to resort to subterfuge?

That was nine months ago. Now Kenny knew the answer to his own question. Turning off the highway and heading into the maze of narrow city streets, he winced as he reenacted that initial interview in his mind. At

Maison Louis's door, a reluctant parking attendant took his wreck of a car. Why hadn't he gone by his always reliable instinct? Yes, the money and the trappings had mesmerized him. This time he would pay attention to his hunches. Maison Louis, how spiffy. Dollars to donuts Forbes needed him badly. But this time he would know better. This time, he wouldn't fall for the hype. Forbes, he knew, had only a sawdust soul.

Forbes, looking solemn and surprisingly gaunt, was seated at a table nursing a glass of milk. As the maitre d' led Kenny to him, Forbes rose. "How wonderful to see you again, Kenny." He seemed to force a smile as he reached to shake Kenny's hand. "It's damned decent of you to come despite… Well, you'll understand after I explain things. I'll tell you what really happened."

But Kenny knew what had happened. So why was he here? Why, again, was he nibbling at the hook? Well, for one thing, still unemployed, he had the time. Tough break. The economy, and particularly his industry, had been hit hard by the recession. For another, what harm was there in hearing what Forbes had to say? To listen didn't imply commitment. But most of all, this was an opportunity for retribution, a chance to vent his resentment. He'd make Forbes squirm for what he did to him.

They ordered dinner, Forbes insisting that Kenny have the works—the frogs' legs appetizer, the special Lobster Casserole Maison Louis, and, later, the chocolate mousse, a house specialty, with espresso, followed by Grand Marnier for sipping.

"If nothing comes of this meeting, at least you'll have a good dinner. I owe it to you, Kenny. Do you realize how sorry I am?"

"Sorry! Hell, Forbes, no one made you fire me."

"Not true, Kenny. Please understand I wasn't a free agent. Things weren't that simple. I was merely the instrument. There were forces beyond... well, the circumstances were such that I had no choice. The whole damn management team in Chicago insisted I 'can' you or else."

Or else what? thought Kenny. Forbes's own demise? Unlikely. Kenny glowed with satisfaction over Forbes's need to justify himself and his apparent contrition. What a difference between this meeting and the one three months before. Never, ever, would Kenny forget that meeting.

The day had begun at six in the morning when Forbes had called him at his new home in Winnetka, to which he and his family had relocated from the East two weeks earlier.

"Take the next plane out of O'Hare and be in my office this afternoon," Forbes had ordered.

"What's up, Forbes?"

"Nothing to worry about. Just be here."

One thing Kenny hadn't needed was another worry. He had failed to sell his house in Worcester before making the move west. The burden of two mortgages had been chewing up his entire salary gain and then some.

As Kenny, sweaty and weary, had arrived at Forbes's Boston office around two that hot summer afternoon, he found his boss staring out at the blue harbor dotted with white sails. Forbes was holding a glass half filled with milk. Turning as Kenny entered, he gestured with his head toward the window and said, "That's where you and I ought to be. Haven't sailed in years. Somehow got away from it." He shrugged. "What the hell."

Forbes opened the center drawer of his desk, reached in, and withdrew a sheaf of handwritten papers. In a gesture of contempt, he tossed them toward Kenny, who had taken a seat facing the desk. Forbes's desktop was always bare. As the sheaf slid into Kenny's lap, he recognized his own handwriting. It was the seventy-five-page report he had drawn up, the analysis of his findings with recommendations, the culmination of all his work of the previous six months.

"How did you get the original?" Kenny demanded, incredulous. "I gave this to the secretary in Chicago to be typed."

"Nobody in his right mind would commit this—this absurdity—to print," shouted Forbes.

Stunned, Kenny sat wordlessly searching Forbes's eyes for clarification.

"When I hired you, I wasn't looking for some…some reformer. Do you realize what you said here?" Forbes stabbed his finger toward the report in Kenny's hands; Kenny remained speechless. "You said that the entire operation is wrong, the equipment is wrong, our manufacturing method is wrong, the whole damn plant is wrong. In other words you said we ought to scrap the whole fucking thing and start over again."

"That's right, Forbes. Everything IS wrong, and that's why it hasn't made money, and it never will the way it is."

"Well, you just can't condemn the whole goddamned scene, don't you understand?"

"Forbes, this report represents my honest opinion. What else can I say? And I've based my suggestions on my own successful prior experience. Isn't that what you asked for?"

Forbes kneaded his stomach with his fist, then re-filled his glass with a fresh container of milk from the refrigerator. "I didn't expect such a radical... Look, take this back and tone it down. Everything can't be wrong."

"But basically everything *is* wrong."

"That's only your opinion."

"Isn't that what you wanted when you hired me?"

"Now understand me, Kenny. Do you realize what it would mean were I to go along with your recommendations? That would be admitting that the entire management and engineering groups that designed the plant and developed the process are all wet. Hell, I'd have a revolution on my hands; I'd have to fire them all and start from scratch. And what do you think would happen if they got wind of it upstairs? It would amount to an admission of major error. Mr. Lord would have our heads, guaranteed. So why don't you go back to the drawing board like a good fellow?"

"Can't you get someone else to give you the recommendations you want? You don't need me."

"No, that won't work. I must have your signature. I can't hire someone else at this stage of the game."

"I'm sorry, Forbes. I wouldn't even know how to go about doing it another way. I wrote what I believe."

"For Christ sakes, Kenny, be smart." A long, heavy silence settled between them. "Think about it. I'll give you until Friday." After downing the remaining milk in his glass, Forbes turned to the harbor scene below. "Just look at those sailboats. Aren't they something?" Kenny joined his gaze. "So clean and elemental. That's where I ought to be." He let out a deep belch. "Christ," he said.

That night on the flight back to Chicago, Kenny had made up his mind to remain firm, whatever happened.

He did not change his recommendations. On Friday afternoon, two days later, the manager called him into his office and handed him two weeks' severance pay. "By the way," the man said, "I read your handwritten report before sending it off to Forbes. You know, you're wacko."

How ironic this all was. Could Kenny ever have imagined three months ago that he would be dining with Forbes, at Maison Louis no less, listening to the man's apology? Never expecting that it was possible, this was the sort of retribution you enact in your mind's eye, the inevitably satisfying "thought murder." But Forbes had his pride. Only one thing could lead him to face Kenny's rancor. Not his conscience, thought Kenny. Definitely not that. He needed Kenny for something and he needed him badly. Kenny watched Forbes's expressions range from arrogant confidence as the waiter hovered about trying to please his obviously familiar patron, to pitiful sadness when he spoke of his recent fortune.

"You were right on, Kenny. The Chicago plant never made it, never could. Of course, I knew it wouldn't. Old man Lord instructed me to clean house, which I did and became everybody's bastard. Then he gave me the gate." Forbes spoke as if he were telling someone else's story, as if he himself hadn't been involved. "They ought to put the place up for sale."

"Are you saying that you agreed with my report all along?"

"I never doubted it. You put your finger on the problem and proposed the only sensible solution."

"Then why in hell…?"

"Politics, Kenny. I had to protect my staff...and, well, myself too. The truth was simply too inconvenient. You wouldn't listen to me." He rubbed his hands across his face, attempting to relax his tense expression. "To admit that everything we had been doing was wrong reflected on our competence, don't you see? I tried to point that out, but you didn't seem to get it."

"But look where denying the truth got you," said Kenny smugly.

Forbes fiddled with a fork on the tablecloth as he fell briefly silent, then, raising his eyes directly to Kenny's, he said, "I assure you, Kenny, it's a lesson I'll never forget."

"Did you know we had just bought a house in Illinois and hadn't sold our other one in Massachusetts when you lowered the axe on me?"

"I had no idea. I'm really sorry about that, Kenny."

"It's been hell carrying two mortgages. We returned to New England only because we were able to sell the house in Winnetka first."

What Kenny didn't say was that the proceeds of the sale plus unemployment insurance—a source of great embarrassment to him—were all that kept him solvent, and perhaps for only another month at that.

"Well, cheer up. I'm about to offer you an outstanding proposition."

"Didn't you give me that line once before, Forbes?"

"Hah, hah. Maybe I did, but things are different now. I'm a senior veep with Decameron Industries—a first-rate company, wouldn't you say?" Kenny nodded. "Well, they've hired me to set up and lead a division to compete head-on with Lord, product for product. And you're the one I want to help me do it."

"Very impressive. Some big deal," said Kenny, still on his retribution kick.

"It can't fail, Kenny, not with Decameron's support and with you a part of it."

"I don't think so, Forbes. It's not for me."

"Why in heaven's name not? I think it's ideal for you—an opportunity not to be missed, Kenny."

"Decameron—they're just another Lord. And you're the same Forbes who canned me for being honest."

Forbes shook his head. "What you're saying is you don't trust me."

"Yeah, something like that."

"Well, I don't blame you. I don't blame you one iota." Forbes motioned to the waiter for the check as he pondered his next statement. "Are you working, Kenny?"

"I've got a few things pending," Kenny replied awkwardly.

"Did I say that your salary would be twice what you were earning at Lord?" Suddenly he had Kenny's attention. "And you'd have your own office next to mine on the thirtieth floor of the tallest building in Atlanta?"

"I suppose that would impress anyone, but..." Kenny was struggling to remain blasé.

"There's an executive dining room, and of course you'd have a company car—a Jag like mine. The company owns a small estate on Jamaica. To use it, you just put in for the three weeks you want. I should mention you'd have the use of our private jet to visit the new plant we'll be building."

It was far beyond what Kenny had expected. He found it hard to stick to his original resolve. Forbes's offer was overwhelming him.

"Sounds interesting, doesn't it, Kenny?"

"I suppose I ought to think about it."

"Yes, I think you should. We could have a great future together." As they rose from the table, Forbes reached over to Kenny and hugged him gently. "You'll be my man, and I always take care of my men." Although Forbes's line sounded familiar, Kenny didn't flinch.

Forbes grasped Kenny's hand in both of his and smiled more warmly than Kenny had ever seen him. He seemed consumed with a sudden joy, perhaps the joy of expiation.

"Let me know what you decide by Friday, okay?"

"Okay, Forbes...I'll let you know by Friday."

Kenny knew that he'd been given the offer of a lifetime. He also knew that he wouldn't turn it down. Yet as he drove away from Maison Louis, he felt increasingly depressed. He wasn't sure how, but he knew that, in the apparent winning, he had lost. Again.

THE FLOWER

My Ma planted some kind of tall plant in an old iron pot, which she had painted black and filled with dirt. All last summer she had it on our front porch where it did mighty well, and even had a single flower for a few days. But one night a frost came and withered the leaves. So Ma brought the plant into the house and set it on the floor beside the fireplace.

When my Pa saw it he said, "What is *that?*" Ma explained that it used to be a beautiful plant and would be again.

"Good grief, why waste your time on that miserable specimen of vegetation?" he asked.

Well, Ma watered the plant every time the dirt seemed even a little dry. But it didn't really get to look better. One morning the stem flopped over the edge of the pot and looked as droopy as a damp rag. Pa noticed too and smiled a little.

About a month later Ma was watering the plant in the pot when Pa said, "Don't you know when you're licked?"

Ma said, "It's far from dead. In fact it's having a baby. See, there's a little sprout showing just above the dirt."

Pa said, "Nah, it's dead."

Then my Ma said, "If it can have a baby, it's alive enough to stand on its own two feet." Pa just scoffed.

Well, last night you should have been here. A flower was born. Pa noticed some color at the base of the plant as he sat down in his chair with the newspaper. When Ma came into the room to tell Pa that supper was ready, he stood, looked over at the flower, and turned to Ma. Then he kissed her and told her he loved her. And you know I felt the same way about Ma after I saw the flower.

HEARD THROUGH A CLOSED DOOR

"What are you studying at the university, Mr. Arnold?" Mrs. Kincaid's voice was mellow, almost melodic. She was a tiny, thin woman with a bony face, her eyes deep set, her gray hair prim and collected.

"I'm a liberal arts undergraduate."

"Ah, so you're getting a well-rounded education. Good, Mr. Arnold."

In 1947, on the south side of Chicago, you could rent a nice room in a family home for six dollars a week. Mrs. Kincaid's apartment was spotless. She showed me a small bedroom off the living room, quite adequate for my needs. It contained a single bed and a comfortable chair and a desk; its sole window overlooked a mixed residential and commercial section of 57th Street.

"At this point I really don't know what I want to be."

"Yes, we have a whole world of choices. So often we make the wrong ones."

"I'll take the room," I said.

"You've made a good choice, Mr. Arnold," she said with a gentle smile. "Tonight…will you be here this evening? Yes? Well, tonight you must meet my husband and daughter. She's also a student at the university."

Eleanor turned out to be a vivacious auburn-haired beauty. Mr. Kincaid was a taciturn, unobtrusive, faded man. Although I rarely saw the daughter after our initial meeting, I encountered Mr. Kincaid each evening as I passed through the living room. He was always seated in his Morris chair reading the newspaper.

"Good evening, Mr. Kincaid," I would always say.

"Eh? Oh, yes, good evening, Hal," he would inevitably reply.

After dinner, to which I was occasionally invited, Mrs. Kincaid usually joined her husband in the living room where she sat in a straight-backed chair and read poetry. Buried in their reading, the couple rarely talked, and when they did it was always in a formal manner. But one evening, through my closed door, I heard Mrs. Kincaid say, "Mr. Kincaid, won't you speak to Eleanor? I've failed. Perhaps you could bring her to her senses." Both husband and wife always addressed each other formally.

After clearing his throat, Mr. Kincaid said, "I don't think I can do much good. You know how strong-willed she is. Once she makes up her mind..." He cleared his throat again.

"She won't listen to me," said Mrs. Kincaid. "You must get involved. At least say something to her."

"Well, I'll try if you insist."

"I do. We must stop her from ruining her life. I...I'm at my wit's end."

I could hear Mr. Kincaid's newspaper rustle, then silence. Distracted by what I'd heard, I speculated on what Eleanor was doing that was so self-destructive: quitting school, drinking, smoking pot, joining the army? None of this sort of behavior was consistent with the Eleanor I had come to know. From my infrequent and casual dealings with her, she seemed sensible and stable. In fact, I had a mind to pursue her.

"Would you like to have dinner with us this evening?" Mrs. Kincaid asked the next morning as I was leaving the house.

"I'd like that very much. Thank you," I replied. I'd have swum across Lake Michigan for a home-cooked meal.

At the dinner table Eleanor introduced me to their other guest, her friend Allan. She had just navigated his wheelchair into the dining room. I extended my hand, which he was unable to take. But his eyes were lively and friendly.

"I do have one good leg," he said with a laugh, "but that would be rather awkward, don't you think?" His body seemed small, withered.

Eleanor helped him rise from the wheelchair, and supported him as he moved to a seat at the dinner table. I went to help, but she waved me off. As Mrs. Kincaid served dinner, Allan indulged in cheerful banter. In the middle of the meal he murmured a few words to Eleanor, who rose, retrieved the wheelchair, and with considerable difficulty helped Allan into it.

I stood ready to give a hand. "I must do this alone," Eleanor said. "Please excuse us," and she pushed the wheelchair into the bathroom off the hallway, closing the door behind them. It occurred to me that Allan was unable to urinate without assistance. Mrs. Kincaid looked at Mr. Kincaid with a pained expression.

One evening the following week, Mrs. Kincaid secluded herself and Eleanor behind the closed door of her daughter's bedroom. After a short while, she emerged looking pale and agitated, and headed for the living room where she sat in her Victorian chair and began reading a book of Emily Dickinson's poetry. She was so engrossed in her reading that she did not notice me enter my room and close the door. Soon, hearing the rustle of a newspaper, I concluded that Mr. Kincaid had arrived. Then I heard Mrs. Kincaid slam her book down on the table, as if in anger.

"He's selfish, Mr. Kincaid, absolutely selfish." Mr. Kincaid rustled the newspaper some more. "How can any man expect a girl, hardly twenty-one, in full bloom, a lovely flower, deny herself the fullness of life simply for his sake? It's selfish, unfair, cruel, dastardly cruel. I will not have her miss all I've missed. I will not, Mr. Kincaid. It breaks my heart."

I heard her sobbing as Mr. Kincaid said, "There, there. It's out of our hands. There, there."

"You always accept," Mrs. Kincaid complained. "I'm tired of your acceptance. One has to protest. Don't you understand, Mr. Kincaid? I've settled for second best and now so has she. I won't allow her to make my mistake. I hate that man for what he is doing to my daughter."

Over the next few months, Allan frequently visited my room. He delighted me. He was easy to talk to, open, well versed in many subjects. We spent long hours in fascinating discussions. I grew fonder of him the longer I knew him. "Everything's possible," he once said to me, "if you don't give in."

In time I became unaware of his handicap; he no longer seemed different from me or anyone else. Nor did he seem to acknowledge being a burden to anyone, least of all to Eleanor. Thus I came to understand how Eleanor would see him as normal.

"I can do anything anyone else can do," he often said with a chuckle. I took that to mean he could do anything that mattered from his point of view. He was studying for the ministry. "I know you might assume it presumptuous of me to think that I can lead others. I believe life is good despite its pain, and often because of it. I'd like to spread that message."

Although he may have won me over, he had not won over Mrs. Kincaid. Her resentment toward him grew more and more venomous. But he ignored it. He spoke to her only with respect and consideration regardless of what cutting remark she might have made. His equanimity seemed to baffle her.

One evening through my bedroom door I heard her complain to her husband, "How can he be so calm? So innocent? Doesn't he realize how much I despise him? And doesn't he see what he's doing to Eleanor?"

"It's out of our hands, Mrs. Kincaid," replied Mr. Kincaid.

One day, without a word to anyone, Eleanor and Allan drove off to Downers Grove, a small town outside of Chicago, where a minister friend of Allan's married them. When Mrs. Kincaid found out, I sensed that she felt wounded and betrayed, although it was not in her nature to explode or reject her daughter for what she had done.

"She could have told me," I heard her say through my door. "We could have given her a wedding. She could have worn the wedding gown that I saved for her all these years. Why has she been so cruel to me? It's beyond me."

"Now, now," said Mr. Kincaid. "She had to do things her way. You know how independent she is."

Mrs. Kincaid was distant, if civil, toward Allan, but she was critical of Eleanor, so much so that the couple, who now lived in their own apartment, rarely visited.

"I know she needs me; she's ruining her life," I heard Mrs. Kincaid say one evening as I lay on my bed reading. "I've told her she's welcome here despite what she's done. Isn't that enough? What else must I do?"

"It's her life," Mr. Kincaid responded.

"How can you be so disinterested, so above it? How can you be so cold?" She sounded as near to anger as I'd ever heard her. "I don't understand you. I never have."

Mr. Kincaid's response consisted of the rustle of a newspaper and silence.

Suddenly, the tension between the newlyweds and the parents evaporated when Eleanor informed her mother that she was pregnant. "It's marvelous, simply marvelous," Mrs. Kincaid cooed. It occurred to me that Mrs. Kincaid may have thought that Allan wasn't capable of fathering a child, that his handicap extended to his organs as well.

When the couple came to visit, Mrs. Kincaid greeted her daughter with a warm embrace. She had become a "new" woman; through my door I often heard her humming in the living room while Mr. Kincaid read his newspaper. "I could almost forgive him his awful selfishness," she said. "I'm happy to see that one good thing has come of their union. Yes, it makes up for much."

During one of their visits, I heard startling news through my door. The four of them were in the living room, and Allan announced that Eleanor had been diagnosed with multiple sclerosis, not a well-understood illness in those days.

"What does it mean?" asked Mrs. Kincaid, her voice trembling.

"Mother, the doctor says multiple sclerosis is not necessarily fatal," said Eleanor. "So don't jump to any conclusions."

In fact," added Allan, "there are usually long periods of remission when Eleanor will seem to be perfectly normal."

"Well, that's some comfort, I suppose," said Mrs. Kincaid. "I pray that they're working on a cure with a breakthrough due at any time."

"Oh, there's a lot of research going on," Allan said.

"What about the baby?" Mrs. Kincaid inquired. "Will this interfere with having the baby?"

"Of course not, Mother."

"Well, are you sure that having the baby is advisable? Could it harm you in any way? That's my first concern. And would the child be normal? I can see many possible issues. We must take them all into account."

"You're worrying needlessly, Mother."

"The doctor is urging us to have the child," said Allan.

"'Us' isn't having the child," Mrs. Kincaid shot back.

"What I mean is," Allan continued, "it might actually be good for Eleanor, and there's no chance the baby will be affected."

Despite listening from behind my door, I felt somehow involved too. Allan's revelation shocked me, and I sympathized with Mrs. Kincaid's worst fears. I marveled at Allan's calmness and optimism. Had he meant that having a child would benefit Eleanor mentally, not physically, by keeping her occupied? I agreed, Eleanor must have the child for her sake. But I knew enough about multiple sclerosis to realize what Allan had not said: that it could lead to total paralysis and early death. I could not help but think that eventually Eleanor would be no less incapacitated than Allan himself. This must have occurred to Allan, who knew so much about everything. Perhaps Allan felt that prayer would help them endure the horror that was bound to come.

During her pregnancy, Eleanor experienced various periods of physical weakness and, as Allan had predicted, periods of remission when she seemed perfectly normal. The family latched on to the latter periods, hoping that they would become permanent. But in fact they were temporary, more so as time passed. A stoic Mrs. Kincaid displayed no emotion as she watched her daughter's life ebb. One night, on the other side of my door, I heard her sobbing as Mr. Kincaid tried to comfort her. But it was Allan who, with his calm and deliberate manner, offered them the hope they needed to avoid collapse.

The doctor had decided to induce labor during a period of remission. "It's possible," Allan told his in-laws the day they took Eleanor to Lying In, "that after she gives birth, she'll go into permanent remission."

"Do you really think so, Allan?" begged Mrs. Kincaid. "Help me believe it will happen. Please help me, Allan."

Allan enabled Mrs. Kincaid to keep hoping. When they visited, she saw how well he managed to do things, and marveled at his abilities. When Eleanor was bedridden, he would rise from his wheelchair, drag himself to the stove, cook for her, and feed her. He had devised tools that enabled him to do with his mouth what other people did with their hands. Mrs. Kincaid watched as Allan, without the use of his arms and with only one leg, answered the phone, used the bathroom unattended, and bathed Eleanor in the bathtub. I, too, watched in astonishment as he wrote a phone message by using a pen in his mouth. I wondered why he hadn't shown such self-sufficiency before Eleanor became ill. Was this because he had had no need to call on all his resources?

The family spent all day and night at the hospital until Eleanor gave birth. It was a healthy baby girl. For the first time in months, they experienced joy as they gazed upon the newborn in her mother's arms. It seemed that this new being had imparted fresh life to Eleanor. But they all knew they would have to wait to see if it would last.

The following evening, Mrs. Kincaid knocked on my door. "I'm sorry to have to say this, Hal, but we'll need your room for Eleanor and the baby when they come home from the hospital. Your room is the closest to the living room, and I'll be sleeping on the couch so I can be close by if I'm needed. We've all enjoyed having you, and I'm sure you'll have no trouble finding another room." I assured her that I understood. "Do you think you could leave by next weekend?" she asked. I said I would. "Please come often to visit," she said with a sincere tone. "We'll miss you." And then she closed the door behind her.

Eleanor occupied my old room for only a month before she returned to the hospital for good. I tried to see her one afternoon, but the floor nurse said that Eleanor was having a bad day.

"Then I'll come another time," I said.

"You can," said the nurse, "but she probably won't know you. The disease has affected her brain. She's like an angry child, and curses her mother and father whenever they come to visit."

Nevertheless, I tried again a few days later and ran into Mrs. Kincaid wheeling Allan down the corridor toward Eleanor's room.

"It's so good to see you, Hal," said Mrs. Kincaid.

"Thanks for coming," said Allan.

"Have you seen her?" Mrs. Kincaid asked.

"Not yet," I replied.

"Well, I'm afraid it would be a waste of time. She no longer knows Allan, or me. It's so heartbreaking, my beautiful daughter only a shell, without a mind."

"How's the baby?" I asked.

"Healthy and happy," said Allan.

"Our pride and joy," said Mrs. Kincaid.

"We have been given a life for a life," said Allan. "I'll see that my child keeps Eleanor's memory alive long after I'm gone."

"Don't talk that way, Allan. You and I must live for the child now."

Eleanor was cremated without a wake or a funeral. Three months later I visited the family. While we talked, Mrs. Kincaid cradled the baby in her arms, bottle-nursing her. I saw that my room had been converted into a nursery.

"She's a real beauty," I commented.

"Looks just like her mother when she was a baby," said Mrs. Kincaid.

A second coming, I thought. Everything about the apartment was cheery and bright. Mrs. Kincaid looked years younger. As I was about to leave, she invited me to wait for Allan, who was due to arrive soon.

"You know," she said, "I was opposed to their marriage. I thought my daughter would be unable to cope with Allan's handicap. I thought he was asking too much of her, of anyone really, and that he had no right to expect such a sacrifice. I had hoped she'd fall in love with someone like you."

"Well, I...I... Thank you," I stammered, thinking back to my early interest in Eleanor before Allan appeared.

"But I was wrong," she went on. "I was wrong about Allan."

"He's an exceptional man," I said.

"Yes, very exceptional. I believe he was meant for my daughter." She sighed. "For all of us. Someone who has suffered as deeply as he has knows how to endure pain and sets an example for the rest of us. You know, he gave us the strength we needed. He gave us more than we gave him." Pausing, she listened. "Oh, I hear him at the door."

He entered in his customary wheelchair, this time pushed from behind by a striking young woman. "Hello, Hal. Good to see you again. I was about to call you. This is Karen." I reached for her extended hand. "Before I take over my pulpit, we're getting married this June and I'd like you to come to our wedding."

"Charmed to meet you," said Karen. "Allan has spoken of you often."

I flushed. How could he be so insensitive to Mrs. Kincaid with talk of remarrying, and so soon. Eleanor's ashes were hardly cold.

"I plan to go back east as soon as school's over in May," I said indifferently.

"Work on him, Mrs. K," said Allan. "Talk him into delaying his departure by a few days."

Pretending not to hear what Allan had said, Mrs. Kincaid cast her eyes aside and concentrated on feeding the infant. Karen reached for the baby, taking her from Mrs. Kincaid into her own arms to continue the feeding. To Mrs. Kincaid this was a painful, symbolic act. I watched Mrs. Kincaid's smile turn to a grimace. Having lost her daughter, the light of her life, she was now about to lose her grandchild, whom she had counted on raising into adulthood. She had expected that Allan's handicap would secure her motherly role. Both father and granddaughter would certainly need her. It was an outrage that Allan would remarry. Who else beside her daughter would ever dedicate herself to his every need except herself? But she underestimated Allan's powerful charisma. Of course, she knew she was no match for Karen who was warm, young, and beautiful. Mrs. Kincaid's treasured usefulness was about to sadly end in a role of simply being a grandmother. Life again had deprived her of a needed purpose.

THE VOW

"Jules, we need you," Virginia implored.

Jules sat at the green kitchen table in a circle of light falling from a shaded ceiling lamp. From a turmoil of papers scattered over the tabletop, he plucked a type-written sheet.

"Jules, thank you for coming with us," Virginia said.

Annoyed, Jules raised his tired eyes, flashed them into the gloom of his wife's dim outline, then dropped his gaze to his preoccupation.

"We've never had you all to ourselves like this," she went on, studying his tense expression. "Not since we built this cottage eight years ago." Her gaze caressed his high cheekbones, thick black brows, and lean body. His hairline was receding, but his face was handsome still, albeit set with resolve.

She sidled behind him, and then, seeing what he was working on, glared at the memorandums bearing cryptic-sounding words: standard cost analysis, evaluation procedure, marginal operation.

"Jules," she tried again. His head jerked up, and his foot stamped the floor as the small cottage trembled on its stilts.

"Shh, you'll wake the children," she warned.

"Well, stop bothering me."

"We'll talk later, then."

"Yes, yes," he said impatiently, and waved her off.

Feet slippered, wearing a flowered cotton bathrobe, Virginia stood in the doorway of the children's bedroom and listened to them moving restlessly in their sleep. Disconsolately she muttered to herself, "At least your body is with us, Jules. It's more than we're used to having".

The children—the boy was six, the girl eight—had gone to bed early that evening, impatient for the next morning. "Oh boy, oh boy," they clamored, their bare feet thudding across the floor, yanking their pajama tops down over their heads as they scampered in a frenzy to their bedroom. They plunged into their pillows, exultant. Their father had promised to go with them to the beach the next day.

"But only for a few hours," he had added. "I have to make the two o'clock flight from Hyannis."

Virginia walked across the room to the children's beds. The boy was uncovered, his blankets contorted. She smiled and tucked him in tenderly, then turned to her daughter. How neatly she sleeps. Virginia nestled her cool lips into the children's silky, moist cheeks. "Goodnight, my loves." They snuggled deeper, as if her voice had seeped into their dreams.

Virginia crossed the kitchen without glancing at her husband, then passed through the dark living room to the screened front porch. The damp, chill breath of the sea stung her thin, weary face. She gazed across the rippled sand, barely discernible in the moonlight, and listened to the crashing surf resounding in the blackness.

Her flimsy bathrobe was no match for the cool evening air, and she shivered. She heard a chair scrape against the floorboards inside. Through the tunnel of the living room, Virginia saw Jules's shadow playing on the kitchen wall. She watched as he gathered his papers and inserted them into a bulging briefcase, then stretched, his hands almost touching the low ceiling. She awaited his footfall, but heard instead the kitchen door creak, then slam. Her husband had walked out into the tangy, dark silence alone.

The next morning was brilliant, as if the world had regenerated in the misty night.

"Hurry, children," she said. "We're all going to the beach. The tide is out, just right for riding the breakers."

From the cottage they could see the green surf rolling onto the shimmering golden sand. Beyond, a blue sea lashed at hovering white blurs of screeching gulls.

"Where's Daddy?" asked the girl.

Virginia's pale gray eyes mirrored the dancing ocean. Ruby lipstick primly coated her clucking mouth. "Now, don't worry. He'll keep his promise."

Hearing his mother's reply, the lad careened through the living room and pounded on his father's bedroom door. "Coming, Dad?"

"I'll be there in a minute." The son thought he heard a hint of excitement in the muffled voice.

As Virginia packed the beach bag, her motions were hasty, almost frantic, with anticipation. Her brown hair, faintly threaded with gray, curled beneath the broad brim of her beach hat. She scuttered about from room to room, rummaging for things that she imagined the family would need for a morning at the beach.

In wrinkled blue swim trunks reeking of mothballs, Jules padded into the kitchen like a shorn dog. Peering at his bowed white legs covered with shaggy fuzz, the children giggled. Jules wore an embarrassed smile. How thin he's become, Virginia thought, gazing at the outline of his ribs slivering like fragile slats under his skin. His arms were slender strands of flab. Where had his once powerful litheness gone, his taut flesh that used to fasten her yielding body to his? When did the dissipation of body and heart begin?

"I'm ready," he announced.

"Oh, Jules, why don't you put on a shirt," she said. "You'll burn to a crisp." She took a shirt from the beach bag and handed it to him. He put it on, looking a bit contrite.

Arms loaded with their motley burdens, the family trudged across the warm sand toward the cool brine. Virginia unfurled a blanket, which fluttered in the sea breeze from her outstretched hands. "Help me, somebody, or I'll fly away." Each took a corner, laughing at its writhing antics as they pressed the ballooning cloth against the sand. Jules's usually hard, chiseled features broke into a broad grin. Virginia couldn't help but notice. The moment felt thrillingly familiar. From the welter of her memories, she found the incident: a blanket, a sea breeze, and a young couple. Did he, too, remember, back before his ambition consumed him, when they shared the dream of a summer haven by the sea? She asked herself, when did those earlier days of simple love and flowing communion end?

The children raced off to a sandbar almost invisible under the water. The hectic crosscurrents plowed onto the strand like a mournful drum roll.

"Isn't it dangerous out there?" Jules asked.

"Not really. The water is quite shallow," said Virginia.

"But when the tide returns…"

"They know when to come in. You needn't worry."

Jules speared the umbrella into the sand, then crouched in its shade watching his cavorting children. "Very enjoyable here," he conceded.

Sitting, arms locked around her knees, Virginia sighed. "You relax so seldom." Her red-skirted bathing suit revealed firm thighs, curved surfaces of brown sheen.

"I can't help it." His face tightened, his deep eyes narrowing to slits in the strong sun.

She groped for a reply that would encourage his, but when her words emerged they were tinged with sadness. "You used to know how."

There were few people on the beach at this hour. Jules stood up and scanned the shore. He counted a half dozen umbrellas whipping in the wind.

"The business is big now. So are the problems. I have no choice." His voice was tight, his mouth rigid.

Rising, she confronted his averted gaze. "We have a problem, too," she said. She watched his foot make a gash in the sand. "And the problem is you."

"Don't worry about me," he said.

"Oh, I don't. I worry about us, and about them." She stretched an arm toward the children.

His eyes burrowed deeply into hers. "This is the way it has to be."

"For heaven's sake, why?" she asked. "Is it for the money? Don't we have enough of that?"

She shuddered, abruptly aware of her folly. Their hours together were scant enough. What pleasure could be eked from them now that he was here in body only? It's too late to make up for what they had lost, she thought with regret.

His intent gaze followed the children disappearing in the foam. His face relaxed when he saw them emerge again.

Had they been in a room together, Jules would have condemned his wife to an agony of silence by walking out. But here on the beach, cowered by roaring space, he seemed compelled to reply.

"I must keep winning," he said.

She withheld an urge to sob. "Why?" Her voice became plaintive. "It's only your pride."

They saw the boy and girl prancing through the shallows toward them, shouting lustily. "Daddy, Daddy, come in. It's terrific!"

Jules welcomed the distraction. Virginia barely had time to veil her emotions with a smile. The children's glossy brown bodies heaved with energy and excitement. How straight their backs, how graceful and free their motions, she thought. Even Jules marveled at their agility.

"Let's ride the breakers together, Dad!" The boy tugged at his father's arms while the girl pushed from behind.

"Not today, son. Some other time."

"When?" Virginia asked derisively.

"Aw, c'mon, Dad," the children bleated in unison.

After letting them drag him along, Jules suddenly sprinted for the water, leaving the youngsters panting behind. "He's going in!" they screamed, waving back at their mother without turning, for their father was offering an indescribable gift.

Perched on her knees, Virginia watched the three figures romping together, fixing the sight in her mind to be savored again and again. She swayed to their twists and turns, barely resisting bursting from her spot to join them.

"There's a big one!" the girl yelled, pointing to a green swell rolling heavily toward them. The three of them waited, poised for the climax. "Catch it at the crest, Daddy!" the girl screamed.

As the huge wave gathered, leapt up, and arched, they flung themselves into it. A boiling froth descended, churning gray and white, flailing their bodies with piercing points of spray and bubbling into their ears.

But when the surge unraveled, only two bodies could be seen gliding into the gentler shallows. Only the children arose, bleary eyed and gasping.

Virginia was running toward them in panic, arms gesticulating, mouth gaping in silent screams carried away by the wind. The children stared about for a sign of their father, and found nothing. Virginia reached their side, hysterical, clutching them to her as if the water swirling at their feet still claimed them.

They didn't see Jules's limp body sliding along the pebbly sea floor toward deeper water. He had dived too early and missed the wave's crucial instant of cresting. As the thunderous torrent poured down, it drove him to the bottom, stunning him. He had tried to rise, to find a footing, but a great tidal recoil had begun, reeling him backward. It had swept him under as he thrashed and fought. Then, realizing he was powerless, for the first time in his life he submitted.

In the murky quiet of the ocean bottom, stark thoughts spun through Jules's mind. Feeling a cold loneliness, he yearned for the warm touch of his wife's hand. He wanted only that before his next watery breath; then he could accept dying. Strangely, his family, those who loved him, now mattered. He was overcome with remorse mingled with fear. He prayed, "Let me some-how survive and I will give myself to my family." He real-ized he really did need them.

Suddenly Jules bobbed to the surface in a trough between gently toppling white peaks. Sating his lungs with delicious air, he lay back, enthralled by the glaring blue sky. As he floated on a swell, he sighted the beach. Barely making out a cluster of swarming figures, he be-gan swimming slowly toward shore.

"Shh, children." Virginia crossed her lips with her finger. Her thin cotton robe hung loosely from her nar-row shoulders, almost to her ankles. The children loi-tered behind her asking about their father as she bent over the stove preparing supper. She, too, was anxious over Jules's prolonged slumber, having regularly visit-ed the bedroom to listen to his breathing. "I'll call you when he wakes up," she told them. "Now stay on the porch and try to be quiet."

A darkening red sky glimmered behind the scrub pines to the west. The wind of the day had died; only the drone of the sea intruded on the land's quiet. The dampness of the evening reached through the cottage's thin walls.

Virginia reviewed the day so full of terror, now calm in its retreat. Jules loved her; she knew that now. How fearful that moment had been when she heard an on-looker on the beach shout, "I see him! See? Out there!" pointing to an object rising on the billows far out, then dropping from sight. Tearing herself from her children's arms, she had plunged into the incoming waves as if by instinct. When she finally reached him, his bulging eyes flickered with recognition. His arms, slowly slapping the water like mechanical rods, never stopped as together they gained on the shore, tossing, rising, then crawling at last to hard sand, where they lay crumpled and exhausted. She heard a whispered "thank-you", and opened her welling eyes wondering whether the runnels she saw coursing down his temples were tears or droplets from the sea.

From the porch, Virginia could see that the sky's red glow was gone now; dusk was deepening to darkness. A low half moon cast a shimmering white streak across the black water. Hearing Jules's soft steps behind her, Virginia turned to the doorway. His drawn face jutted from his open white collar.

She walked over to him and took his hand. "How do you feel?" she asked.

He smiled wanly. "Never better."

"Would you like some supper?"

"Yes, that would be good."

While she stood at the stove stirring broth, her back to him, he sat at the table, hands folded on the scratched surface. Then his eyes caught his briefcase on the floor in the corner. In a moment his bony fingers began fidgeting, drumming against the wooden tabletop. He squirmed, legs twining and untwining.

"I know you planned to leave today," Virginia said cautiously. He got up from the table and walked over to his old leather briefcase and retrieved some papers. "Couldn't you stay the rest of the week with us, Jules?"

He dug his eyes into the documents as her voice waned to a background chant.

"We could do things as a family. Did you know there's a beautiful freshwater lake nearby? It's a wonderful place to swim. Unless, of course, you've had your fill of water." She grimaced at her bad joke. "And we could take a side trip to Provincetown and visit the art galleries," she continued. "The children would love that. Do you know our daughter has a flair with a paintbrush?" Virginia's face was serene, eyes glittering with joy, gaiety in the chatter spilling from her brimming heart. "We could go out to dinner…the four of us. Perhaps tomorrow night. It's been years, Jules. Would you like to…"

The springs on the screen door squeaked. "Jules!" Swinging around, she gaped at the quivering screen door, at his vacant chair and empty soup bowl. His papers were gone. A dripping spoon hung from her limp hand as she raced to the porch in time to see his car's tail lights fade into the gloom.

"Time for bed, children," she murmured. But they couldn't hear, for her voice merged with the moaning sea and was lost.

THE WATERFALL

"Hey, another one is coming in. Look fellas, look!" shouted one of my mates.

From our campsite atop a barren hill, we could see the ships arriving in the bay below. They moved slowly up the inlet and tied up to the docks we had built.

"Do you think this could be the one?" I asked.

"Naw, that one's too small to hold our battalion," said another mate. "I'm beginning to think they're gonna let us rot out here. Cripes, the war's been over for two months already."

A third mate chimed in. "It wouldn't be so bad if it wasn't so damn hot. It's really kinda nice here except for the heat."

"Amen," I said.

The top of our hill was part of the crest that rimmed one side of a verdant valley. The valley floor, a vast grassy field dotted with random clumps of trees, extended for three to four miles to an impenetrable tropical forest which terminated at the foot of a cone-shaped mountain that rose into the sky like a backdrop. In the early evening, the mountain was a gateway to the sun before its golden light disappeared behind the peak.

"It ain't only the heat," my complaining mate continued. "What gets me is the waiting. Always waiting. I'm goin' nuts from boredom."

Disappointed, we all turned our backs on the bay and headed for our tent, where we would lie on our cots even in the heat of the day, as the broiling tent roof seemed to be pressing down on us. All of us, that is, except my friend Jerry, who lingered and stood gazing up the valley toward the mountain. In fact, he had ignored the ship coming in.

"C'mon, Jerry. Let's go back to the tent," I said.

"Have you ever seen the mountain in the early morning?"

"Yes," I replied, joining his gaze. "It's really beautiful, all golden when the sun first strikes it."

"It's the waterfall that gets me," he said. "You've noticed it, haven't you? Look, it's glistening now in the sun, about three quarters of the way to the top."

Against the mountain's hazy green flank, I observed a streak sparkling like polished chrome.

"When the sun drops behind the mountain, the waterfall becomes invisible," I said.

"Have you ever watched the sun sit on the mountain peak in the evening," he said, "then set behind the peak and radiate a red halo? It's magical. It's mysterious. How do you suppose it happens?"

"What happens? What are you talking about?"

"The waterfall. The water. How does a waterfall come to exist so high up a mountainside?" Jerry's eyes fastened on the threadlike cascade, silent in the distance. It disappeared into the forest, but then it reappeared again as a fast-flowing ribbon on the valley floor and finally emptied into the bay.

"Let's go back to the tent, Jerry, before we get sunstroke."

"Not yet. I'm waiting here for Dolores."

As he spoke, I spied the woman walking toward us up the hill. She glided like a moving statue while balancing a bundle of laundry on her head. As she drew near, her dress appeared brilliant white against her smooth olive brown skin.

"Jerry," she cried, waving her arms. "My *magunda lalaki.*"

"What is she saying?" I asked.

Jerry waved back and blushed. "It means 'handsome boy.'"

"Is that so?" I said, grinning, causing his blush to deepen. "Hey, Dolores," I shouted, "do you have my trousers?"

Going around either in my underwear or stark naked, I hadn't worn trousers for a week. Since we were scheduled to embark for home any day now, no new clothes had been issued to replace the ones that were worn out.

"Yes, here they are," she said as she approached. She put down the basket and handed me a neatly folded stack of washed clothes. I envied Jerry as Dolores smiled at him with love in her eyes.

"Are we going swimming today, Jerry?" she asked.

Jerry usually walked Dolores back to her thatched hut by the stream several miles deep into the valley where the field verged on the forest. There the two would swim and play in the cool current through the heat of the afternoon. Later, after the glare of the sun had eased, Dolores would begin the laundry, beating her customers' clothes against a smooth rock on the stream bank while Jerry napped in the shade of nearby palms. His afternoons were idyllic by any measure. No wonder he had no interest in the arriving ship. Who in his circumstances would be in a hurry to leave such a paradise?

"I won't be swimming with you this afternoon, Dolores," said Jerry. She lowered her eyes in disappointment. "But I'll walk you back to the hut." Her dark eyes brightened with delight.

"What's wrong, Jerry? Aren't you feeling well that you won't swim?" she asked.

Jerry laughed. Dolores's concern amused him. "I'm fine. I'm going on a trip. But don't worry, I'll be back."

"Where on earth are you going?" I asked.

"To the waterfall," he replied.

"Jerry, you promised you wouldn't. Please don't go," Dolores implored.

"I'm sorry," Jerry said, "I've got to do it. I've made up my mind."

"I'm begging you not to go, Jerry. You know there are still Japanese back there, and savages," she pleaded.

"She's right, Jerry," I said. "It will take a week or more just to get through the forest and up the mountain. In only a couple of days you'd be AWOL."

"Look, I've been watching that waterfall for months. I won't rest until I discover its source."

"I told you where it comes from," said Dolores.

"You know its source, Dolores?" I asked, surprised.

"My people say there is a big lake in the mountain."

"I don't believe it," said Jerry. "The waterfall is too far up. There isn't enough room for a lake. Anyway, the lake is nothing but a Filipino legend. No one can tell me they've seen it or know anybody who has. If there's a lake, which I doubt, I'll confirm it myself."

"You'll never get back in time to board the ship, if at all," I warned. "When the ship comes in to take us home, you'll miss it."

"I'm willing to take that chance. I can't go back to the States without knowing. My duffle bag is already packed with food. I'll put on some clothes and we'll start, okay Dolores? We'll walk together as far as your hut, and then I'll go on alone."

I persisted. "If the commander hears of this, you'll end up in the brig."

"I don't care. After I'm back they can punish me all they want. At least I'll have the answer."

"Let me go with you to the lake," said Dolores, embracing him.

"No way, Dolores. It would be much too difficult for a woman."

"I could stand it better than you," she said, indignant.

"Anyway, I have only enough food for one, so that settles it." Jerry was adamant. "I'll tell you all about it after I return."

"I don't care to know," she said. "I'm happy about the lake whether or not there really is one."

The two went to our tent, where Jerry put on jeans and a blue chambray shirt. Wearing a pith helmet to protect his head from the sun, he led the way down the path with Dolores following. After reaching her hut by the stream, he plunged into the jungle alone.

I never saw Dolores again. She no longer visited our camp seeking clothes to wash. Perhaps when Jerry said good-bye at her hut, she knew it would be the end of their relationship. Whether she lost him while he searched for his fountainhead, or whether she lost him when he returned to the States, lose him she knew she must.

Two and a half weeks later, Jerry straggled into camp. His clothes were in tatters and his body and face had fresh bloody scratches. He had lost a considerable amount of weight. He was immediately taken into custody by the company lieutenant and confined to the brig. I next saw Jerry two weeks later at the summary court martial, which the lieutenant requested I attend, hoping that I could enlighten the court as to why Jerry had disappeared, and to where. Jerry had refused to offer any explanation.

The commander was seated behind his desk, flanked by the lieutenant, an ensign junior officer and a warrant officer. Guards escorted Jerry into the steaming Quonset hut and left him in front of them. Jerry appeared rested, even contented, albeit much thinner. I sat next to the guards off to the side along a wall.

"What has this boy done?" demanded the commander to anyone who would answer, it seemed.

"He went AWOL for eighteen days, sir," the lieutenant said.

"Let's see...they call you Jerry," said the commander, rifling through some papers on his desk. "Where did you go, Jerry? To Manila to have a good time?"

"No, sir," Jerry replied standing at ramrod attention.

"At ease, lad. I thought everyone who went AWOL went to Manila. Well, if not Manila, where then?"

"To the mountain, sir."

"To the mountain? What mountain?" demanded the commander as he searched the face of each officer to his left and right.

"The mountain at the back of the valley, sir," said Jerry.

"Did you know this?" the commander asked the lieutenant.

"Yes, sir. I learned it from that man over there a few days after he went missing." He pointed toward me.

"And you didn't send any men after him?"

"No, sir. I thought it was too risky. We might have lost a few men just to save one damn fool...I mean one man, sir."

"I see," said the commander, appearing mollified.

"Tell me, lad, why did you trek up that mountain? Why would you do a damn fool thing like that?"

"I don't think you would understand, sir."

"Understand! Who are you to say who would or would not understand? You're a mighty audacious youngster. Now you'd better answer my question, do you hear?" The commander's face had turned beet red.

"Yes, sir." Jerry shifted from foot to foot.

"Well, I'm waiting."

"I just wanted to learn the source of the waterfall, sir."

At this the ensign burst out laughing. One of the guards jostled me as the commander's jaw dropped in astonishment.

"You mean the waterfall on the side of the mountain, of course," said the commander, motioning toward the window behind him.

"Yes, sir. You know it, sir?"

"I'll ask the questions, young man. Yes, I've seen it. You say you were seeking its source?"

"I was curious as to its source, sir. There's a legend..."

"I've heard it. The natives believe it's a lake."

"Yes, sir."

"I think you've done a foolhardy thing. You risked your life, you risked missing the ship back to the States, and you risked marring an otherwise perfect record in the Seabees. Did you realize this before you left?"

"Yes, sir, I did. But I just had to find out before I went home."

"I see." The commander turned to his officers. "Well, gentlemen, what punishment do you think he should receive?"

"I'd confine him to the brig until we board ship for the States, sir," said the warrant officer.

"And you?" he nodded to the lieutenant.

"I think he deserves that, sir."

"All right then, to the brig he goes." The commander made a short sweep with his hand. "You're all dismissed."

The guards took Jerry by each arm to lead him out as the others left the room.

"Just a minute," said the commander. "Leave the lad here. Wait outside until I call you."

The commander turned to the window behind his desk and gazed at the valley spread before him. He studied the mountain in the distance and the narrow streak down its side, sparkling like tinsel in the sun. He remained silent while Jerry stood at attention before his desk. Then he turned, faced Jerry, and searched his eyes.

"Tell me, son, did you find a lake up there? I'd like to know."

NOT A CHINAMAN'S CHANCE

"I presume you're the plaintiff," Judge Donovan said, looking at me from his elevated paneled bench. I clutched the arms of my chair as I sat at a table on the main floor.

"Yes, Your Honor," I said, pleased to know the proper address from having watched many courtroom dramas on TV.

Across the aisle at a table to my right sat the defendant, a slender man of Chinese extraction. The courtroom was softly lit. It had a hallowed quality.

I had filled out a form called a Statement of Claim and Notice of Trial at the office of the third district court in town. In eight lines of ruled space I wrote: "Via UPS on 8/27 I received my computer damaged, which defendant allegedly repaired. Its hard disk and floppy disk drives were inoperable and its case was broken. Defendant refuses to repair machine to original condition or to replace it. Cause of damage: machine was incorrectly assembled and poorly packed in its carton."

None of this betrayed the anger I felt toward Jim Yee, the president of the Dependable Computer Company.

We'd had a bristling phone conversation when I had advised him of the dire state of my computer.

"Don't bother me," he had said with a slurred Chinese accent. "I too busy."

"You mean you won't fix it? You don't see your responsibility in this?"

"You not ship computer to us in proper carton."

I knew that the carton had arrived in good condition; the computer was the problem. It was a phony excuse.

"The carton has nothing to do with it," I said. "Your technician failed to assemble and pack the machine correctly."

"Look, I just back from out of town and I got more important things to do. I not talk with you."

"Well, then maybe you can talk with my lawyer," I threatened.

"Your lawyer! Listen, I going to hang up, see. So bullshit." Click!

Judge Donovan, a ruddy, moon-faced man with wire-rimmed glasses, smiled as he laced his comments with satire.

"I suppose, if you're the plaintiff as you say, it would make sense for you to start, if you don't mind."

"Your Honor, may I read a letter I had written to Dependable Computer to explain what happened?" That way I wouldn't have to deal with stage fright or worry about leaving something out.

The judge nodded.

Somewhere in the midst of my recitation, I sensed that it wasn't convincing. It lacked the intense anger I'd felt. Sticking only to facts, the letter lacked conviction. I looked up. The judge appeared bored, but he waved me to go on. I finished and sat down.

Before the hearing, I thought I'd win hands down because the evidence spoke for itself. As my wife and I and a group of twenty or so litigants waited in the lobby to have our cases heard, I scanned the crowd for Jim Yee, whom I had never met.

"Do you think he'll really show?" my wife asked, as convinced as I that the case was open and shut in my favor. "Why would he bother to travel more than two hours and spend most of a day defending an unjustifiable position?"

"Jim Yee would," I said, spotting an Asian male in the crowd. "That's our man over there."

"How do you know?"

"He's puffing nervously at a cigarette and pacing like a fiend…that has to be the man I argued with over the phone."

I sensed his drive, his determination to be right. I asked myself, "*Why do most Asians and Jews in America excel at everything they do? What are they trying to prove?*"

Jim Yee must have seen me looking at him. He approached me as I stood hunched against a wall.

"You the plaintiff?" he demanded.

"That's right," I said.

"How come you so insistent? Don't you know you should go to UPS and file claim?"

"You mean the computer was insured?"

"'Course it insured. I told you before."

"This is the first time I've heard it," I said. It was a smoke screen. "Anyway, how can I file a claim when I didn't ship the package?"

"'Course you can. Person who receives always files claim."

"No, Jim, the person who ships, who contracts with the freight company, has to file. I have no paperwork, no information on when it was shipped or if it was insured. Can you give me proof of insurance?"

"You file claim."

"Look, when I used to be in business, I shipped by UPS a lot and…"

"We don't make your computer anymore. Is obsolete. What do you want from us?"

"Either fix it to its original condition or replace it."

"You goddamn crazy," he fumed, and zigzagged across the lobby, stopping only to light another cigarette.

"He's heading for a heart attack," said my wife. "Why is the president of a company spending time fighting for fifteen hundred dollars?"

"He's the kind of man who can't tolerate losing," I said. "I feel sorry for him."

In Jim Yee I saw myself, refusing to submit, proud, needing to succeed.

The judge asked me, "What is the name of the computer?"

"It's a Dependable computer, Your Honor."

"The name of the computer is Dependable?"

"Yes, Your Honor."

"Then it would seem obvious that they are the proper people to return it to, wouldn't you say?"

"I had, Your Honor," I replied.

"All right, now let's hear the defendant."

Jim Yee's defense was long and incoherent. "I want you to know what I think. I think this man is trying to build a fake case. That's what I say, a fake case. He is computer consultant who purchased machine for re-sale. He purchased it for niece. I have records to show this. I warranty computer for one year but it not under warranty anymore, so what does he expect? I am not responsible after warranty is over. I must tell you I am president of Dependable. I have been in business many years, and I know how to assemble computers from long experience. Now this man tells me I don't know how to assemble computer. He is building fake case, you see."

I was fuming. What's a warranty got to do with it? At no time had I asked Dependable to repair the computer for free. Jim Yee had laid down a smoke screen. Wouldn't my factual presentation dispose of his claim?

"What do you have to say?" the judge asked me after hearing Yee's little speech.

"I am not a computer consultant, never have been. I'm a writer. And I don't have any nieces, only a nephew."

Judge Donovan grinned as Jim Yee muttered, "Niece and nephew are same in Chinese."

"Well, at least you have a sense of humor," said the judge, congratulating Jim Yee.

"Is that all, sir?" the judge said, turning to me.

I nodded. That was all.

The courtroom became quiet as the judge shuffled some papers.

From nowhere this ridiculous thought crossed my mind: "*At Gettysburg, men died in beautiful rolling green fields under a blue sky.*" Well, wasn't I dying without a chance to win on the battlefield of the courtroom?

Then the judge turned to Jim Yee. "Do you have anything more to say?"

"As I say," Jim Yee reiterated, "he is trying to make fake case. What does he want? New computer? We don't make his kind of computer anymore. It now old fashioned. New computer would cost, let's see, fifteen hundred forty-two dollars. So you see, impossible. I tell him collect from UPS since he pay freight. We never pay freight. It insured. But no, he want new computer. Impossible. That all I say."

I spoke up: "Your Honor, in my letter, in the part I didn't read, I requested that my machine be replaced with an identical machine or an equivalent one."

The judge nodded. "Okay, gentlemen," he said. "I shall take your testimony under advisement. You will be notified of my verdict."

Adolf Eichmann, master organizer of the death camps during World War II, never had a chance when he was tried in Israel. The evidence was overwhelming. But even if it weren't, the need for Jewish retribution was. The judges had made up their minds in advance.

The whole truth had not been told. Although I accepted the judge's dismissal, I offered him my letter for his review.

"If you wish," he said.

Jim Yee, not to be bested, offered some papers as well.

Addressing Jim Yee, the judge asked, "Are you related to Yee, the chairman of International Computer?"

That Yee was a famous industrialist and philanthropist. Jim Yee was a nephew. The judge seemed impressed. I turned to the rows of benches where my wife sat. She smiled weakly.

"I didn't do a very good job, did I?" I said as I sat beside her. "I know I've lost."

"I should have gone up there with you," she said.

"He put up a smoke screen. I didn't know how to deal with it. I figured the judge would see through it. But he didn't."

"You asked me to go with you," she said, "but I was too nervous. The two of us would have done better."

"It was my responsibility, not yours. Don't blame yourself."

"But I do."

I placed my arm around her waist as we walked to the exit door.

"Why didn't I defend myself better? Why didn't I challenge Jim Yee's testimony? I don't understand."

"You're too hard on yourself," she said. "Maybe the judge will go by the facts."

"No, I know I lost." I paused for a moment. "I think I wanted to lose. I don't know why I think that. I'm a mystery to myself.

Through the rest of the day and that evening, I beat on myself.

Did Christ defend himself? Did Socrates, Galileo? Silence is defiance.

Although I hadn't been entirely silent, I hadn't defended myself enough.

At dinner I had no appetite. Watching TV, my mind wandered to the courtroom drama. I hashed it over again and again, imagining what I should have said. I envisioned myself in the same league as Edmund Burke and Mark Anthony, my words making Jim Yee flinch and Judge Donovan applaud.

As we lay in bed later that night, I said to my wife, "I let you down. I'm sorry."

"Why do you say such a thing?"

"You deserve a man who stands up for himself."

She reached to embrace me, but I pulled away. "I'm sorry," I said. "I'm too preoccupied right now. I want to be left alone."

Weary, feeling down, I fell asleep without waiting for the late news. At 3:22 in the morning I awoke from a frightening dream in which I pounded the sheets and beat my head with a clenched fist. I sat up shaking.

As they pray, Jews strike their heads against the Wailing Wall in Jerusalem.

Why was I turning against myself, even in my dreams?

"What's wrong?" my wife whispered.

"Go to sleep," I said.

"It's the Dependable thing, isn't it?"

"I can't seem to drop it."

"Want to talk about it?"

"So I've lost fifteen hundred dollars. Big deal."

"I don't think the money has anything to do with it."

"It's that I didn't defend myself. Something about the judge made me want to give up. He was powerful and I felt weak. I didn't have a Chinaman's chance."

"Did you think he was prejudiced?" my Gentile wife asked.

"You mean against Jews?'

"Yes."

"He's Irish Catholic. In my grammar school most of the kids were Irish Catholic, and I was often the butt of their Jew hating. I got in a fistfight once with a bully who called me a Christ killer."

"Did you defend yourself?"

"I knocked him out. Or rather he passed out when his head accidentally struck the brick wall of the school building. He never bothered me after that."

The Jews of the Warsaw ghetto battled the Nazis until their deaths. But most Jews meekly boarded the cattle cars and let the Nazis take them to concentration camps to be exterminated. Two Jewish paths to dying.

"I've never understood why you turned your back on your religion," she said.

"I don't believe in God. Any god," I said.

Karl Marx, a Jew, said religion is the "opiate of the people." Freud, a Jew, had no use for a god.

"It's not necessary to believe in God to be a Jew. Being a Jew can't be denied, but I reject the Jewish community."

"God's chosen people," said my wife.

"Yeah, chosen to be the world's victims. When things went bad for the Gentiles in France during the Middle Ages, the Jews were blamed and massacred. They were kicked out of Spain in 1492 for their success. My grandparents fled the Cossack pogroms in Russia. It goes on through the Holocaust. But I share the pain no matter what I believe…for my self-respect. I can't escape."

My wife lay silently next to me. Through the glass doors to the balcony we could see the bare tree branches swaying in the wind in the dawn light. The ugly, beautiful, unjust, innocent, mindless outside invaded the room.

"I didn't ask to be born a Jew."

My wife reached over and covered my hand with hers.

If a Black man in America had the chance to be white, would he take it?

"I'm ashamed…of being a Jew, a Christ killer. All my life I've wanted to be accepted as an American, nothing else. I blame my people for being victims. I hate them for it. I hate myself for being one of them."

I curled up like a baby in the warmth of my wife's embrace.

"Until now, I never knew I was ashamed. I never knew I hated Jews. I never knew I hated who I am."

"Let it pour out," my wife whispered.

"That's why I had to do better than anyone else. I'd show them I'm as good as they are. And I did. I'm a success."

We lay wrapped together in silence for a long time.

Decades ago, Israel defeated the invading Egyptians and Syrians in six days. It was a victory that made every Jew in the world proud. It made me *proud.*

"Christ," I said, "all my life I've had it all wrong. I'm as good as anybody. I *am* worth something."

Thanks, Judge Donovan, you son-of-a-bitch.

The following Monday I received a Notice of Judgment in the mail. It said, "The court found judgment in favor of the defendant. This means that the defendant does not have to pay the plaintiff any part of the claim or costs in this case."

So the verdict. And so I lost. And in the losing, I discovered myself.

A LONG, LONG SLEEP

At 2 a.m. on a starry November night, Reverend Miller stood in the frosty air waiting for Ann to answer the doorbell. Not wishing to wake the sleeping children, he had pressed the bell only three times, and only briefly. But now he pressed it hard for a good thirty seconds. At last, the lock clicked and the door opened a few inches. He heard Ann's sleepy voice.

"Who is it? Forgot your keys? Is it you, Don?"

If only it were, thought Reverend Miller. Two hours earlier he had said good-bye to the young couple, the last to leave the gathering at his home.

"Feeling better now?" he asked, addressing Don as they departed.

"Oh, I'm all right. Just a little indigestion," Don said.

"You shouldn't have had all those drinks," Ann said, ushering her husband out the door. "You know how drinking disagrees with you."

"Drive carefully, now. God bless you," had been the minister's parting words.

On recognizing her visitor, Ann swept open the door. The minister stepped in with a rush of cold air, snapping her alert.

"Don, where's Don?" she said. She looked as though she was trying to locate him in her mind.

Then she remembered. "Go to bed," he had said. "Don't wait up. I'll be right back." She had heard the car tires crunch against the gravel as he backed out of the driveway to take the babysitter home.

Turning her eyes to the kitchen clock, Ann gasped. She had been asleep for two hours. Feeling Ann's wide eyes following him, Reverend Miller sat down in the maple captain's chair beside the kitchen table.

"Please sit down," he said to her.

She sat on the edge of the chair opposite him and stared into his tense face. Her jaw worked before words came.

"What's happened to Don?"

The minister reached for her hand across the table. "His car hit a tree," he said. Her hand clenched his like a tight cord. "Ann, he didn't make it."

She withdrew her hand, suddenly limp, and placed it with her other in her lap. They sat saying nothing for several minutes, she gazing off into blurred space, he searching her eyes for a sign of awareness.

A shuffle of feet sounded and a little curly haired girl, rubbing her squinting eyes, entered the kitchen.

"I'm thirsty, Mommy," she said as she crept onto her mother's lap.

Ann hugged her to her breast as her eyes filled up. She rocked the child back and forth.

"I'm thirsty, Mommy," the girl said again.

Ann set her on the floor, walked to the steel sink, and filled a glass with water. Between sips the child asked," Where's Daddy? Asleep?"

"Yes, asleep. A long, long sleep."

The child returned the half-full glass to her mother. "Come, I'll put you back in bed."

As she lifted the child into her arms, she turned to Reverend Miller.

"I'm all right, Reverend."

"I'd like to stay for a while, if I may."

Ann nodded and disappeared into the dark hallway with the child in her arms. After she tucked her in, she kissed her, then bent over the next bed and kissed her older sister. "You're all that's left," she whispered, and headed back into the kitchen to be with Reverend Miller, who sat with her waiting for her tears.

"I don't understand. God is so cruel," she said.

The reverend searched for an answer. "It's not for us to understand, but to accept."

"Never, never." And then the tears came, and he drew her close. Above it all, he knew, people have only one another. He could offer only his presence and his compassion.

A VISIT TO PARADISE

One guy in our tent was hard to figure. As I remember, I was the only one who thought so. The rest of the men were sure he had a woman, which would explain why he disappeared from camp every time we had liberty. Sure, everybody disappeared from camp when they had liberty, but when they came back, they talked about it. You knew where they went and what they did. The stories were always colorful because usually the guys got drunk and raised hell or they visited a prostitute. Even if they did neither, they always said they did.

Whenever Fred came back to camp after liberty, he never told anybody where he had been. When anyone asked him about it, he'd laugh and say, "I've been out looking over the country." Once when he came back, one of the guys asked, "How was she?"

"Very nice, very nice," he answered, and then went back to reading.

Fred read practically all the time. He didn't play cards with the rest of us. He didn't talk about women. He didn't knock the officers. He didn't gripe. He worked like a son-of-a-gun no matter what he did, even digging ditches. Because he seemed apart from us, we probably would have hated him except that he was always congenial. Nobody gave him much thought. Except me.

I was a kid then, about nineteen years old. I figured Fred was lonely, so I tried to become his friend. I didn't do this wholly to make him feel good, though. I expected to get something out of it, maybe a new way of looking at things. For instance, Fred read books. I'd never read a book that a teacher didn't require. Fred had a volume of Shakespeare in his footlocker. I can remember seeing *War and Peace* and *Walden*. He had *The Magic Mountain*; before I returned to the States, I had read it. It was the first book I'd read of my own accord. I've been reading ever since.

We never became close friends...friends who could speak to each other about what was on their minds and in their hearts. We became just friends. Maybe that's why, when he left camp on liberty, he didn't invite me to go with him. And for some reason I don't understand, I never asked to go. I guess I sensed that what he did away from camp, he wanted to do alone.

I didn't think he had a woman, though. It didn't fit him. And if he did have a woman, it wasn't the way the others had women. Fred would have had to love the woman. No, I figured that Fred had something else going on when he left camp. It had to be something in the same league as his books and his need to be alone. I looked for clues. They were probably there, but I wasn't sharp enough to notice them. He actually gave me the biggest clue—I can say that now in hindsight—a couple of weeks before I found out what he was really doing. He got into an awful fight with Whitey, and what he said about it gave him away.

Whitey, I should tell you, was a mixed-up guy. That's the best way to explain him. He never knew what he was doing or why he was doing it. He didn't care much about anything except getting back to the States. He raised more hell when he was on liberty than anybody else in the battalion. I think he had the clap at least a half dozen times; and when the doc asked him who he'd caught it from, he refused to tell. "I love her, Doc, I love her." That's all he'd say, and then he'd go back to her and catch it again. We called him Whitey because his hair was as white as a poodle's. It hung down over his eyes like a poodle's, too. Back then there were no "buzz cut" requirements while overseas. I used to wonder how a man could go through life seeing the world through hair.

Whitey did have one deep secret that I should mention. He had a liquor still, which he spent weeks pounding together out of scrap sheet metal. The din of his pounding kept us awake at night. He pounded only at night when everybody had hit the sack so nobody could see what he was doing. It was supposed to be a secret, after all.

He kept the still somewhere in the jungle and fed it pineapple and grapefruit juice, which he stole from the commissary. No one could ever find the contraption. Sometimes even Whitey couldn't find it, and he'd return to the tent all scratched up from his frantic searching in the thick brush with his gallon can empty. Usually, though, he'd return with the can filled halfway; we could hear the stuff sloshing inside. Then, already half lit, he'd lie on his bunk and lift the can to his lips. With some of the liquid running down behind his ears, he'd guzzle and gurgle like an ecstatic baby.

One afternoon, two Filipino girls came by to deliver our laundry. They were quiet, polite kids who did a good job for us, and we left them alone. They always amazed me. They'd walk up the hill to our camp in their white dresses in the high afternoon sun, which beat on them like a blowtorch. Yet when they got to us, while we dripped with sweat just lying in our bunks, they would appear cool and composed.

That afternoon Fred was lying in his bunk, reading as usual. I was sitting on my bunk, bent over my footlocker writing a letter. Two guys were playing poker at the table in the center of the tent. Whitey was drinking, but he stopped when he saw the girls enter. The girls walked over to me first and gave me my stack of washed and ironed laundry, and I paid them. Then they went to Fred who put down his book to take his laundry, and he paid them, saying "thank you" in English.

Next they approached Whitey, but they hesitated. It was hardly perceptible. But then one of the girls moved closer to hand him his laundry when Whitey's arm shot out like a snake's tongue and grabbed the girl's arm.

"Come in here with me, you Gook," he said, pulling her on top of him in his bunk. When he tried to rip off her dress, she screamed. The other girl went for Whitey and began beating him in the face. When the poker players saw her beating their buddy, they pulled her away. It took both of them to do it.

I was sort of paralyzed. If I hadn't been, I'd have run for help. What Fred did snapped me out of it. He smashed his book to the floor, leapt to Whitey's bunk, and pulled the first girl away from him. Whitey stood up looking stunned. Fred yelled something to the girls in their native language. The one held by the poker players wriggled free, and both girls fled. The three men stood there facing Fred.

"Why in hell did you do that?" Whitey demanded. Fred didn't answer; he just went back to his cot where he sat calming himself. "You know what Fred is, fellas?" Whitey said, "a gook lover."

"Yeah," one of the other guys said. "Did'ya hear the way he spoke their language? Where'd you learn it, Freddie? Say, I thought you were beginning to look pretty damned dark for a GI."

Whitey lay back in his bunk again and lifted the gallon can to his lips. "Damn. When we gonna get out of this hellhole?" he muttered.

"You've made it hell, Whitey," said Fred. "You've made paradise hell."

And that was the end of that. Whitey drifted off to sleep. The poker players went back to their game. I tried to start my letter for the fifth time. And Fred lay on his bunk staring at the hot, sagging tent roof.

Two things about this incident had been clues to where Fred went and what he was doing on liberty. One was his mention of paradise, although he didn't refer to any definite place. The other clue was his speaking the native tongue, Tagalog, which was unusual for a GI because he couldn't have learned it anywhere but in the islands. A GI might pick up a few phrases from the laundry girls, or the other kind, so I didn't give it much thought. At the time, I considered what Fred did for the girls more significant. Who knows what Whitey might have done once he got started? Same for the poker players. I thought about it so much that I never did get my letter written. Fred had done a courageous, noble thing; those three guys could have clobbered him without much trouble. After all, Fred didn't seem the sort of guy who went in for fights.

I dropped my letter, walked over to Fred's bunk, and sat down. "Fred," I said, "I'm sorry I wasn't in there helping you."

"That's okay," he said without lowering his gaze from the roof.

"That was a pretty good thing you did," I told him.

"That was a pretty lousy thing *they* did," he said.

"I was scared, I guess."

"So was I," Fred said.

"They're not so bad," I said.

"Who?" he asked.

"The gooks," I said.

"No, they're not so bad…the gooks."

I had the feeling he was making fun of me. "I mean the Filipinos," I said.

He lowered his gaze and looked at me. "Do you know any of these people as friends?" he asked.

"No," I said.

"Well, they're just like friends everywhere."

"I would think so," I said.

"Except that they're warmer than we are, more accepting. We give them our laundry; they give us their hearts."

"As I said, I really don't know any."

"That's a shame," he said. "You really ought to."

One thing led to another, and soon he was mentioning people by name, and the names of places, becoming more animated than I had ever seen him in the three years we'd been together in the outfit. When he talked about the Filipinos, he used the words "humility," "childlike," and "simple." And when he talked about Americans, he used the words "arrogant," "uncivilized," and "lost."

Maybe because I listened and seemed so interested, he asked, "How'd you like to come with me on my next liberty?"

"Sure," I said. "Maybe it'll give me something to write home about. I don't know what to write about most of the time." In addition to being curious about where Fred went on his liberty, I figured the experience would give me that new way of looking at things.

Early on a Sunday morning, just as the sun was rising over the rim of the mountain range on the opposite side of the bay, Fred and I, carrying rucksacks on our shoulders, began our trip inland. When I asked him where we were headed, all he said was, "You'll see. Even if I told you, it wouldn't make any difference."

We walked along the shore of the bay for nearly a mile until we reached a cluster of native huts. The Filipinos were already up. The women were starting fires for cooking and the men were out in the bay fishing in their dugout canoes.

After Fred spoke to one of the women in dialect, she called her husband who came out of the hut, shook Fred's hand as they smiled at each other, and then led us to his canoe, or *banca* as he called it, beached at the water's edge. We climbed in, and he took us across the bay to Olongopo, a good-size village. We got out of the canoe, walked inland a little way to a two-lane concrete highway, and tried to hitch a ride. Soon an army truck heading north picked us up. We sat in the back watching the countryside fall away behind us. We crossed the Zambales mountain range, where we had seen the sun sneak out earlier. Beyond the mountains we dropped down and entered an enormous flat plain dotted in every direction with clumps of low trees. The clumps grew denser and, eventually, in the misty blue distance, became a forest. Then another mountain range appeared.

"Pampanga, the breadbasket of Luzon," Fred said. "Rice, sugarcane. Very rich land. But there's nothing growing here now except grass. The natives don't have seed."

The road was very straight and smooth. "Nice road," I said.

"For us, yes, the way we're traveling," Fred said. "But not so good a few years ago for some other Americans. This is the road they walked in the Death March from Bataan."

"No kidding," I said. "A nice concrete highway like this?" Somehow my words didn't come out right. I felt a little ashamed. Fred made no comment, for which I was grateful. We traveled for some time before he spoke.

"See that tree, that mango tree there beside the house?" I nodded. "An American from the March is buried beneath it."

"Yeah?" I said, very impressed. I asked myself, now how did he know that?

As if he had heard me, he answered. "Friend of mine buried him." After a pause he added, "Died in her arms."

"Her arms, her arms, her arms." The words kept repeating in my mind, because they caught me by surprise. I hadn't thought of a woman in connection with what he had been saying.

After we rode for an hour beyond Olongopo, Fred beat his fist on the cab roof, signaling the driver to let us off. The driver stopped and shouted up to us, "You mean here?"

We jumped off the truck. "Yeah. Thanks, fella," Fred said.

"What's out here?" the driver asked. "You're in the middle of nowhere."

Fred laughed. "This is the place," he said.

Shaking his head, the driver zoomed off in his ten-wheeler, leaving us standing at the entrance of a dirt road that headed into a dense clump of trees. The road was hardly more than a path, dotted here and there with puddles of water.

As we walked, Fred began going faster and soon I had to run to keep up. "Let's slow down, Fred. What's your hurry?" I said. Though he slowed down, I could see that he wanted to get going.

A group of kids, some half naked and some completely bare, were running to us. As they drew near, I could hear them yelling, "Fred, Fred! Americano! Co-musta, Fred?" When they reached us, they jumped all over him. He called them by their names and said something to them in Tagalog. They kept trying to get into his rucksack, so he stopped and opened it and gave each kid some gum and a candy bar. Waving their loot above their heads, they ran ahead of us shouting Fred's name. In a few minutes we entered a small village of thatched huts on stilts. But there was no one around, only the kids.

"Where are the adults?" I asked. Fred pointed to a small church at the end of the village street. As we walked toward it I could see that it was in bad shape, its corrugated metal roof patched with thatch matting, its masonry walls full of holes.

Approaching, I could hear a man's voice coming from the church, but couldn't make out his words. The kids had become suddenly quiet. Upon entering the building, we saw a hundred or so people seated on benches, some of which had backs and some not. The speaker on the dais stopped talking as the people all at once turned their heads toward us. From every direction I heard, "Psst, psst." Everybody was inviting us to sit beside them. The speaker, who I could tell had to be the clergyman, spoke perfect English without a trace of an accent.

"For the benefit of our American visitors, I shall continue my sermon in English." Then he said something in his native language. A murmur spread throughout the room and everybody nodded their heads, signifying, I guess, that they approved.

The minister talked about his gratitude toward the Americans. His speech was flowery; and everyone was staring at me. I was too uncomfortable to pay attention to his every word.

After the sermon, a plate was passed around. Fred dropped a couple of pesos into it, and I added an American half dollar. What a stir that caused. As the plate went around, everyone looked at it as if they were collectors finding a rare coin. When the plate got back to the minister, he retrieved the coin and held it up for everyone to see. Then he looked straight at me and said, "Thank you, my friend. Can you tell me how much this is worth?"

"A peso, I think," I replied.

"That's right, Reverend," Fred said.

"May I, with your permission, replace it with a peso," the reverend asked, "and retain this coin as a souvenir, a remembrance of your American generosity?"

Embarrassed, I nodded. The congregation sang some church songs in their own language, ones that I knew in English. The minister said a prayer which ended the service. The people crowded around us, chatting with Fred, until the minister broke through and shook Fred's hand.

"You've had a long trip and you need a cool drink. Come to my house, and you must introduce me to your friend."

Well, you'd think I was running for mayor. I must have shaken the hand of everybody in that village.

"Is that what a half dollar does?" I asked Fred.

The minister heard and said, "No, that's what being an American does."

Then Fred piped in, "Isn't it more, Reverend Sangco? Isn't it what being *you* are does?"

The reverend shrugged his shoulders. "I am nothing."

So I was right. Fred didn't have a woman. Or I should say that this village, these people, were his woman, because I saw that he loved them and they loved him.

Back in the States, I found myself thinking of Fred more than any of the men I served with. I wanted to share him with all the young men and women in the world today by writing about him here. I hope you'll think of him too once in a while. He was really something, and so was the reverend, and so were his people.

GOD TOOK MY DOG AWAY

Today God took my dog away. Last night a man phoned saying that a car had hit my dog in front of his house and he wanted my parents to come pick him up. My Pa doesn't get excited often, but this time he did. When he tried to put on his coat, he couldn't find the sleeve, so he threw the coat on the floor and rushed out without it. He wouldn't let me go with him. He said it probably wasn't serious so there was no sense in my going. In a way, I was just as glad because my heart was pounding so hard I could barely stand.

In a little while Pa came back with Pup in his arms. My Ma gently put Pup on a pillow that she had placed on the floor near the kitchen radiator. The dog looked good to me, except that his furry coat, which was short and usually smooth, was roughed up a little. His eyes were closed most of the time, and when he opened them he didn't seem to see. I thought I saw tears come from the corners. Every so often he whimpered. I tried hard not to cry.

Pa called the vet, who came right away. They told me to go into the other room while the vet looked Pup over. I told them I wouldn't. Pa yelled at me and grabbed me by the arm and pushed me into the hallway, closing the door after me. I stood there and listened through the door. When I heard them stop talking, I opened the door and saw the vet ready to leave with Pup in his arms.

I wouldn't let him take Pup away. I stomped and screamed and began hitting the vet. He said he was taking Pup to put him out of his misery. I didn't care; he couldn't have him. So the vet placed Pup back on the pillow and stuck a long needle into him. I slept beside Pup on the floor all night and prayed to God.

When I woke up in the morning, Pup was dead. My throat got so tight I could hardly breathe. I cried all through the day every time I thought of my dog. But each time I cried I felt a little better, and tonight I'm crying a lot less. God took my dog away and I don't know whether to hate him, or love him for giving me Pup in the first place. Pa said that if God gave Pup life, he had the right to take him away, and I suppose that's fair. I hope tomorrow I'll be able to forgive Him, but today, no matter how hard I try, I can't.

SUCCESS AND FAILURE

Everybody who was anybody in the community was at the dinner honoring the Businessman of the Year that Saturday night. The mayor, the senators from the state capital and Washington D.C., the chairwoman of the school committee, the local radio talk show host, the publisher of the city's morning newspaper, and the spouses of all sat behind a long table extending the width of the stage. Bradley Hazelton and his wife, Norma, sat next to the mayor in the center. They gazed down upon a few hundred friends and lesser luminaries who sat at round tables on the main floor.

After the meal, the mayor rose and spoke into the microphone. He said that Brad, the guest of honor at this dinner, was the model whom every American businessman should emulate. He recounted how Brad had taken over his father's small furniture manufacturing business in an old factory building by the harbor, and in less than a decade, with hard work and dedication, had grown the business into the city's largest employer. Beyond that, Brad's generosity to the community, his substantial donations to the Boys Club, the art museum, and city beautification, was unprecedented.

Brad rose to accept the plaque honoring him as Businessman of the Year. As he stood before the microphone, he surveyed the audience before him, smiling broadly. His eyes swept across their faces, meeting, for an instant, the proud stares of his two sons and daughter. He had done it all for them, he thought. Their work would ensure the long-term survival of the business; they would broker his immortality. He was in his mid-fifties and had lately become aware that he had less time ahead than he had lived.

But the eyes he most searched for were those of his aged father. There, seated at a table in the rear of the hall, he found him. After his father had a heart attack, he had beseeched Brad to join him in the business. "It'll be your show," he had promised. Brad, disenchanted with working for other companies, had been easily persuaded.

During the first few years, the business remained small because his father, a product of the Depression, would never take a risk. Brad, on the other hand, was a risk taker. Finally, he had confronted his father. "Pa, if we don't increase our sales staff and advertise more, we'll die." He and his father were alone in his father's office after the workers had gone for the day.

"No, we won't," his father responded. "I've gotten along pretty well over the years without spending money for such things. We've got good customers; they'll stand by us."

"Maybe so, but I don't want to work for the same salary indefinitely. I've got to see some growth."

"In my day, I was lucky to have a business and make ends meet. It's still enough for me. Anyway, it's my money you'd be spending."

"No, it isn't," Brad replied instantly. "The company would borrow from the bank."

"Go into debt? Not at my stage of life," said his father.

"But I'd sign for it personally. It wouldn't affect you."

"It's my business. No debt! Do you understand?" His father pounded his fist on his desk.

"I thought it was *our* business," said Brad. "Remember, you gave me an option on half the stock." His father remained silent. "Look, Pa, I'm not happy here. We're worlds apart. If you won't let the business grow, I'd like to strike out on my own."

His father looked shocked. "You mean that, Brad? You'd leave me after knowing that I could be gone in a flash?"

"I'll stay, but only if you'll let me run things my way."

"I don't want to lose you."

"I'm sorry, Pa. It's my way or not at all."

"Then I don't want to know anything you're doing. I'll have to retire."

"You could keep your finger in. Just don't interfere."

"No, I'll retire."

"Are you sure that's what you want?"

His father sighed. "It's about time, I suppose. I know you'll do things right. Just show me the financials every quarter."

"Sure, Pa. Every quarter, and you can watch the bottom line grow."

From then on, Brad's father had steered clear of the business except for the quarterly board meetings when the financial statements were reviewed and the company's strategy for the future was discussed.

The evening that Brad was chosen as Businessman of the Year, he figured his father would be proud of him, although his father was too far away from the stage for Brad to see his grinning face clearly.

"Thank you, Mr. Mayor. Thank you everybody," said Brad. "I'm overwhelmed by this honor. I'm not sure that I deserve it. Really, instead of me, it's our able and dedicated employees who should receive it."

There were shouts from the floor: "No way, Brad. You did it, not us." They came from the company's key employees seated at two of the tables in the rear.

"I suppose I can take credit for some sleepless nights when I wondered whether we'd make it or not," Brad said, turning toward Norma, who was nodding her head vigorously, making everyone laugh.

"And to think Dad only finished high school," Brad's son Binkley whispered to his brother, Ken. They were seated with their wives at the table nearest the stage.

"Yeah, so he puts us through college," said Ken, "then doesn't listen to a word we say."

"He's still the boss," Bink said. "It's his company."

"You can say that again," said Ken. "*His* company."

"I want to thank my sons," Brad went on, "for making the success of the past few years possible. It's really their company. And I owe much to this community for its moral support." He paused for a moment, then added, "And I owe much to The Main Street State Bank for the dollars they have lent us." Again laughter. "Thank you, thank you everybody."

At eight o'clock Monday morning Ken dropped by his father's office. Brad raised his eyes from *The Wall Street Journal* spread before him and turned to his oldest son, who had taken a seat beside his desk.

"I think you ought to know we're having a cash flow problem, Dad."

"Is that so? Well, I'm sure it's only temporary. Nothing to worry about," Brad said, returning to the newspaper.

"Maybe so, but some of our creditors are demanding payment and we don't have the money."

"Call the bank for chrissakes, Ken," said Brad, annoyed at what he considered a routine matter. "Why bother me with this? You know what to do. Use the credit line."

"I can't. It's extended to the limit."

"Okay, okay. I'll talk to the bank."

"I don't think you'll get very far. I tried and they seem pretty adamant."

Brad's face flushed as he pivoted in his swivel chair. "You don't ask the sons of bitches. You tell them. We're the best customer they've got."

"It's the receivables, Dad."

"I've told you, forget the receivables. They're okay."

"No, they're not. A lot of them are ninety to a hundred and twenty days old."

"They're good customers, aren't they?" Brad said in a challenging tone.

"Yes, but..."

"Then there's nothing to worry about. I've given the customers extra terms, see."

"That may be, Dad, but we can't afford to do that," Ken said cautiously.

"Listen, you stick to your bailiwick, the books, and don't go poking your nose into my affairs. I said I'll talk to the bank."

"Okay, Dad," Ken said with a shrug, and he rose and walked out of the office. This time was like all the other times, Ken thought. He could never bring his father around to his way of thinking.

On the morning of the annual board meeting the women in the office were excited. They wore fancier dresses than usual, cleared their desks of accumulated papers, and put on their best smiles. They prepared coffee and sweet rolls for the board. From the beginning, the members had always partaken of the women's hospitality, and always kidded them about their looking younger as the years passed. The board consisted of two lawyers, an independent accountant, two of Brad's friends who were CEOs of other companies, Ken, the company's accountant, and Bink, vice president of production.

It was always a morning of optimism, and the conviction that whatever mistakes had been made during the preceding year would soon be set right by these competent and authoritative individuals.

On this particular morning, an uncommon visitor, Glen, vice president of the company's bank was in attendance. After the board reviewed the financial statements and registered the gravity of the situation, all eyes shifted to Glen.

He stood before them with a grim look on his face. "We're calling in the loan, Brad. You've broken through the limit established in our agreement."

Brad's face paled. "Why would you do this? We're your biggest account. If we fail, you'll fail with us."

"Maybe so, maybe so. But if we do, it will be only partly your doing. Listen Brad, our other customers are in the same shape as you. The bank's assets are currently way below our liabilities."

"My god, Glen. And you'd still let us go bankrupt?"

"Yes, we would. At least we'd get something."

"Damn this economy," Brad exclaimed. "My father went through it, and now it's my turn."

The board members had listened silently, as if in shock. Brad turned to each of them, but not one had anything to say. He knew they were helpless, just as he was.

So the company went bankrupt after three generations of ownership and management. Ceasing to exist, its buildings became vacant shells. Brad still had his private wealth that could last him and his wife the rest of their lives. The loss of the business was a blow, but worse, his damaged pride, his lost sense of having succeeded and provided for the welfare of so many in the community, was unbearable. He felt worthless, too old to begin again, especially with the economy in ruins.

He remained in bed for days on end. His wife Norma took on all the responsibilities of running their lives. She had never seen him like this. "You can't keep staying in bed," she said. "Snap out of it!"

"Leave me alone," was all he would say.

She was frightened. He had simply given up, and she failed to understand.

One morning after a couple of months, he rose from their bed, got dressed, had a hearty breakfast, and read his *Wall Street Journal*. Norma was relieved, thinking that at last her husband had "returned to the living," as she put it, and that all would be well again.

But Brad had not truly alleviated his depression. He was simply going through the motions of normalcy. One day, when Norma returned home from shopping, she found him hanging by his neck from a beam in the garage.

He left a note apologizing for his failure and asking for his family's forgiveness. His last words were, "I can no longer tolerate myself. Please understand."

DINNER WITH DADDY

Daddy wasn't there when I arrived at the restaurant. After waiting in the foyer for about fifteen minutes, I began to worry because he was always prompt, compulsively so. It was beginning to snow and he had a three-hour drive into the city from his retreat in the mountains. Why did he choose to move so far away? He lives in the middle of nowhere.

"I need to talk with you, Daddy, but it's not an emergency," I had said on the phone earlier in the day after hearing the weather forecast. But he had insisted on meeting me anyway.

"A fire should be extinguished before it gets out of hand," he had replied.

I had told him on the phone that my mother, whom he had divorced two years before, had revealed something about him that had disturbed me a lot. I haven't slept well ever since.

He hadn't asked me what it was. He just said, "Don't judge me, Honeybunch, until you've heard both sides. Okay?"

My mother was bitter after he left her. She said she'd take him back because she still loved him and he said he still loved her, but he told her there was "not a chance." And that only made her more bitter. She called him a "self-centered bastard."

I felt I had to defend him because he was my father. My mother didn't seem to acknowledge that anymore.

"He's *not* self-centered," I said. "He's not like that at all."

She let loose a tirade detailing all the bad things he'd done to her while they were married. Well, I was there during most of the marriage, wasn't I, and I hadn't seen him do any of those things. Maybe he had done them in the privacy of their bedroom or when I wasn't looking.

Then she said something that hit me like an earthquake.

"Your father was unfaithful; he carried on with other women for at least half our marriage, and for three years he kept a mistress. You didn't know that, did you?"

"Daddy did that?" I said in disbelief.

I had figured that my father was no angel. But I imagined that he was more virtuous than other men, certainly wiser, and always did the right thing. You might say he was my dream man. I guess I was the classic teenager who was in love with her father and envisioned marrying him, if not for the small matter of his being married to my mother. And I imagined that he wanted to marry me. Of us three kids, my two sisters and me, I was Daddy's favorite. He didn't call me "Honeybunch" for nothing.

My mother's description of Daddy's infidelity was very convincing. She gave specifics. "The woman was the receptionist in his office. You know who. Only after I called her and told her to keep her hands off my husband or there'd be consequences did the thing end."

For a few weeks I could hardly think straight. I couldn't concentrate on my job, I'm a junior accountant. How could my father have deceived my mother—deceived all of us, in fact? Everything I believed in somehow seemed false. I felt empty.

It hit me all the harder because ever since the divorce, Daddy and I had grown closer than ever. I visited him often at his getaway, where we would go on long walks and talk about life. And we would go swimming in the summer and skiing in the winter. I never had him to myself like this when we were a family. I'd come to know him as I never knew him; beyond loving him as a daughter I had grown fond of him as a friend.

To my relief, at twenty minutes after the agreed-upon hour, Daddy walked in to the restaurant. He looked classy with his pewter-colored hair, his mustache trimmed neatly, and his face crinkled into a loving smile.

"Hi there, Honeybunch," he called to me as he dusted the snow off his coat.

When he embraced me, I felt happy. I couldn't believe he had done the bad things that my mother said he had done. Actually, I had essentially said that to my mother.

"If Daddy is such a despicable person, why do you want him back?"

"Because I love him," she had said sadly, as if she couldn't help herself.

Daddy asked for a booth in the corner so we could talk privately. He ordered wine for himself. I don't drink or smoke, or do anything bad, for that matter. My friends keep telling me to lighten up. I wish I could.

We engaged in small talk for a while: how was my job, how was I feeling, how was my love life? He never asks about my mother, which is fine with me because she has told me not to talk about her, even though she always wants to know about him.

At last, over dessert, he said in a jesting tone, "So tell me, Honeybunch, what's the terrible thing I'm supposed to have done?"

"You've had a mistress, Daddy. Mom says you were unfaithful to her."

He nodded, and his expression grew serious.

"I thought that's what you were getting at on the phone," he said. "Yes, it's true."

I waited for him to say more, to defend himself. Instead he stared across the room in silence.

"Is that all you're going to say?" I demanded.

"No, no," he said. "I want you to know, to understand." He laughed uncomfortably. "I thought I'd know what to say, but now I don't know where to start."

"Well, why did you do it?"

"The fact is your mother and I weren't happy together during the last fifteen years of our marriage. I guess we did a good job of keeping it from you kids."

"But she says she still loves you."

"Yes, I suppose she does in her way. And I still love her. We raised a family together and we had some great times. Didn't we?"

"Then why…?"

"I needed love and approval and support; I needed someone who respected me for who I was and what I did. Everybody has a right to find happiness, and I found it in my woman friend. Still, I loved your mother. Even though my friend begged me to leave your mother, I refused because I couldn't hurt her and I couldn't break up our family. Do you understand?"

"But Mom forced that woman to leave you."

"Is that what she told you? The truth is, I ended it of my own accord. She had nothing to do with it. Did you know that when your mother learned about the woman—I had told her the truth in hopes of bringing things into the open and saving our marriage—your mother wanted to leave me? Only after I pleaded with her for the sake of the family and promised to end the affair did she agree to continue our marriage. But it was never the same after that. Your mother is GOOD in capital letters, a morally perfect person. She said she would forgive but never forget. It turned out she did neither. She never trusted me again. I can understand that, but understanding doesn't make it any easier to live with."

What he said about my mother, her goodness, was like opening a door into a room I'd never entered. I realize that my mother clings to me, to my sisters as well, but mostly to me because I happen to live close by. When I avoid her, which by her definition is not phoning every day and not being with her most weekends and holidays, she makes me feel that I'm letting her down, somehow abandoning her. Then the guilt sets in. Because she is so good, so innocent and "victimized," because she loves me so much and gives me money and gifts, I can't ignore her with a clear conscience. And for this reason I find myself angry at Daddy. She used to be his responsibility and now, by leaving her, he's dumped it all on me.

My mind was racing. Maybe if he had found another mistress, he could have stayed with my mother. Now I understand him because I find myself in the same situation. He had to leave. And now, I know, so do I.

By this time the restaurant had filled and people were seated at tables near our booth, so we had to talk quietly not to be overheard. Through the large window I could see giant snowflakes falling like cotton balls.

Daddy spoke with such earnestness, his words seemed so weighty, that I had to flip them back and forth in my mind.

"I'm amazed that you two ever got married," I said.

"It wasn't always the way it became," he said, sighing. "For the first ten years, things seemed perfect. I don't think either of us was ever happier."

"So, what changed?"

"Life played a dirty trick on us."

Keeping me in suspense, he paused to let me absorb his cryptic statement.

"Yes, it was a goddamn dirty trick. We both changed, your mother and I. Neither of us remained the person we had been when we married. In the beginning, when I was struggling in the world and needed her, we were fine together. But when I went into business and became successful, and my life no longer revolved around the two of us, I stopped depending on her for moral support. I had found my own strength. She grew unhappy. The business replaced her, or so she thought. And the more unhappy she became, the more I gave myself to the business. In retrospect, I can say we should have split then and avoided much of the pain we both now feel. It would have been easier for each of us, especially your mother, to have started over when we were younger."

"But you sold the business and retired. There was nothing to come between the two of you anymore. And then you left. I don't get it, Daddy."

"She wouldn't let me forget my infidelity. The toughest thing I've ever done was leaving your mother, knowing that she would suffer from terrible loneliness, knowing that I would feel guilty for the rest of my life. How could I abandon and leave unprotected someone as innocent and good as your mother?"

As Daddy talked, I became overwhelmed by confusing thoughts and feelings. Somehow his explanation confirmed rare moments of awareness that had been flashing like lightning across my mind, but I had ignored them. And then, like a sudden vision, I understood a new aspect of myself. I reached across the table and placed my hand on Daddy's.

"As a child, I assumed the responsibility of keeping you and Mom together. I know now that's what I did."

"Are you saying you knew we weren't getting along?" he said dumbfounded. "I thought your mother and I had kept the tension between us pretty well hidden. It was an unspoken conspiracy. Come to think of it, it was the glue that held us together."

"I knew something was wrong between you. Even as a kid, I sensed it."

"Kids know, don't they?"

"I did," I said.

"I suppose no one can hide the truth for long." He paused. "But the fact that you took the responsibility of keeping the peace..."

"I felt I had to. If you and Mom didn't stay together, I thought I would die, literally. And that's why I've always been so good, so moral. By being good, I was setting an example. I thought that somehow it would make both of you be good to each other."

"My god, Honeybunch, what an awful load you took on. All those years…"

Tears began to fill my eyes, but I tried to hold them back. People would see; this wasn't the place.

"Forget the others," he said. "Damn the rest of the world. Just let your tears flow."

He came over to my side of the booth and held me and stroked my hair while I sobbed quietly into his shirt.

"My poor, poor child."

I was crying for myself, for the child who had tried to do the impossible. I knew now how much he loved me. How could I have imagined that I would lose his love by confronting him about his infidelity? So what if he wasn't perfect.

Suddenly I felt at peace because I understood him and, in so doing, I understood more of myself.

We gathered our coats and walked out into the falling snow. The city seemed soft and hushed. The passing cars were silent; the voices of passersby muted. The whole world seemed fresh and beautiful. He reached his arm over my shoulder and pulled me closer to him as we walked.

"Thanks," he said.

"For what?"

"For opening up to me. If people would talk with each other, I really believe we could solve most problems."

"Thank you, too, Daddy."

"For what?"

"For listening and for telling the truth."

I suddenly felt free. No longer would I see Daddy as my mother would have me see him, even though I could understand her bitterness. For the first time since I have been a child I felt inner peace.

HEARTSTORM

Jack's heart raced. Pain stabbed his chest, and he felt as out of breath as if he had just run a hundred-yard dash. "What a damned lousy time for this to happen," he thought. "Couldn't it have waited until the business had straightened out?"

After Felicia drove him to City Hospital, Jack hobbled into the emergency room and announced to the nurse behind the desk, "I think I'm having a heart attack."

The nurse rose abruptly from her station, grabbed a wheelchair, and told Jack to sit down. Then she rushed him into a vacant cubicle and helped him onto a white-sheeted gurney.

"Everything will be fine," she said, seeing the panic in his eyes. "Just take off your shirt and lie down." She emanated a crisp, clean fragrance and a matronly competence. He was sure she noticed the excess rolls of flesh about his midriff as she listened to his heart through a stethoscope, then took his pulse. "Your pulse is very fast, but strong," she said calmly. "I'll get the doctor." Then she drew the curtains around the gurney, enclosing him in seclusion and peace.

"Damn," thought Jack. "The bank better not hear of this." Why had he borrowed to the hilt? To expand the business, of course. Used every asset he owned as collateral. Had to. Then sales fell off and interest rates skyrocketed.

The first symptom had struck as he was leaving for lunch with Felicia, one of his office workers.

"Is anything wrong?" she had asked, observing his hesitation as he slid behind the steering wheel of his beloved Jaguar.

"It's nothing. I'm okay." But after they had driven a short distance on the highway, he pulled to a stop on the shoulder. "I think you'd better drive."

"What's wrong? Please tell me what's wrong."

He massaged his left arm; his round face was pale and glossy with sweat. "I'll get over it. I've had it before. It's nothing. Just drive."

"Oh, Jack," she pleaded, abandoning the more formal "Mr. Sampson" address that she used at the office. "I'm worried. Please let me…"

"For God's sake, drive."

At the restaurant Jack tried studying the menu, but he was too distracted by his increasing discomfort. The waiter took Felicia's order, a small antipasto. In her mid-thirties, Felicia worked hard to maintain her svelte figure. She knew that was how Jack Sampson liked her. Didn't his wishes influence everything she did?

"Just water," Jack said to the server, who had waited on them often. "A little indigestion…maybe I'll have something later."

"Would you like an antacid tablet, Mr. Sampson?" asked the server.

Jack rose from his chair. "No, thanks. I think I'll go out and get some air."

It was really the past-due payment on the loan principal that had given him indigestion—if indigestion was actually the cause of his discomfort. The bank hadn't yet contacted him. It surely knew that the checking account balance was zero. The bank was bound to close in. After all, the agreement stipulated that if the balance fell below a threshold figure, then... The consequences were too devastating to contemplate.

In a few minutes, finding no relief being in the fresh air, Jack returned to the table. "Take me to the hospital," he told Felicia. "Believe me, nothing's wrong, but I ought to be checked out." He waved to the waiter to bring him the bill.

Felicia drove to the hospital in silence. Were she to reveal her concern, she knew he'd bark at her. At the swinging doors to the emergency entrance, he instructed her to return to the office. "And don't tell anybody where I am."

"Call me, won't you?" she pleaded.

"It'll be nothing. Just routine. You'll see."

She was approaching hysteria. She embraced him and kissed him fervently on the lips.

"I'll let you know how things go. I'll call. Okay?"

"I couldn't go on without you," she murmured.

"While we're waiting for the doctor, I need to ask you a few questions," said the nurse. "Name?"

"Who, me?"

The nurse smiled. "No, your shadow."

"Jack Sampson."

"Age?"

"Fifty-five and not counting."

"Weight?"

"One seventy-five, most of it around the middle."

"Blue Cross account number?"

"Call my office. No, don't call my office. Call my wife. She has it. No, I'll get it for you."

"Married, it would seem?"

"Unhappily."

"Any children?"

"Seventy-five employees."

"Employer?"

"My wife."

"C'mon, Mr. Sampson."

"Consolidated Plastics, here in town."

"Occupation?"

"Failing businessman."

"Your personal physician?"

"Me...myself."

A youthful doctor wearing a blue lab coat breezed into the room. "How do you do, sir? Sit up, please." He reached to shake Jack's hand as he perused the answers on the questionnaire. Then he took Jack's pulse and applied his stethoscope to his patient's chest. "Well, well, a strong, even beat, sir. Describe your symptoms, Mr. Sampson."

Jack described the chest pain, the fast breathing, the racing heartbeat, the ache down his left arm, and the dizziness. He mentioned pulling off the highway, losing his appetite, and needing to leave the restaurant for some fresh air. He didn't mention Felicia.

"Tell me, Mr. Sampson," said the doctor, "have you been under some stress lately?"

"Hell, no. Absolutely not."

"I see."

"Everything's fine. I mean until this thing happened."

The goddamn bank. Couldn't they give him more time? Sure they could. He'd guarantee that they'd get theirs. But how? There was no way. Banks don't have a heart.

"Look at the monitor, Mr. Sampson." Jack stared at the graphic representation of his heartbeat on the small screen. "I see nothing wrong," said the doctor. "There's absolutely no evidence of any trouble."

Trouble? Hadn't he signed the notes personally? Everything he owned was on the line. That was the trouble.

"You mean it wasn't a heart attack?"

"Not that I can tell."

"Then what in hell was it?"

"An anxiety attack, Mr. Sampson. You had the classic symptoms."

"Never heard of an anxiety attack."

"Some of the symptoms mimic a coronary occlusion."

Relieved, Jack grinned. He'd been given a second chance. Maybe it was a sign. Maybe the bank would give him a second chance too.

"Y'know, Doc, I can't afford to get sick. If it had been the real thing…"

"I suggest you see your personal physician, get to the bottom of your problem…"

"Hey, Doc, I told you I don't have a problem. And I don't have a personal physician."

The doctor shrugged. "Rest here for an hour," he said as he headed for the door. "Then you can go."

Go? Go where? Go bankrupt?

The nurse pulled back the curtains, exposing Jack to the rest of the world. While she took his pulse again he tried to sit up, but she gently pressed him down.

"Lie here awhile and rest. Doctor's orders."

Jack basked in her solicitude. How comforting it was. He let himself relax and closed his eyes. When was the last time he hadn't been in charge? He couldn't remember.

"You're like my husband," said the nurse. "What is it with you men? What are you always trying to prove?"

Smiling through closed eyes, he was amused at her homespun view of what drove him. He wasn't out to prove anything. It was more than just the bank lowering the boom. The creditors were hounding him. Three banding together could throw him into bankruptcy. And there were other forces: the business downturn, the high interest rates. Out to prove something? Hah! He was trying to survive.

"What am I trying to prove?" Jack almost shouted. "Just that you can beat it, sweetheart, just that you can beat it."

He fell into a childlike sleep. It was desperately needed. For weeks, his nights had been torments of wakefulness.

In an hour the nurse awakened him. "Your wife is here, Mr. Sampson... Do you hear me, Mr. Sampson?"

Jack nodded, eyes closed, still luxuriating in his languor.

"I'm here beside you," said his wife. Opening his eyes, he gazed at her. She bent down and pressed her cool lips on his cheek. "Get dressed and I'll take you home." Jack bolted upright and took his shirt from her outstretched arm.

"No, you won't. You're taking me to the office," he said, his voice hard as steel.

"But you've had a..."

"A what? What did I have?"

"Well, I'm not sure. Everyone is rather vague." She looked to the nurse for an answer.

"Ask your husband," the nurse responded.

"I'm fine. Can't you see? Absolutely wonderful."

Oh, if only he could weep. If only he could collapse and wallow in the acceptance of possible failure. What a supreme luxury that would be. But then wouldn't the world come to an end?

"S'long, sweetheart," he sang, taking the nurse's hand and then turning and bounding from the room. "Let's go," he shouted to his wife as he swaggered down the corridor toward the swinging doors. "The lions are waiting."

WHERE THE TALL BUILDINGS ARE

Pa likes to take me with him on his long business trips so he has company and I can see what the USA is like. Last week he took me to Chicago.

After we got settled in our hotel there, Mr. Slide called on us—he's an old business friend of my Pa's—and took us on a sightseeing trip around the city. The buildings sure are tall, taller than the ones in New York. Pa took me there once too.

Mr. Slide must like buildings because that's all he talked about. As we drove around in his big car, he showed us a tall white building and said, "Chewing gum built that place." He pointed out others. "Soap built that one." "Insurance built that." And then, "The market built that." "Merchandising built that." He just went on and on. I could see he liked his city and was very proud of it. And I could see my Pa was very impressed because he'd say, "No kidding, chewing gum?" "No kidding, soap?"

I was impressed, too. The only thing is, I wouldn't like to live in a place like that, but I guess a lot of people do because there were crowds and lots of traffic.

After we drove around some more, Mr. Slide asked if I liked what I saw. I said I liked all of it, but one thing seemed to be missing. He smiled and asked me what that was. I said, "A place that God built."

"Oh, we got churches, son."

"I don't mean that, Mr. Slide. I mean you don't have a place like the woods in back of our house where you can hunt squirrels."

Mr. Slide stopped the car, and burst out laughing. He swept his arm in front of him. "These are our woods, boy, and we're hunting in them every day." Pa laughed too.

PARTNERS

Three tall middle-aged men, each of them wearing a gray overcoat and spit-shined black shoes, entered the small foyer of the Enterprise Corporation. One of the men passed a business card to the female receptionist sitting behind the pass-through window.

"Mr. Palais, please," he said. Then he turned to his friends and nodded toward the worn floor tiles and the soiled leather chairs.

"Julius," the receptionist said softly into the phone, "three gentlemen from Consolidated American are here to see you."

"Julius?" the first man whispered. "Now isn't that cozy."

The second man dabbed his forefinger on the surface of the coffee table, which held several outdated issues of *Time* magazine. He examined his finger. "Dirt," he said with obvious disdain.

The door alongside the pass-through window opened. Julius Palais, whose forehead extended to the middle of his scalp where gray streaked hair began, stood there grinning. "Gentlemen, gentlemen. Hang your coats on the rack over there." Seeing no spare hangers, he shouted to the receptionist, "Marsha, get some hangers, quick." Turning to the visitors, he threw up his hands in a gesture of futility. "The office help takes them home. What can you do?" He extended his stubby hand, and one by one the visitors returned his grasp.

"No calls," he barked at Marsha, "I'm in conference."

The three men followed Julius single file between rows of gray metal desks, with the din of old-fashioned typewriters assaulting them. The room was hot, the air hazy from cigarette smoke in spite of the glare of too many overhead fluorescent light bulbs. A half-dozen young men were snatching at ringing phones, listening briefly, then slamming down the receivers and, with their neckties flying, jumping up from their desks while yelling orders to their colleagues. Passing through this bedlam, the quartet entered Julius Palais's office. As the door closed, a welcome hush enveloped them.

"I'd like you to meet my partner, Leo Galatin," Julius said, directing their gaze toward a figure sitting hunched over a corner table strewn with papers. Julius's own desk across the room was bare.

Leo rose from his chair, pushed his steel-rimmed spectacles back from their perch at the end of his nose, and extended his hand slowly, as if he abhorred motion. "How do you do," he said, limply shaking each visitor's hand.

"Leo Galatin, you should know, gentlemen, is the financial wizard behind Enterprise," said Julius. Gazing at Leo in mock awe, the men smiled. "When your company acquired us," he added, "that was good for everybody." Leo, tall, thin, and slightly bent even when standing, observed the men, but didn't speak.

"Consolidated American is your company now, too, Mr. Palais," said one of the men.

"Of course, of course. What I'm saying is that when you got Leo, you got a real bargain, something that no ledger can show."

Impassive, Leo studied the men. "Now Julie," he said, "you can't deny you've been Enterprise's inspiration, while I've been only the moderating influence."

The men fidgeted in their chairs with their heads lowered, not meeting Julius's eyes, or even one another's. Then the first man cleared his throat. "We presume you're ready to acquaint us with all the details of your operation," he said.

"I suppose, certainly," Julius replied, his tone seeming tired, resigned, tinged with annoyance. "Ladd asked that we hold nothing back, and, of course…"

"Mr. Ladd indicated that you'd be cooperative."

Leo sat drawing circles on a sheet of paper, lightly at first, then darker, until the point of his pencil snapped.

"Of course, we'll cooperate," said Julius." As you say we're all employees of Consolidated American now." He looked over at Leo as if seeking his assent, but Leo ignored him and reached for another pencil. "Our interests are identical," Julius emphasized.

"Do you mind if we tour the plant before we start?" the second man said.

"I'll take you through," said Julius, bounding from his chair.

"We'd rather go by ourselves, if you don't mind."

After they left, Leo tossed his pencil onto his desk and nodded slowly. "The time has come, Julie, the time I've been expecting. We've had a year's reprieve; now, as I predicted, they'll be moving their boys in."

"But they need us, Leo. They'll need us for a long time. You and I took twenty years to build this business. Do you think they can learn how to run it the way we can? Never. They'll always need us. Dammit, they're a cold bunch of bastards, aren't they?"

Julius recalled the discussion that he and Leo had had when they agreed to sell the company. He recalled saying, "I'm tired. I'm tired of the fight. The big boys don't give us a chance. If they don't gobble us up, they destroy us, so let's get gobbled up and come out with a bit of change and a salary for the rest of our lives. My God, Leo, we're fortunate. We've got it made."

"Got it made?" Leo had challenged.

"Sure, without question."

"Who's got it made? What does that mean?" Leo had replied. "We sold because we knew we were doomed, so now we play it safe. I didn't agree to sell for the money, Julie. I like my work, and I expect them to keep their promise and leave my position intact."

"Got it made, got it made." Had his own words come back to haunt them? Julius wondered. What are promises but fragile intentions. The image of Leo's fear loomed as a terrifying specter before him. Should he feel the same way? Could it be that the promise, solemnly demanded, casually granted, would be obliterated without a qualm?

Julius spun through the brass revolving door into the glassed lobby. His body bent slightly forward at the waist, his eyes aimed dead ahead, he rushed into the throng of gray-suited men and doll-faced women. The crowded elevator rose silent and smooth, flicking off the floors in a bank of numbers above its door. Julius tightened his grip on the calfskin briefcase bearing his gold-embossed initials. As the door rolled open on the twenty-fifth floor, he jostled his way out, and entered the reception area, with its plush carpeting and a soft glow emanating from the ceiling. No fluorescent lights here, he noted.

"Good morning, Mr. Palais," said the sleek, smiling receptionist.

Julius nodded, removing his hat as he swept past her into his new office. He dropped his briefcase onto a couch, then moved behind his enormous desk and lowered himself into a black upholstered chair. Gilt-framed oil paintings lined the wall over the couch. His desk was an unbroken expanse of teak except for a single piece of paper lying in the center and a black phone with a bank of buttons. Behind him, a wall of windows, now spattered with raindrops, commanded a spectacular view of the city.

Julius swiveled in his chair and gazed down at the miniature life below. They're toys, he thought, nothing but toys...black figures dashing amid the neon, little bugs racing down the slick canyons. He stared across the void between his window and the blue-tinted windows of another tall building off to the right. Rows of white-shirted men were bent over their desks. Work, you lousy paper shufflers. Dictate your stupid memos. Complicate it, screw it up. That's all you're good for.

He turned back to his gray-carpeted office with its paneled walls rimmed by soft indirect lighting. He studied his black phone, his clean desk, the symmetrical grain of the teak surface. "You goddamned paper shuffler. That's all you're good for," he repeated. He had used these words often when criticizing Leo Galatin.

And Leo, lifting his eyes from the legal documents spread before him on the table—Leo always worked on a table— would respond, "Without paper we'd have no Shakespeare, or theory of relativity." Then, with a faint smile, he'd look over his thick glasses, "or money."

Leo, Leo, Leo, my good old friend Leo. Julius stared at the black phone. How he would like to talk to Leo as in the old days, just pick up the phone and discuss a business problem or, as he did occasionally, talk about what was in his heart. His hand hesitated on the receiver and then withdrew. The unrelenting image of Leo pleading, frightened, careened through his memory.

"I'll try, Leo," he had said. "I'll do all I can on your behalf. I'll go to Ladd and I'll tell him he can't do this to my partner."

"Be firm, Julie. If you'll insist…"

"Insist! Why, I'll tell him if he fires you, he'd better 'can' me too."

"You mean that you'd quit?"

"Exactly."

"No, no, I wouldn't want you to go that far."

Julius had reached his arm across Leo's narrow shoulders and hugged him. "We started this business together, and we'll finish it together."

Julius had kept his promise. He had phoned Jack Ladd.

"Listen, Jack, I'm calling regarding Leo." Julius paused as Ladd explained the necessity of having to let Leo go. "Well, I can understand why you want your own finance man," said Julius, "but…" Ladd interrupted, reducing Julius to silence. "I see. Then there's no chance you'd take him back? Sure, I'll be at the strategy meeting. I've got some ideas I'd like to propose. Thanks, Jack."

Julius had placed the receiver in its cradle, leaned back in his chair, and let out a hoarse scream. Then he reassured himself that he'd get over not keeping his promise to Leo to quit if Leo were fired. He'd get over his cowardice, get over despising himself. After all, in business isn't it every man for himself?

The rain streamed in silvery strands across the small oval window beside Julius's seat. As the plane lifted off into the starry void above the clouds, the surge pressed his body into the resilient womb of upholstery. It had been a year since his company had been absorbed, and Julius had looked forward to a peaceful flight well above the fury down below. Up here he was removed from his withering, cruel responsibilities. He sighed. What a pleasure it was to place his destiny in another's hands for the next two hours.

But his escape would not be total after all...would not, in fact, last more than the time it took the engines to relax as the aircraft reached altitude and the passengers replaced their tension with neighborly small talk.

"Julie, it's an amazing coincidence, our meeting here," said the man with gold cufflinks who was sitting in the adjoining seat.

But Julius Palais could not reply with equal fervor. He regretted that he couldn't because Paul Pandolfo, although a business competitor, was a friend. That evening Julius did not want to be alert in a guarded conversation. Slowly turning his head from the dark reflection of himself in the window, Julius said, "I fly to Chicago a lot these days. We were sure to meet sometime."

"Well, I've been wanting to talk to you for a year, ever since you made the deal with Consolidated

American," said Paul. "I almost called you the day I heard of it, but I figured you had plenty on your mind. So I said to myself that I'd meet up with you someday and we'd have a good talk." Paul cast his eyes toward Julius rather casually to hide his intense interest while searching for a reaction.

"How do you find things these days?" inquired Julius.

"Good, good under the circumstances." Paul shrugged. "What can you expect with competition the way it is? Hell, you know. You make a living, pay the overhead. I'm the last person to complain."

"I guess the banner years are over," Julius said, twining his fingers, then dropping his hands to his lap as he turned to the window and gazed into the blackness.

"Yeah, no doubt the glory days are over. But hell, Julie, you don't have to struggle anymore the way you worked it." Paul's tone was admiring, although he was clearly prodding.

Turning his head swiftly from the window, Julius fastened his eyes on Paul. "It was better when we struggled."

Paul chuckled and bounced his knee against Julius's. "Cut it out, Julie. You want pity? Hah. Look, I'd sell out in a minute for any decent offer."

"Why?"

"Why?" Paul stared incredulously at Julius's impassive face. "I'd sell for the same reason you did. I'm tired. I'm tired of the fight. The big boys don't give us a chance. If they don't swallow us, they destroy us, so I'd rather be swallowed and come out with a neat bit of change and a salary and retirement benefits for the rest of my life. My god, Julie, you're a fortunate guy. You've got it made."

"I suppose I have."

"Sure you have. What's wrong with you?"

"Got it made." The haunting words reverberated in Julius's agonizing memory.

Leo had once asked, "What does 'got it made' mean? We sold because we knew we were doomed, so we played it safe. We secured our careers. I'm not agreeing to sell just for the money, Julie. I like my work and I want their guarantee that my job will be kept intact."

What are promises but the most fragile of intentions? The image of Leo's stricken face when he had been rejected, again loomed terrifyingly before him. Julius's promise, solemnly demanded, casually given, had been quickly obliterated without a qualm.

A CAT'S TALE

Even after more than two and a half years, I remember him vividly.

Anybody could see that he was hungry. He was lean, and his face looked gaunt. I was hunting for grasshoppers in the backyard (grasshoppers and snakes were my passion then), and those that I offered him he ate with relish.

I invited him (should I admit a bit forcibly?) into our house. The grasshoppers must have taken the edge off his hunger, because before he consumed the milk and meat scraps we offered him, he sauntered around familiarizing himself with his surroundings. He poked under the sofa and the beds, tried to pry his way into the closets, and examined cracks to see whether he had missed anything. Finally he ate, and then fell into an enviable slumber.

We put him out that night, never expecting to see him again. But bright and early the next morning he was sitting at our back door, already looking better. How could we not let him in? After a few minutes of deliberation, my family agreed to accept him as our steady boarder.

As a rule, the first thing one does when getting a new pet is to name it. We tried endlessly to come up with a suitable name. My mother had little to offer. She had already used up all the names that suited her on her two sons. Finally, and unanimously, we decided to call him just plain Kitty, mainly because he seemed to respond to that name, if spoken in the correct tone, and repeated. My mother did that quite well.

Kitty wasn't especially handsome, nor, for that matter, was there anything outstanding about his physical appearance. His size was far from spectacular, although his face was pleasing, not cross looking like many tomcats I knew. His emotions were clearly obvious: anger, boredom, joy, and supplication. Because of his almost human-like expressions, we came to treat him as a member of the family.

The four of us, Dad, Mother, my brother, and I, had distinct relationships with Kitty.

My father's was the most complex, at least in his opinion. He was never one to make a row over cats and dogs, as the rest of us were inclined to do. In fact he downright disliked animals. A furniture upholsterer, he said that animals annoyed him when he was conducting transactions in the homes of pet-loving customers. So he was definitely against our taking in Kitty. Only because the rest of us were so enamored of Kitty did he allow the cat to live "out of his pocket," as he put it.

One evening after work when Dad was sitting in his cigar-perfumed chair reading the newspaper, he eyed my brother gleefully ruffling Kitty's fur. Down came the paper as Dad proclaimed that my brother was sure to contract bubonic plague or some other dangerous disease surely carried by cats. And when Dad rose in the morning and stumbled out of bed into the kitchen, he often exhibited an air of false wrath and made motions to kick Kitty. I admit, though, that I never saw him follow through with his threats, and one day I even caught him red-handed slyly petting Kitty's fluffy fur and murmuring in a monotone that outdid Kitty's purring. Even though he was obviously embarrassed by this exposé, he offered no explanation and simply assumed a look of indifference.

Kitty seemed to like Mother best, perhaps because she was always tactful with him, but more likely because she was the one who usually fed him. He would always lapse into ecstatic purring while under the influence of her gentle caresses. But even though my brother and I were rough with Kitty, he seemed to forgive us.

After a few weeks we took Kitty for granted, expecting his silent begging at mealtime and feeling sure that he would strut in the back door each morning, his fur coated with dew. We accepted all this as part of our daily routine, even during mating periods (he was not "fixed"), when he inevitably appeared with cuts and bruises and we would nurse him back to health. He was quite a scrapper, although he seemed respected by his feline admirers and given wide berth by his enemies. He was the only cat I knew who could walk through the field behind our house without some jealous rival pouncing on him.

Often I expected that one morning we would not find Kitty at our door. That morning finally came. I remember the date well because it was during the week of Pearl Harbor. A little while after noticing his absence, we got a call from a nearby neighbor. My mother answered the phone, her voice first rising to a high pitch with delight, then dropping to an almost imperceptible whisper. On listening, my heart began pounding, as if it knew something was wrong. The click of the receiver hanging up resounded in a thickening atmosphere, then silence, then the words, "Kitty was just run over by a car."

It didn't seem possible. At age fourteen I hadn't yet suffered the loss of a loved one, feline or otherwise. "Impossible," I kept repeating.

The neighbor brought Kitty to our house, and my mother gently placed him on a pillow on the linoleum kitchen floor. A flicker of life remained in his limp body. My mother dribbled water around his mouth with an eye dropper, but he couldn't seem to lick it off or swallow.

I went off to school that morning in low spirits. During sixth period I was told that my mother was on the phone and needed to talk to me. She wanted me to know that the Animal Rescue League had just taken away Kitty's body.

I contained myself until I got home from school, but halfway through dinner I felt a thickening lump in my throat. It was followed by a flood of tears.

Late the following morning, new linoleum was laid on the kitchen floor. The arrangements had been made the week before. Our Kitty, and the old linoleum so familiar to him, were both gone forever.

I wrote this story on July 1, 1944, when I was serving overseas in the military in the jungles of New Guinea. I enclosed the story in a letter and sent it home to my mother. My younger brother, then a high school student doing poorly in English, submitted my story to fulfill an assignment, for which he received an A. In fact, the story was subsequently published in his school's newspaper. I considered that outright plagiarism, but I've since forgiven him for his transgression.

SUMMER BREAK

Sometimes with the best intentions and all innocence we can't win. Fate has devised an evil conspiracy
against us. And when it is abetted by the determination
of a young woman and the mindless system of the tax
bureau, all hope of rescue is lost.

After her freshman year at State College, my daughter took a temporary job selling bibles door-to-door during the long, sultry North Carolina summer. Although
just nineteen years old and shy, she was determined to
earn enough to support herself during the subsequent
school year. Having heard that the money was good if
she was willing to work hard, she was hoping she could
even earn enough to study in Paris for the second se-
mester of her junior year.

Concerned about her knocking on strangers' doors
in a strange city, and her working long hours (supposedly sixteen hours a day, six days a week), her mother
and I tried to dissuade her. When that didn't work, we
decided to be supportive, focusing on the job's advantages. In addition to the good money, the company's information sheet pointed out that the experience would

contribute to character development. Our daughter would not be an employee but an independent contractor, an entrepreneur. (No mention was made that this exempts the company from paying social security taxes and health insurance.) The rewards would be directly proportional to her efforts. She would learn firsthand how the American way works.

The company invited the parents to attend a meeting given for the New England recruits. The meeting was supposedly designed to inform, but seemed designed mostly to inspire. Young men, bright eyed, eager, impeccably groomed and wholesome looking, and young women right out of TV ads spoke to us of their great past successes. Some had earned over $10,000 in previous summers.

The featured speaker, silver haired and golden voiced, wearing cuff links and looking wise, stirred us to such a pitch that we gave him a standing ovation. Was there now any doubt, either in our daughter's mind or ours, that she would emerge from the experience a richer, more self-sufficient, more well-rounded person? Evidently there was, but we kept it a secret from one another. Like the parents of any kid about to leave the nest, we simply hoped for the best.

In a friend's car, she and her fellow entrepreneurs drove nonstop from New England to the company's headquarters in Atlanta. No one wanted to spend money en route for a motel room and decent meals, so they stopped only briefly for fast food, and not much of it at that.

At company headquarters, recruits from across the country received a week of indoctrination on how to convince potential buyers that they needed this publisher's bibles.

Thus, ostensibly prepared for any eventuality, our daughter's team then drove nonstop to a small mining town in West Virginia. But because the coal industry was depressed and most everyone was unemployed, there were few customers. Hearing that the economy was thriving in the land of tobacco, our daughter left her team and moved to Winston-Salem, North Carolina. Arriving hungry and exhausted, she began looking for a place to stay. Failing to find one, she and another girl bedded down that first night on the bare floor of the living room of an apartment occupied by five men who were also in the program.

Later that week, a phone call interrupted our breakfast. An unknown voice indicated that our daughter wished to speak. Coming on the line, she immediately broke into tears and explained that she had been unable to work the phone herself because she couldn't see; her eyes were bandaged. Having left her contact lenses in too long during the previous long day of knocking on doors, she had temporarily lost her vision and had been rushed to a local clinic. Under doctor's orders not to uncover her eyes for at least twenty-four hours, she was confined to a strange apartment in a strange city, left alone until late evening, and dependent on strangers to lead her and feed her. Our hearts ached.

She recovered, thankfully, and with a newly acquired girlfriend (who turned out to be promiscuous and a committed pot smoker), she finally located a sparsely furnished apartment owned by an unsympathetic, demanding landlady who charged an outrageous rent.

"Look for another place," I insisted.

"But, Dad, I don't have the time. I'm knocking on doors by eight in the morning and don't get home until ten or eleven at night. That's what is expected of us."

Morning after morning at seven, the ringing phone replaced our alarm as she called seeking encouragement, unloading her frustration, always weeping from exhaustion after working grinding fourteen-hour days. This had to be akin to slave labor, I thought. She described doors slammed in her face, and prospects promising to buy if she returned in the evening and then refusing to see her when she showed up. For the first time in her sheltered life, she witnessed human cruelty: husbands beating wives, mothers beating daughters. As she rode the streets on an old bike she purchased to make her job easier, rednecks reached out of their truck windows to pinch her bottom. One Sunday a policeman in a cruiser stopped her and asked to see her vendor's license. She didn't have one and was cited.

"Fly home," we said. "We'll wire you the money. You don't have to suffer like this."

But she wouldn't give up. Although Sunday group meetings were held in her area (to which she had to travel four hours) to restore daunted spirits by repeating the company's indoctrination message, instead they further depressed her. She said they were little more than pressure sessions and pep talks. The recruits were to wake up at 6 a.m., stand before a mirror, and repeat "I feel happy! I feel healthy! I feel terrific! You gorgeous thing, you, don't you ever tire?" Then they were to take a cold shower, all the while singing more propaganda in the form of "The Bookman Song:"

It's a great day to be a bookman.
It's a great day I know.
It's a great day to be a bookman everywhere I go.
Goodbye no-nevers, goodbye doubts and fears
It's a great day to be a bookman...be of good cheer.
I feel happy. I feel terrific. I feel GREAT!
There you go! Have a ball.

Toward summer's end, we learned from company reports sent to parents that our daughter ranked among the top 10 percent in her sales category. Despite all the hardship, perhaps because of it, she was beginning to feel good about her achievement. She thought that maybe it was worth it after all. She saw that the sweetest success is hard won.

But problems began to surface. For three months she had taken deposits on book orders; now the time had come to deliver the goods. But a customer in the car rental business who had promised to lend her a car gratis reneged on his offer when she came to collect on his promise. She rented a car elsewhere, but as she drove from the rental lot, she collided with another car and was found to be at fault. Because she hadn't taken out insurance, she had to make good on the combined damage to both cars of over $600. But she was feeling rich, having made almost $3,000 selling books after expenses—more money than she had dreamed possible—and she accepted having to part with the $600 with admirable equanimity. Certainly with more than her parents could have mustered.

Our daughter's summer break would appear to have ended happily. Not so. Enter the State Department of

Revenue. To my surprise, our daughter had to pay $148 state tax, about 36 percent of her federal tax, on an income of nearly $3,000, a sum far below poverty level.

More than a year later, she received a notice from the Department of Revenue penalizing her $14.21 for late payment of taxes. After informing the department by letter that she had actually paid her taxes six weeks early, she got a call from a state revenue agent—a call that I inadvertently intercepted at our family home. I informed the agent that my daughter was a student away at college but that I was familiar with the situation and offered to help. When he asked if I had her power of attorney to discuss the matter, I knew she was headed for a serious bout with the "system."

She then called the agent long distance. He read her the law, although not in lay language that a twenty-year-old would understand. At issue was her failure to submit an estimated tax return. She had reasoned that she could not possibly have done this until later in the year when the company sent her a check for the summer's work so she knew what she had actually earned. She thought that, having had negligible earnings during the prior year, she had no basis for an early estimate. But after talking with the agent, she felt that it wasn't worth fighting the system for the small sum in question, so she paid the penalty.

But the department wasn't satisfied; a new notice arrived with an additional "demand charge" of $2.00 and interest of $.59. In its relentless efficiency, the department collection costs had now exceeded the sum sought. She again figured that there was no point in fighting it. Although there was a live person, a revenue agent representing the state, he was no more human than the digital automaton that was pursuing our hapless daughter.

Even more complications continued to surface. Our daughter had forgotten to include the casualty loss of the car accident on her federal and state tax form. It turns out that no tax at all should have been paid, so she plans to file an amended form next April. Will the state refund the original penalty, the demand charge, and the $.59 interest? Ah, well. If only I had some assurance that the department was going after the big fish with as much zeal as they have after my daughter. As for her, she will probably leave the state after graduation. Thank heavens she plans to write books, not sell them. For her graduation present I'm thinking of giving her the wherewithal to relocate to New Hampshire or Florida, where there is no state income tax. Isn't that also the American way?

HOME

The plain in tropical Pampanga province is flat like the Great Plains of the United States, except that it is rimmed by a range of forested mountains. The grassy green expanse darkens to deep blue near the foot of the mountains. Clumps of trees sprinkled across the plain hide small villages, each with its great hacienda mansion surrounded by peasants' hovels. The town of Guagua and the village of Lubao are simple paradises, not easily forsaken for all their poverty. An American friend from my outfit lived in Lubao in 1945 while World War II was winding down.

A two lane concrete highway cut northward across the plain. Americans taken prisoner on Bataan knew the highway; many died on it and were buried by the Filipinos beneath mango trees that grew beside the road. Now, months later, ten-wheelers pounding along it cause the earth to rumble and vibrate. One day a ten-wheeler stopped near an isolated clump of trees. My American friend jumped from the truck and waved to the driver. "Thanks for the lift, Joe." Every American in the military is called Joe.

From the highway a dirt road plunged into the vegetation. Muddy puddles breeding mosquitoes filled the potholes. He hopped over them as he worked his way down the path and into the dense, dark growth. A rucksack hung from his shoulder. On the breeze he heard the strumming of a distant guitar from the flooded fields where the villagers were planting rice seedlings. Lubao was the home of people with bare feet and kerosene lamps, where the huts lining the dirt streets were on stilts so they would stand above the water during the rainy season. Lubao's inhabitants were generous and hospitable. Never mind that technologically Lubao was a void; its people were humane, and their lives were rich and full. The young American revered Lubao and its people. Once there, he never wanted to leave.

The big ten-wheel truck rocked along at fifty miles an hour. I sat in the back curled up against the cab. The hot tropical wind eddied around me as the sun evaporated my sweat. The two-lane concrete highway faded swiftly away behind me and joined the vast flat green plain that extended toward the mountains.

I had come from our military base by the sea, beyond the mountain range. When I had left the camp the commander had asked, "Do you know where he is?"

"Yes, sir," I answered.

"Where?"

I wouldn't answer.

"You're supposed to be his friend, aren't you?

"Yes, sir"

"You want him to return to the States, don't you?

"Yes, sir"

"Where is he, then?"

I remained silent.

"Then to hell with him," the commander had said, turning his back to me. He looked out the window into the deepest reach of the valley where a mountain rose high in the distance. Even from where he stood he could see the silver streak of a waterfall cascading down its flank. "He won't be punished, y'know. No point now. We're all going home."

"Yes, sir"

He turned to me."Go get him."

"I'll try, sir."

"You'll get him."

"Yes, sir"

When the ten-wheeler had traveled forty miles northward from the sea, I pounded on the cab roof, searing my hand on the hot metal. The truck stopped by a dirt road that disappeared into a clump of trees. I jumped down into the dust.

"What's out here?" the driver asked.

"A friend," I said.

"Out here?"

"Thanks for the lift, soldier," I said.

"There isn't anything out here, fella." Then he put the truck into gear and roared away.

On the opposite side of the highway the green plain lay like a vast carpet in the sun. The dirt road was dark and damp. I welcomed the cool reprieve from the scorching plain. The road led to the village of Lubao.

About a month earlier I had visited this small village. It had a schoolhouse and a small church with a corrugated steel roof. The village breathed its own life and practiced its own religion. Although its people were familiar with the outside world, they preferred isolation. They knew Guagua and Olongopo and Manila, but they always returned to Lubao. They came back to its sleepy muddy stream that meandered behind their huts. They came back to the rice fields where the cool artesian wells kept the earth soaked. Lubao was a serene and safe place.

Americans always passed Lubao by. They didn't even know it existed because it couldn't be seen from the highway. However, the people of Lubao liked Americans and were grateful to them. On my first visit there, I was welcomed. Even if I hadn't been a friend of their best American friend, they would have fed me until I could hold no more, and given me a sleeping mat and a blanket for the night.

I never returned to Lubao voluntarily; this visit was a mission. Had I returned after my first visit, I could not have resisted making a third visit, and a fourth, and more. I would have found a home there even though my real home was nine thousand miles away. In Lubao I was simply an impersonal G.I. tourist, seeking no part of friendship or love. I did not allow myself to fall under the spell of its simplicity and ease and beauty. Instead, the great offerings of Western civilization awaited me. My ambition and my dreams were clear.

As I came within sight of the village, the kids spied me. The half naked older ones and the naked little ones flocked around me. They grabbed at the rucksack hanging from my shoulder and I gave each of them a candy bar and a precious stick of gum. Delighted with their loot, they sprinted ahead announcing my arrival. I aimed directly for Reverend Sangco's house. He greeted me at the door with a smile and an extended hand.

"Come in my boy, and be cooled."

"Thank you, Reverend."

Indeed, the house, made of bamboo, was quite cool. The mahogany floor shone from a coating of wax.

"Sit down and let us give you some cool water. You must be thirsty after your trip."

I sat on an upholstered bamboo chair, the only one of its kind in the village. Reverend Sangco's wife, nodding meekly, silently in greeting, handed me a cup of water. A gentle breeze from the watery fields drifted through the room. It smelled fresh and strongly damp. And it carried the dainty strains of a melody from a guitar.

"We are very happy that you are paying us another visit," said the Reverend.

"I'm also glad to see you again, Reverend, but I have come for a purpose."

The Reverend's English was simple and precise, his voice deep and gentle. He spoke without a trace of an accent. He said that the Great Books that lined his shelves had taught him English. And before the war, he had learned how to pronounce the words in conversation with a friend, an American missionary.

The Reverend searched my eyes awaiting a further explanation of my mission. The very fact that I had a mission might have surprised him, too. No one ever comes to Lubao with any purpose other than to be in Lubao. This village offers no drama, only poverty and happiness.

"My outfit is leaving for the States in a few days, Reverend."

He nodded, as if my statement were a natural law. His wife asked him a question in dialect and he replied to her quietly. She sat down slowly on a wooden chest placed against a wall and stared at the floor.

"He's been here a long time now," I said.

"Yes, he has had a long leave," said the Reverend.

"No," I said.

"Ah, yes, he told me."

"He had only a weekend pass and he knew we were going to be shipping out soon."

As the Reverend sat silently absorbing what I had just said, his wife continued staring at the floor, her lips mumbling something I couldn't fathom.

"Where is he, Reverend?"

I saw pain in his eyes.

"In the fields planting the rice seedlings with Angelina. It is the time."

"Angelina, Angelina," the Reverend's wife moaned.

The sun had hidden behind the trees and the village had sunken into shadow. After an hour, the people came in from the fields and entered their houses. The dogs barked and the pigs and chickens that roamed under their houses became noisy. Life had returned to the village.

Angelina entered the house first, and he followed. When she saw me she curtsied slightly and smiled. Slender, with long black hair that curved around her shoulders, she was a quiet girl.

He halted almost imperceptibly when he saw me.

"What are you doing here," he demanded in a hostile tone.

"Visiting," I said. "I didn't think you'd mind."

He shrugged. "It isn't my village. I don't own it."

But from his tone I think he thought he did.

"Well, let's have supper," the Reverend said. He called in dialect to his wife, who had left the room. Then my friend also called to her in dialect. The Reverend and he began to argue, my friend heatedly. The Reverend finally acceded to his demands.

"The Reverend had instructed her to serve you C-rations," my friend explained.

"Yes, the food of your country," said the Reverend enthusiastically.

"But I told him that you wouldn't appreciate it," my friend interjected.

"I'll eat anything you wish to serve me," I said addressing the Reverend.

The Reverend beamed. All of us ate C-rations that evening, with my friend glowering at the Reverend throughout the meal. But the food would be less reason for him to be unhappy than hearing what I would have to say next.

"I have orders to bring you back to the base with me," I said.

"Forget it. I'm not going. This is my home now."

"They won't let you stay here."

"I know that, but they'll never find me."

After I returned to the base without my friend, the commander called me into his office.

"I see you didn't bring him back. Why not?"

"I didn't find him, sir."

"You didn't find him, you say?"

"That's right, sir."

"I say you did. You found him didn't you?" The commander insisted. He knew well the bonding that took place among the men.

And I knew he knew. "That's right, sir."

Whether or not my friend returned to the States was irrelevant now that the war was over. Furthermore, I couldn't force him to return to the base.

"I see," said the commander. "We move out tomorrow. One man more or less doesn't matter, does it?"

"No sir, it doesn't"

"Tomorrow we're going home, son."

"He's already there, sir."

DEAR PEN PAL YOSEF

My Pa and I went to Washington D.C. today. It's the most beautiful capital in the whole wide world. Oh, excuse me, I'm sure yours is just as nice. We visited the senator from our state. He's the man who represents us in the Senate and does any favors we ask, which he has to do or else we'd kick him out. He seems like a nice man and I wouldn't kick him out just because he *didn't* do us a favor. But Pa says that's the way it is. Well, Pa and the senator got to talking about something called the national debt.

"What's the national debt?" I asked. The senator put his arm around my shoulder and said, "Son, that's the money your government owes the people, and it's a mighty big pile, yes sir."

I looked up at Pa. "But you always told us to never borrow."

"Not exactly, son," Pa said, winking at the senator. "I said never borrow unless you can pay it back."

"Oh," I said, "you mean the government is going to pay it back?"

"Yes sir, boy," the senator said.

"When?" I asked.

The senator glanced at Pa. He looked as though he had a stomach ache. "Any time the people want it, boy," said the senator.

"How much is it?" I asked him.

"More than a trillion dollars," said Pa.

I don't know how much more than a trillion dollars is, but I know it's a lot. So I said "Wow, the government sure is rich to have that much money."

The senator sat down behind his desk. "Well," he said, "we don't have quite that much money, son."

"Not by a long shot," Pa said.

This was getting interesting. "Then how's the government going to pay it back?" I asked.

The senator got up and shook Pa's hand. Then he said, "Drop in again, sir. Always glad to meet my constituents." He looked at me and patted me on the head. "But better leave him home next time."

I don't know why he didn't like me. I thought he was a nice man and I'll vote for him when I grow up.

THE CRISIS AT HEMISPHERE PRODUCTS

The crisis had begun. Hemisphere Products, a subsidiary of General Industries Inc., had been losing money steadily for the past two years, and every attempt to correct this condition within the framework of the existing organization had failed.

During the early months of the losses, Hemisphere's management had assured the management of General Industries that the losses were merely a temporary setback due to a seasonal fluctuation in orders. General's management had accepted this explanation as reasonable, since those early losses did occur during the months of historically low business activity. However, after the slow season had passed, Hemisphere continued to experience losses, whereas its competitors seemed to be thriving.

Hemisphere's management began looking for reasons. It was not an investigation into the facts. No, it was one of soul searching, because for the past twenty-five years the company had operated under a formula that had been successful. The formula was deeply entrenched in the company's culture. After all, they thought, what new facts remained to be discovered?

Absolutely none. What did the company's executives not know? Nothing.

So Hemisphere's management investigated itself. Clearly, someone or some number of executives, were not doing their jobs. At first the staff began meeting once a week, then twice a week, then daily. Each person aired his or her complaints, proposed minor changes, and denied his or her blame for what was happening. Some expressed themselves in a polite, controlled way; others expressed indignation and anger. But names were never mentioned, only situations. No one ever stated true thoughts, only cautious, conservative, safe proposals. The meetings were designed to simply please an audience of the actors themselves.

However, privately, many executives had a clear opinion of what had been happening and why, and a radical solution. The consensus was divided. One group, by far the larger, blamed the workers. The group concluded that the workers had been taking advantage of the company with their unreasonable wage demands and lax habits that had resulted in products of poor quality. The more extreme members of this group implied that there had been worker sabotage, thus it was easy to blame the union, which must be relentlessly fought.

The second group blamed top management. They spoke of the incompetence, the inflexibility, the senility of their leaders. The top man must be removed and replaced. Needless to say, among this group were several who considered themselves qualified to fill that position.

This was the prelude to a top personnel crisis. A major change was about to occur. The forces set in motion were more powerful, more inhuman, more calculating, and more final than any that had been proposed at the meetings. Some executives began preparations to take cover. Others were ready to stand up to any change in top personnel. Still others were laying the groundwork for their escape to a competitor.

The personnel crisis then began playing itself out.

Meet Hemisphere's general manager, Irving Handleman, known as I.H. to his employees and business associates. He is also a vice-president of the parent company, General Industries. Now fifty-eight years old, he had founded Hemisphere Products twenty-five years earlier with a partner, Bertram Michaelson, who had died from a heart attack on the very day that I.H. had secured the company's first big chain-store order.

"Bertram was a production genius," declared I.H. nostalgically, "and no one since has proven his equal. I loved him and I shall miss him to the end of my days."

The truth, were it known, is that I.H. and Bertram had often come to blows, merely tolerating each other because of their mutual dependence. Indeed, the day Bertram died, he and I.H. had had a brutal argument, which some suspect had contributed to the heart attack.

I.H. was a shining example of Horatio Alger's American dream. His family was almost poor, at best lower middle class, and couldn't afford to send him to college. His first job was as a postal clerk, which after a half dozen years he quit to form Hemisphere with Bertram's money. Today I.H. is worth several hundred million dollars, more or less. The day his net worth struck nine figures he celebrated so lavishly that the monetary attainment lasted only a few hours. But since money begets money, he regained that celebrated figure within a few weeks.

Here are a few more pertinent facts about I.H. He had a son, Walter, an only child, who at thirty-one years of age had hung himself. Having been brought into the business against his will, Walter, a sensitive young man, detested all of the positions he had been assigned. His ambition was to be an artist. To become one, however, required a financial subsidy, which I. H. refused to provide. I.H. would say, "Walter is ridiculous, brilliant, but an idealist, impractical. He wouldn't survive a minute without my support." Shortly after Walter started at Hemisphere, he began drinking, and eventually, sank into a deep depression.

Shaken by his son's suicide, I.H. kept asking himself, "Why, why, why?" Of course, were the truthful answer offered him, he would have denied it. I.H's wife, Elsa, went temporarily mad, and ever since, has been quite high strung and occasionally out of touch with reality. Indeed, so shaken was I.H. over his son's suicide that he became disenchanted with the most important concern in his life, Hemisphere Products. He blamed the company for Walter's death, which led him to sell out to General Industries for a goodly sum. But he did agree to manage the business for the next five years. Eventually, as the pain of his son's death subsided, he rededicated himself to the success of Hemisphere, although he often forgot that the company was no longer his.

As Hemisphere's financial crisis deepened, the president of General Industries summoned I.H. to its headquarters in Chicago. General's president, Alex Quick, was a calm, quiet-spoken man. Only thirty-five years old, he had inherited his position after having received the essential preparation for taking over, namely the right schooling, experience within the company, and most important, the indoctrination, that is, the proper management style and the company's business philosophy. He shared ownership with 104 other members of the Quick clan. By the way, the Quicks are Mayflower descendants, and it had been rumored that the Leif Erikson expedition had accidentally left a Quick behind in Rhode Island. With whom that Quick had multiplied had never been settled, so no one in the family ever mentioned it.

"Good to see you," said Alex as I.H. swept into his office and held Alex's hand in both of his a bit too long.

"I suppose you're concerned about Hemisphere's losses," said I.H., who had plopped himself in a chair in front of Alex's desk.

"You don't waste time getting to the point, do you I.H.?"

"What's the use in beating around the bush? I know why I'm here just as much as you do."

"Well, I *am* concerned, and I'd like to know why bad things are happening, from the man who's responsible."

They're due to a host of factors, Alex: from the economy, to the union, to the damn administration in Washington."

"Just a minute. Are you saying that you have no responsibility here?"

"Of course I have some responsibility," I.H. said, annoyance in his voice.

"Not some responsibility, I.H., all the responsibility. You're top man. That's where success or failure begins and ends."

I.H.'s face flushed. "Are you saying that outside influences don't matter, that what happens in our market doesn't matter?"

"When you come right down to it, yes," said Alex, thumping his hand on his desk. "You adjust to what's happening, you take action and stop the losses even if you have to cut your staff and production employees down to the bone."

"That would be unwise. I need to keep things intact, I'll need everyone in place for the rebound, Alex. Don't you understand? For the rebound! You don't get it, do you?"

"We can't continue supporting the financial hemorrhaging that's been going on, I.H. Are you aware that Hemisphere's competitors have stanched their losses and are now back in the black?"

"How do you know that?" asked I.H. astonished.

"We have ways."

"If they're profitable, as you say, then we will be, too."

"When?"

"Soon."

"How?"

"I'll revise our strategy. That's what I'll do."

"Sorry, I.H. That's not good enough. It's gone too far for too long."

"What does your kind know? You go to a famous B School and you think you have all the answers."

"What we learn in B School, I.H., is that success or failure lies with the top man, and you're failing. You've let it happen."

"Godammit, I built Hemisphere. I made it prosper for a quarter century and…"

"You didn't do it alone, I. H. Are you forgetting Michaelson?"

"Are you saying…?"

"It's time you retired, I.H."

"Wait a minute. Look, Alex, I can fix it."

"It's too late, I. H. We've already hired your replacement. It's already done."

"What?"

I.H. looked incredulous. Then, as the reality started to sink in, he hung his head in defeat.

The two men sat silently for a few minutes. Finally I.H. raised his eyes. He looked defiantly at Alex. "I'll start over again and destroy Hemisphere. You hear me?"

"Best of luck, I.H. Now, I've got to get back to work." Alex pressed the intercom. "Please show our visitor out."

As the secretary entered, Alex rose and stepped from behind his desk to shake I.H.'s hand. "I wish you well, I.H. I mean nothing personal. It's strictly a business decision."

I.H. did not take Alex's hand. Instead, he took a swing at him, delivering a blow to his chin, toppling him over. "*This* is personal," said I.H., and he stormed out of the office.

THE THIRTY-SEVENTH YEAR

When Jessica picked up the ringing phone from a sound sleep, it was eight o'clock in the morning, certainly not an appropriate time to receive a phone call. All her friends knew that they must never call her, or she them, before nine.

"Who is this?" she demanded, sounding annoyed.

"It's Dan, Dan Temple."

"Who?"

"We met at the art museum party. Dan Temple. Don't you remember me?"

Searching her memory, she recalled meeting a retired businessman with whom she'd had a fascinating conversation. That was about a month ago. They had talked about what was happening in their lives, which appeared to be on a somewhat parallel course. He had just sold his company to devote the rest of his life to writing, and she had just quit her job at a newspaper to become a full-time artist.

"What do you want?" she asked.

"May I take you out to dinner?"

"What? I can't say. It's very early, you know."

"Should I call you back later?"

"No, no," she said, becoming more alert.

"I'll repeat the question, in case you didn't understand." He laughed.

"Aren't you married?" she blurted out.

"Yes, but I left my wife a month ago. We're headed for a divorce."

"I see. Well…"

"It's just a dinner, Jessica. I think we had a great conversation when we last met, and I'd like to find out more about you. You're under no obligation to ever see me again."

"Well." She paused. "When did you have in mind?"

"This evening."

"You don't waste time. Okay, I suppose that would be all right."

"How about dinner at Oscar's? I'll pick you up."

"No, I'll meet you there."

"Don't worry, Jessica. I'm safe." Dan laughed again. "Give me your address and I'll meet you outside your house at six-thirty."

"Oh, all right," she replied. "It's Five Gull Lane in Fairport."

"Six-thirty at your house tonight," he said and hung up.

Jessica immediately dialed her friend Margaret, who had introduced her to Dan at the party. Margaret, a psychotherapist, had known Dan for several years and had actually been counseling his wife.

"I just got a call from Dan Temple," said Jessica. "He asked me to have dinner with him. I agreed, but I wonder whether that's wise. He tells me he's left his wife."

"Really?" Margaret said, surprised. "He told you that?"

"Was he lying to me? Is he safe? I mean, can I trust him to behave himself?"

Margaret delayed replying as she digested the news about Dan. "I don't think you have to worry. He's a good man in an unhappy marriage."

At Oscar's, Jessica and Dan had a table overlooking Fairport's harbor. As the late September sun was setting, the surface of the water turned orange. "There's a scene for you," Dan exclaimed.

"Yes, it *is* beautiful. I should have brought my paints with me," said Jessica, laughing nervously.

Jessica was curious about the part of Dan's past that he hadn't yet told her, about his role as the CEO of a manufacturing business. She wondered why he was interested in her, a woman who had accomplished little, and no doubt was a good generation younger than he was.

Dan, on the other hand, had no interest in discussing what he did before selling his business. Instead, he wanted to talk only about the major change that was occurring in his life, and to marvel at the similarity of her decisive change as well.

"I sold my business for enough money to last the rest of my life," he said. "But you have no nest egg to rely on. That takes courage, more than I would have had. I admire you for it."

"I remortgaged my house," she said. "I have enough money to last me a year. And I expect to sell some paintings."

"But what if your money runs out in a year and your art doesn't sell?"

"I'll get a job. I don't see that I'm taking much of a risk," she said matter-of-factly.

As they finished their meal and rose from the table, Dan noticed that Jessica had hardly eaten. The fact was, she had been too nervous to eat. She had felt that surely she was out of her league dining with such a high-powered businessman, obviously a millionaire. What could he see in her?

When they arrived back at her house, she thanked him for a lovely evening and quickly opened the car door to leave.

Dan noticed her nervousness. "May I see some of your paintings?" he asked. "Trust me, Jessica, I just want to see your work, and then I'll go. I promise."

Hesitating, but finally giving in, Jessica led Dan through her house to a crowded back room. In the center was an easel with an unfinished watercolor, and in one corner a large drafting table holding a short stack of drawings and a few more watercolors. He was surprised by the small number of pieces. But he studied each one at length, and when he was finished he made a move to leave.

"What do you think?" she asked with some trepidation.

"Well, you don't have much to see," he said. "I thought you were devoting yourself full time to your art."

"I'm having trouble. I never think my work is good enough. Do you like what you see?"

"It's competent, Jessica, but it's awfully tame. The work has no spark. Forgive me for being so blunt."

"No, no, I appreciate your honesty. I need that. I need someone to critique it."

"Look," said Dan, "how would you like to spend this Saturday afternoon with me? We'll have lunch and I'll show you around Harbortown. Bring whatever you need to do your art. There are some great places to paint or sketch, wonderful scenes of the sea, marvelous old houses with terrific landscaping. What do you say?"

She agreed, and a few days later she drove her car to meet him at his designated spot on Main Street. It was a glorious sunny day. Dan got in the passenger seat of Jessica's car and directed her through the streets, pointing out various shops and historic homes. Suddenly she pulled to the curb. Gesturing toward a small garden house under a magnificent maple tree in fall foliage, its broad limbs shading an expansive lawn, she told him she'd like to do a pastel of the scene. As she opened the hatchback of her car and retrieved a large pad, he said, "I'll just go for a walk while you work. When should I return?"

"I don't know. Give me an hour. Would that be okay?"

"Back in an hour," he said.

When he returned, the hatch of her car was open but her art supplies weren't in evidence. He assumed that she had completed her work.

"May I see what you've done?" he asked.

"You don't want to. It's not very good. Really, it's nothing."

"Will you let me be the judge?" he insisted.

She retrieved a rolled-up pastel from the open hatch and handed it to him. "It's just an exercise."

He carefully unrolled it, astonished at how imaginatively she had portrayed the scene: splashes of brilliant orange foliage arching over an old-fashioned garden house set on a dark green lawn.

"What do you plan to do with this?" he asked.

"Nothing. Throw it away."

"May I have it?"

"Sure, but why? I think it's worthless."

"Not to me it isn't. I think it's beautiful."

She shrugged. Was he just trying to impress her?

After lunch in an outdoor restaurant, they went in separate cars to Dan's rented house by the harbor. They walked up and down the streets of the neighborhood and gazed at the boats. He pointed out his catboat bobbing at its mooring.

"Do you like to sail?" he asked.

"Only when there's not much wind."

"My god, a landlubber," he laughed.

She shrugged. "But I'm willing to try sometime, if you'll take it easy."

They spread a blanket on the shore of the harbor where they sat and talked until late afternoon. She told him about her career as a primary grade art teacher in Georgia.

"The administration kept cutting back the hours for art classes, so the kids had hardly any time to learn. I took a sabbatical, came to Maine, and never returned to Georgia."

"That took guts," Dan said.

"I had to do it, Dan. I couldn't stand it anymore. So I found a job working as an illustrator for a newspaper here. Still, my story must be pretty ordinary compared to yours."

"Not at all. I struggled for years working in all sorts of jobs, a waiter in restaurants, an office clerk, an inspector in a factory, a salesman. They were all dead-end jobs, and I felt like a failure."

"But you finally succeeded," she said admiringly, surprised that he had endured such a struggle.

"It's one thing to take advantage of an opportunity when it comes along. That's luck," he explained. "But it's more important to create your own opportunity."

"But how can you?"

"You gamble. I saw a chance to go out on my own where most would have passed it by. I bought into a losing company and gambled that I could turn it around. Eventually, after nearly failing, I won."

"I could never do that," she said flatly.

"But you can. You're doing it. Like me, believing in yourself, you're gambling on your ability to succeed as a painter."

Jessica saw now that Dan was an ordinary man after all, just as she was an ordinary woman. He was without pretension. How similar their fortunes were, his in the past, hers yet to be won—or lost.

The following weekend, they went to the local beach and just sat, she sketching on a pad, he reading a book. From time to time they cooled off in the ocean, where they cavorted like children. He had invited her to have dinner at his place, which intrigued her because she knew no other men who could cook.

While she showered, he inserted two TV dinners into the microwave. When she came to the table, she was wearing a robe he had loaned her, his robe. She had thought that wearing his robe was a bit too familiar, and a bit too soon. But she had begun to trust him more than she doubted herself. As he served the dinners, she began laughing.

"I'm not much of a chef," he apologized with a grin.

"Really?" she said, smiling back at him. He reached for her hand, and she let him take it.

After they finished eating, he asked, "Do you like opera?"

"I don't know opera," she said, almost apologetically.

"Then let me play *Madame Butterfly* for you on the stereo. Why don't you sit on the couch," he said as he rose to place the long-playing record on the turntable.

He joined her as they listened. The music overwhelmed her. She stretched out with her head in his lap. "It's so sad, so beautiful," she said. "I could cry."

Dan lowered his head to kiss Jessica on the lips. She raised her hand to his cheek and returned his kiss. That evening she made no motion to leave. When he asked her to stay over, she said yes. And so began the first phase of their falling in love, although neither knew that yet.

The next morning Jessica returned to her house. Dan returned to his writing, although not to the novel he had been working on. Instead, he began the first in a series of letters to Jessica.

But the smooth path of their relationship suddenly took a strange turn. Dan's letters seemed to border on the absurd. They appeared so nonsensical to Jessica that she wondered what had happened to the man who had admired her art and introduced her to opera, the man to whom she had given herself. On the last day of October, this is the letter she received:

Hi there, Jessica,

My boss, DT (he's a laugh y'know), has asked me to drop you this line on his behalf. He has the crazy idea that you may have forgotten the directions to his pad on Sanford Lane in Harbortown which I share with him and his erotic art. Enclosed is a map that will set you straight in case you weren't. Straight that is.

My name, by the way, is S.S. (Strong Shoulders) Peeooter. I'm DT's IBM clone, his alter ego, his mind-reader (I specialize principally in his mind) and his most intimate adviser. In the old days, American men blamed their wives for everything that went wrong, but that's old-fashioned. Nowadays, they blame the computer, Computero sapiens. That's me.

Through the grapevine I hear you're a nifty gal. Well, I hope the grapevine works in reverse, because I'm pretty hotsy-totsy myself. Don't breathe a word of this to DT, but I've got to admit I'm smarter than he'll ever be. And I'm a hell of a lot handsomer. You should see my keyboard. Just touch one of my buttons and watch great things happen. Touch one of his, if you can find one, and, well, good luck. Fill the monitor screen of my heart and my cup runneth all over the place. I can move blocks of text for you, paragraphs, entire pages, the world—almost, that is. In fact, what I can do when all my disks are whirring and all my silicon chips are sparking like the finale at a rocket show on the Fourth of July, what I can do when all my gigabytes are gigging away full force, well, I can tell you, it'll beat any professional backscratch. You see, I can do anything you ask, make words and figures, even forecast the future—given sufficient data, of course. Oh, sure, some things I can't do like love, laugh and cry, but that's old-fashioned too. Nowadays, you humans don't go in for that kind of stuff.

And that's why when you visit 165 Sanford Lane, you'd better forget him. Go for me. How about it? You'll find me easier to take, much less complicated, that's for sure, and so incredibly more cooperative that it's no contest between him and me. Do you know he's just gotten over mourning a loss, a loss of his own making, a loss of love? Now, no computer would ever be that stupid. Do you know that he's so vulnerable? If I let him, he'd give the whole damned store away. Thank God we computers are logical and know how to practice restraint. So you see, being with me is the simpler option.

The grapevine also informs me you're seeing a shrink. See what happens when you've got emotions? We computers, I'm proud to say, don't need shrinks. In the first place, shrinks cost a bloody fortune. In the second place, they keep you all stirred up inside (If you're not screwed up now, just wait). And in the third place, they get you so hooked on them that you'll keep goin' to them forever. DT thinks (Remember I can read his mind) you'll discover the little girl in yourself, then learn how to keep her in her place. You'll also discover God, the real one, if the shrink is good at leading you way down into your soul. DT claims he never believed in God, the one that everyone thinks is in heaven, until he found HIM someplace else—inside himself. What bunk, what a crock! As for me, I think all you humans are nuts. That's what's so hotsy-totsy about me. I'm so refreshingly sane and simple. How about it, kid?

Here's to making your acquaintance, and more
S.S. Peeooter

Jessica didn't know what to make of this weird letter. Dan had revealed a worrisome side of himself. Their relationship, which seemed to hold promise, now seemed too risky. She wished he would stop sending letters like these, but not ready to call it off completely, she sent him the following note, a lone paragraph.

My dear S.S. Peeooter,

Well, my dear, in all honesty I have never considered a Computero sapiens an interesting being for a friendship. You are full of charm, I must admit. With all your "flattering" comments regarding DT, I cannot quite figure out why you would want to saddle yourself with another humanoid. Perhaps there is some deep, dark void that electrical circuits simply cannot completely fill. Could this be true??? Be careful how you answer. DT is watching, ready to point his finger and say "Aha."

Jessica

Peeooter responded immediately.

Have I missed something?

To respond to your remarks, my dear, in all honesty I think you ought to seriously consider the likes of me as a very, very best friend. Please ponder my advantages:

1) Computero sapiens are no sexual threat. Just think, you can take me to bed with you and have a full night's sleep.

2) You can depend on my "charm" (thank you) day after day after day because you control me, and do I love it.

3) Unlike Homo sapiens, whose motives are suspect (like lusting after you perhaps—you never know), mine are as pure as Ivory Snow. After all, how could I have bad thoughts when they aren't even mine? They would only be yours, which I know come from Procter and Gamble.

4) I'm great for hugging. See how my monitor is easy to put your arms around? And where, tell me where, could I possibly be kissed?

5) You and DT simply never stop talking, especially him. Me, you can shut up anytime you wish by typing Abort or Quit. Try doing that with him and see where it gets you.

6) DT likes the way you paint and draw, but what you want is criticism. Real honest stuff. He's too blind about you right now to see anything wrong in anything you do. He thinks every mistake you make is simply one more step in your growth. But ask me and I'll tell you every time you botch it. But you must tell me what you want me to say. I'll be glad to rub it in real good, make you cry if that would make you feel better. Nothing like going on a good self-hate binge every once in a while. He hasn't the guts, even if you asked him.

7) God rested on the seventh day. So will I. Let me leave you with this thought: there's not much difference between the way my electrical circuits work and yours. Of course, yours may give you more thrills, but mine are more dependable because they're made in Japan. So make your choice: dependable me or thrill-seeking DT. No contest, eh? I'm waiting.

What to make of this? Jessica was at a loss. When the weirdness continued, she phoned Dan and told him to stop.

"I'm serious, Dan. I don't appreciate this kind of thing."

Three days later, on November 8th, another letter arrived.

My dear Jessica,

Last night, only four and one half hours ago, you threw me a curve. You made me face up to what I was really saying— and doing—when I wear the Peeooter disguise. I had already learned that you are one to always reach for the truth, and now I know that you demand the same of your friends as well. Here, then, is the letter you ask of me, undisguised, straightforward, un-tempered by humor, honest and from my heart.

Unable to sleep after I spoke to you on the phone, I watched TV until 11:30, then dozed off. At 2 a.m. I awoke. My mind was oddly alert, completely preoccupied with thoughts of our talk, of your comment that Peeooter reminded you of a ventrilo-quist's dummy. And then I let my mind simply wander without trying to make sense of it. After a half hour the sense surfaced. There is a saying: "The beginning of wisdom is silence. The sec-ond stage is listening." I was silent and I listened. So here I am, eyes wide and shining, at the keyboard, ready to let the chips fall where they will. Why not? I can't sleep, so let my heart take over.

I'd like to preface what I'm about to write with a request: please don't be alarmed. You will be as free and your world will be as safe and secure after you read this as it was before. I may as well begin with the shocker and get it over with. What

I learned lying there, what I had been covering up, denying to myself, was that I am in love with you. But being in love with you frightens the daylights out of me, hence the disguise. When I analyze what Peeooter is saying, I realize he's telling you I'm not worth much. Fearing rejection from you, I'm rejecting myself instead. But that's the immature little boy in me. My adult self wants to win you over to that wiser side of me.

The truth is I didn't plan to fall in love, nor did I really want to. It wasn't in the script. I thought that once I broke away from my marriage, I would have a few pleasant friendships and noncommittal companionships, and concentrate on writing. Having left one long complicated relationship with a woman, I wanted to keep all future female relationships simple. But it seems I have no choice. As John Fogerty's song goes, "I Can't Help Myself." The only way I could become disenchanted now is to find that you aren't what you seem to be, and that's mighty unlikely.

Let me, if I may, talk about what being in love with you means. Right away I should explain that I've never been in love before, not like this, but I have loved. What is love but to place the welfare of another person ahead of your own. They are different feelings, and a healthy being in love will blossom into full-fledged love. The fact is, I haven't known you long enough to love you fully in the latter sense, but I can predict that it wouldn't take all that long to love you and care deeply if we continue to see each other. So now you know the risk. And now you also know why we could sleep in the same room together without your having to fear my violating your wishes. Sure I desire you, sure I want to consummate what I feel for you through making love to you. Hell, I'm a normal male. But my desires are subordinate to my respect for you. I would do nothing that would kill your respect for me. To make a conquest is abhorrent to me. How could I possibly use someone I'm in love with?

My being in love with you has a quality that surprises me. I don't mind in the least that you're not in love with me. I want only to give, and I seek nothing in return. Actually, I'm somewhat in awe of how beautiful it is. I honestly believe that your not being in love with me is an accurate assumption. You are much too cautious to let yourself succumb to such foolishness so early. And it is foolishness, but oh is it sweet. I don't think I've ever felt less demanding of a person I'm with than I am of you. All I seem to want to do is watch you, listen to you, tell you about myself, and let things be. Somehow I have the impression that you're on the brink of something exciting in your life, and I want to be near you to share the unfurling.

I also believe that I'm onto something exciting in my life, too, and I'm already over the brink. It began with my declaration of freedom, and it now concerns my declaration of love. And I'm productive again. I see my writing developing, and me becoming more prolific and powerful. God knows where things will go from here. However, I'm conscious of certain salient facts that condition my thinking. One is that more of my life is behind me than is ahead. Another is that I've been on the wrong track for most of my life, not in a materialistic sense, but in terms of human relationships and values. For the rest of my life I want to concentrate on quality, not quantity. Our society is preoccupied with quantity (and, boy, was I sucked in), and look at the mess we're in. You are so refreshing to me because quality is all that matters to you. I look to you as a model to follow.

Let me tell you of a dream I had last spring that explains this attitude so well. In the dream I visit a car dealer to learn the status of a new Plymouth I had ordered. He advises me that the car won't arrive for several weeks yet, then he shows me an old Cady completely reconditioned that's available immediately. Indeed, it's a beauty, soft deep velour seats, a glittering dashboard, a sleek hulk of a car. Everything is newly minted and the price is right. I consider his offer for a few moments because, I must confess, I so admire the Cady that I'm tempted. But no, I turn him down. The small Plymouth will do just fine. I'll wait.

I don't think I need to interpret this dream for you. I want less in order to have more. I'm willing to leave half my net worth from my old life behind. I'm willing to try to support myself solely from my writing if need be. Not that I want to suffer if I can avoid it. What I wish for now I can't earn or buy. I can get it only by being strictly myself, by expressing myself honestly. I know I can't buy your love or impress you with materialistic nonsense. How does the song go? "I Can Only Be Me." That's the only way I realize I can have you, and if that's not enough, if my little Plymouth won't do, then I shall have lost. I've lost before. I can more easily accept losing now. But maybe I'll win. I figure I've got a 50/50 chance.

I happened the other day to be reading some beautiful words about happiness by Nathaniel Hawthorne. "Happiness is a butterfly, which when pursued is always just beyond your grasp, but which, if you will sit down quietly, may alight on you." So here I am trying to sit down quietly, although from habit I can't keep my feet still. And as Scott Peck writes in "The Road…" delayed gratification is what makes winning and having all the more precious. I have learned patience, learned to wait, and I shall wait for you if you'll allow it.

Your newest, your loving friend,
Dan

This letter changed everything for Jessica. Just think, here is a man who gives but demands nothing in return. In all her thirty-seven years she had never met a man like Dan. There had always been a catch, a quid pro quo, in her relationships with others, even with her family.

She and Dan began dating every weekend, going to plays, chamber music concerts, movies, the beach. Their compatibility seemed strong and satisfying. And Dan couldn't resist expressing his thoughts and feelings in more letters to her, perhaps because it would have been embarrassing, or corny, to voice them. After all, wasn't Dan now a committed writer? Wasn't this the medium through which he could always be strictly himself? A week later this is what he wrote:

My dear Jessica,

Thank you for a beautiful evening. I found it and you fascinating. Two things fascinate me. One is the gradual revelation of your personality style (not your past, which is not so much fascinating as interesting) as I see you in different situations. The other is the way you think, what your values are, what you dislike and admire.

I feel I now know why you "like" me and I know why I "like" you. I have qualities that you look for in men and you have qualities that I look for in women. And neither of us wants to repeat past mistakes that we've made with the opposite sex. The hope is, that while we can't escape those unconscious determinants that lead us to preferences with respect to the other sex, we both would wish for the most compatible and benign personality among those preferences. In other words, you seem to prefer a controlling individual (which I am), but you would hope that such a person not be too controlling and that he respect your space. And I, preferring a woman who can enjoy my tendency toward taking over (which you admire), wish also that you be independent, your own person and free to express yourself always. It's a balance of opposites within ourselves, really. You like being controlled, yet you must control your own life. I like controlling, yet I must be generous and giving.

But my dear Jessica, I sense some of the things that are bothering you about me. One, I feel, is my sixty-five years of age, and this is quite understandable. It bothers me too, for your sake. Still that's not really an issue that we would ever have to face unless we got serious, which neither of us wishes to be, at least at this time. And I have some thoughts on how to deal with that issue if it ever became necessary. The other is the possibility of my getting back together with my wife. Had I a choice, were my wife to miraculously become the compatible woman I seek, I would instantly go back to her, of course. In that relationship, a thirty-year infrastructure, so to speak, is already in place. With another woman I must start all over again, not that I find that so difficult to contemplate, but why begin anew if the old is still sound. Unfortunately, as I said last night, I believe that her problem is so deep-seated that it will take possibly years for her to deal with it constructively. Meanwhile, I can't simply vegetate. I'm bound to form another relationship. This is a very sad but unavoidable truth.

In any case, at this stage of our friendship, I believe along with you that we have a lot to offer each other. If I can painlessly provide you with the motivation to paint, I shall have given you a lot, I think. And whether you know it or not, my eyes fill up when I see you read my stories and seem to enjoy them and offer suggestions on improving them. You see, my wife hates them, refuses to read them. You put a finger on precisely where I'm weakest in my stories: I explain the obvious, I'm afraid my reader might not have gotten the point. I want so badly to communicate, don't I? Again you brought up the issue of my jolting obviousness in "Sailing Free". You don't let go easily, you follow up, don't you? Well, your persistence has borne fruit. Facing the problem anew (which is within myself, really), I gradually began to understand your reaction, went back to the story this morning, and tore out the offending line. Now

213

I see how this makes the ending so much more powerful, too. Thank you, my friend. Keep doing this for me. Before closing, I must ask you a most important question, perhaps the most important question I shall ask you in a long while: did I leave my New Yorker *in your car?*

I love you,
Dan

As if he couldn't stop communicating, the very next day Jessica received the following letter.

Dearest Jessica,
My mind is filled with so many ideas, rushing like a roaring waterfall, that I can't stanch the flow. I want to pour them out to you, but I know your reluctance, your caution, perhaps your fear of any involvement with me. So I won't call, I won't impose myself, I won't unload on you. But I can write, a fair substitute, and you can read about my thoughts at your own pace, which is more moderate, saner perhaps, than mine. And perhaps you're beginning to have a glimpse into my style, a glimpse into why my personality can be intolerable. My feelings are always close to the surface, which I know can be hard for some to take.

I'm on a high these days, alone and on a high. I never dreamed I'd be this way alone. But I find I have so much, more than I ever knew I had. I'm writing like a storm. And I feel, I know, that "El Presidente, El Morro" is a superior piece of writing, a new level of art for me. Within hours of completing it, I began another short/long story in another style. I'm experimenting and so excited by it.

And I also have you as a friend. And I'm in a thrall over you because you have done so much for me in so short a time. I have been reluctant to look into the future because of the certain pain I know it holds. Yet, I can't hold back; after all, I'm moving into the future at every breath. I'm also afraid to take a look because I know I have an uncanny knack at forecasting.

Doctor Loy, in his book "The Sphinx and the Rainbow," *a recent study on the brain and forecasting, shows how certain minds can see into the future with startling accuracy. From this book I learned why I was so successful in business: I had sufficient insight into the future that I made the right decisions time after time. Even when I decided to sell the business, it turned out to be the perfect time, at the company's and the economy's performing high. And most remarkable, I predicted a revision in the tax laws three years ago and sold under the old more favorable laws before the recent change.*

With some trepidation, having allowed myself to look into a future we might have, I find a beautiful scenario. You will grow to love me as I love you. We shall live together for a short while. Then I'll buy some land that you will help me choose (not hard to imagine, right?), and we'll have a half cape built on it that you will help design, including an artist's studio facing north; and then after you have made peace with yourself through therapy, you will marry me.

But there are two unknowns, into which I have no insight that can affect this scenario. One is your capacity to produce under conditions of affluence. You would have no money worries for the rest of your life and you would be free to pursue your art unhindered by such pressures. The question is, are such pressures necessary for you in order to create. If you resolve your need to do with less (which may be based on a feeling of not deserving more), you will become a renowned artist, perhaps noted for painting some of the finest houses in America, dramatic landscapes, and telling portraits.

The other unknown is your sexual style, since you have hidden from me all clues to that part of your psyche. My marriage has been unfulfilling, especially sexually, because my partner has been extremely inhibited. She sees having sex as being exploited. It is one of the reasons I sought satisfaction elsewhere. In my opinion "the joy of sex" comes from partners having imaginative new experiences together. Sex is not a grim business, but rather play to be enjoyed. And, in my opinion, this is the only reason that a couple (it needn't especially be a man and a woman) should live together before marrying—to find out whether they are sexually compatible. Without this compatibility the relationship is doomed, yet so many, especially women, ignore it and subject themselves to empty sex.

So there you have it, dearest Jessica. As I said this weekend, you won't become bored by associating with me. Letting it all hang out, that's the only way I'm going to live from now on. If the time comes that you're willing, boy, could we have a fun life together. Don't be afraid to let your own imagination run free.

All my love,
Dan

As their dating continued, their comfort with each other grew, so that eventually on most weekend nights, Jessica slept over at Dan's and they usually made love. She told him she enjoyed receiving his letters, now that they were not so weird, and she enjoyed helping him with his stories. She thought he was an extraordinary writer, that his stories ran deep and dealt honestly with human relationships, that they were personal which made them universal. She thought that his stories showed how men and women of all ages who were faced with challenging situations coped, won, or lost. He had also begun writing a novel about his war experiences.

But Dan was simply filing his stories away. Why? He had told her it was because he feared rejection. His issues were not unlike hers. She painted solely for her own sake, having no ambition to share her work with the public. In fact she was seeing a psychotherapist in order to understand her lack of direction, her failure to be productive, and to explore her childhood past. She knew that some of her issues revolved around having been uprooted when she was a young teen, and suddenly compelled to live with a crude, hostile stepfather. Her mother had been doting, but had failed to come to her defense.

Meanwhile, Dan was seeing a psychiatrist, a woman older than himself, whom he addressed by her first name, Marion. In addition to trying to understand why he didn't share his work with the public, he also wanted to understand the dynamic that led to the failure of his marriage. About that he learned two things: there are no angels and no devils in a marriage, and when the emotional needs of either person change, the marriage is bound to get into trouble.

In a large, vacant room in the attic of Dan's rented house, Jessica installed her easel, and occasionally painted landscapes of the surrounding countryside. She based her paintings on notes and sketches that she had made and sometimes photographs of a particular scene. Most of her work consisted of small conservative watercolors; many were drawings of cottages around town. But no matter how much she tried, she felt that her paintings and drawings failed to match what she imagined they should be. Although Dan sympathized with her, he was at a loss to advise her.

"I see what you mean," he once said. "They don't have much life. I think they simply need more color, more vibrancy."

"But I'm using color," she exclaimed, frustrated. "Why isn't it working?"

For days at a time she remained in her own house working at her art, struggling to discover what was missing, how to transfer what she imagined onto the canvas. Meanwhile, Dan wrote to her.

My dear Jessica,

You have been gone only a day and I'm writing you. God, I'd give anything to cherish and adore you for the rest of my life the way I do now. Why can't I if I work at it? Trouble is I'm no longer a naïve, lovesick youngster. I don't trust life as much as I used to. But there's a quality to our relationship that doesn't follow the pattern I'm accustomed to, which makes all this seem so out of the ordinary. Being skeptical of mystical events, I hesitate to call what's going on between us one of those events, yet I have a sense of something subtle and hidden directing us.

Several things cause me to think this way. One is the incredible ease with which I have come to love you, as if I had known you elsewhere. Do you believe that people have had lives prior to their current one? I never have thought that, although Shirley MacLaine is convinced from her own experiences that it's true. Everything you do seems so familiar to me, the way you think, your habits, even your humor. And you yourself have mentioned how comfortable you are with me.

Another thing that strikes me as uncanny is the way we met, so casually, yet we accepted each other immediately. I have a strange feeling about this. Did I, or did fate, know that I was about to leave my marriage? At the time I met you, I had no idea of what I was going to do. Did I store you in my mind waiting for the appropriate time to approach you? Why did I think of you "out of nowhere" the night I decided I needed com-

panionship? Did you accept my dinner invitation because of some force beyond yourself even though under normal circumstances you would have been more cautious? You, too, have said you've wondered about your response to my first call. And now we seem to have a wonderful compatibility in personality, sexuality, style, and our life stages.

But let me now reveal a zinger. Something about your age has significance. It's been bugging me for days. Many years ago I wrote a play entitled "The 37th Year" about a man whose life had reached its peak when he was an ace basketball player while in college. From that point on, he endured a steady decline. Now, in his thirty-seventh year, he's about to reckon with what happened, and change direction. Marion, my psychiatrist, has remarked that the thirty-seventh year is a good time in a woman's life to initiate change. I may have told you that the first ten years of my marriage were, to me at any rate, idyllic. The change, the destruction of the marriage, began in the tenth year, my wife's thirty-seventh year. In a sense you are now, in your thirty-seventh year, providing me a continuation of my conjugal happiness. My bliss picks up with you where it left off with someone else so long ago. Incredible, isn't it?

And now I have a chance to make my story of more than twenty-two years ago a happier one—with you. Our collaboration restores the creativity that had atrophied in the years that followed those first ten. Whatever it is, whether something within ourselves, or outside, I feel an inevitability about us that will result in a remarkable blossoming of productivity in the expression of our respective art forms. Our collaboration sets us on the road to mutual understanding so that we can more fully appreciate the art that we shall individually produce later on. I never knew life could be so sweet.

All my love, always,
Dan

In the months that followed, Dan's divorce was set in motion. It was extremely bitter because his wife hired a female attorney who seemed to demonize men. His attorney set him up in his law office to study the state's divorce laws, and allowed him to participate in designing their strategy.

Rick, a close friend from Dan's high school days, had just retired and moved into town from Boston. Rick's wife had died. Often Jessica would invite Rick to join her and Dan for dinner at Dan's house. On some mornings the three of them would meet for breakfast at the local diner.

"Jessica is such a beautiful person," Rick said to Dan one day. "Where did you find such a jewel?"

"It was destiny, Rick. I believe that."

But Dan was wrestling with deep feelings of guilt over his divorce. It became so overwhelming that it began to affect him physically. He grew thinner and thinner and couldn't sleep. When his wife pleaded with him to return to her for one last try, he felt obligated to do so. He thought he owed her.

"I have to assuage my guilt somehow, Jessica," he said. "I can't live with myself."

"You know it's not all your fault, Dan," she tried to reassure him.

"Intellectually, yes," he replied. "But this guilt is deep within me. I can't rid myself of it. I made a vow thirty years ago. I must live up to it. Do you understand?"

"Yes," she said, "I do. You have to resolve this, even if I never see you again." Tears filled her eyes as they clung to each other.

She and Dan had now known each other for six months. They had lived together through the fall and winter, and now it was over. On the day of their final conversation Jessica retreated to her house and, after a sleepless night, wrote the following letter:

My dearest Dan,

After seeing you last night, perhaps my loneliness for you seems stronger this morning. "Seems" is the key word because I don't believe it has been less.

Filling my coffee maker I got a quick mental picture of you preparing the Krups. This time you are alone. My heart aches for your loneliness. I so want you to be happy and at peace.

My mornings shared with you were my favorite times. It was wonderful to come down the stairs and see you there. The bathrobe hugs and morning smiles were very dear to me. I can see you sitting in your chair, cross legged in your leather mules, as we talk with each other and listen so patiently and lovingly.

Coming out of my bedroom into an empty kitchen, I feel dull, strong pangs in my heart. These may pass as I start my day, but right now, they aren't leaving me. As I contemplate my own need for affection, I feel, at first, so sorry that this may have contributed to your sense of becoming swallowed up by me; but then I find it quite tolerable for two reasons. It may have been my very behavior that spurred this discovery to "come to a head" for you before years would have passed, while at the same time I believe that you have a great need for the same feelings of affection and love that I do. And our love met and united us and was very, very satisfying. I am so glad I was there for you and could pass on my strength to you.

The second reason is that I am confident that through my own self discoveries in therapy I can indeed become a truly healthy and balanced woman, and no longer driven to crave such extreme dependence and have such an all-consuming emotion of loneliness so constantly. (I know I may still have weak moments of need, but that's perfectly fine with me.) I think you'll agree that the same experience is true for you.

My hope for us to return to each other and enjoy a healthy, loving union is based on my confidence in my desire and ability to grow and continue my self-enlightenment regardless of these painful interludes. And it's based on my utter faith in you, and my confidence in your true desire and ability to resolve your deep inner conflicts and alter your "path." (And it's based on believing that you truly love me.)

We must both leave behind our built-in tendencies to punish ourselves—perhaps more my tendency—and to abandon true love instead of basking in it. What is it the doctors say: "Where there is life, there is hope." I pray for the grace to help me through these difficult times, and I pray for the same for you, too.

Your Jessie

Dan replied immediately.

My dear, dear Jessie,

As I read your letter I share your pain, and I see in it the beauty of your soul. Your love is so terribly overwhelming and pure. I agonize over not being able to partake of it. But that is my lot, the way it has been all my life.

My psyche is like looking at a finely drawn, richly detailed Velasquez painting in which I begin to see small components and the way they form the central motif. My discoveries continue even before the next meeting with Marion.

For all the pain our separation causes you, a separation of my choosing, I take some solace in knowing that it is honest and actually spares you the prospect of harder suffering down the line. As I now examine my trip through life, it seems I have left a wreckage of pain in my wake.

I perceive something tragic and sad when I think of myself. How awful it is to be able to love, but to fear being loved. All my life I have felt lonely, not knowing why—until now. It is your very giving and loving nature that drives me away. I have, from childhood on, doomed myself to being alone. And yet, at the same time, I yearn to be loved—but not enough to overcome my fear. So in a sense, I'm living my childhood over again, banishing myself to isolation.

From this I'm sure you can see how limited and troubled our future together would have been. Thank God you have been spared the damage I am capable of causing. Please bear this in mind when your heart fills with pangs of longing.

Yet, I realize I am more than that lost, lonely child within. I'm capable of being responsible, of caring for and protecting others, and most of all I'm courageous enough to seek and face the truth. So take heart; I'm not turning against myself. What I've done is done and I have the rest of my life to correct the error. I expect to do it through writing and, eventually, through living. But I'm far from doing it yet.

Enclosed is "Turned Tables" *based on a dream I recorded six years ago. I thought you might be interested in what I did with it. After a while I saw the dream as a short short story. A not very happy one, it turns out.*

Be patient. I'll be in touch when I'm ready to deal with us on a constructive adult level.

Your loving
Dan

And Jessica responded with a note right away.

My dearest Dan,
Thank you for your letter, and story. I loved it. I wouldn't change it in any way. I'm doing okay. Don't worry about me,

my love. I'm keeping busy one day at a time. New discoveries in-crease my inner strength. My life goes on. But surely you know, my sweet, patience has always been one of my strong points. Feel my warm hugs.

Your Jessie

As Dan and Jessica remained apart, Dan couldn't yet bring himself to return to his wife, even though he was riddled with guilt over their separation. Meanwhile, Rick frequently visited Jessica to offer solace. It pained him to see her suffering, and it pained him to see two souls so in love, so perfect for each other, torn apart. Yet he understood Dan's dilemma. At the same time, Jessica's mother begged her to come home and stay with her, knowing that Jessica needed the daily presence of her love and support.

Dan appreciated Rick's consoling visits to Jessica. At frequent visits Rick kept Dan informed on Jessica's state of mind. Dan had told her so in the following letter that he had written and mailed before receiving her note.

Dearest Jessica,

I cannot bear not having more words between us, connect-ing us, at least for this afternoon upon Rick's departure. I am so grateful to him for giving you and me his time and friendship and letting me know how you are bearing up. I think of him as my surrogate. He and this letter sing my heart's pain to you.

He and I have had good hours together. His presence has helped. I took him to Judy's Breakfast Nook this morning where there were memories of we three and our cheery conversation, and, as before, we bantered with the boss herself. We visited WFCC, our favorite radio station across the street, and met a young man, an actor, who works there. He offered the name of a qualified person who would gladly read any original play I might write. You recall some years ago that Playhouse Ninety had accepted one of my scripts if I would change the ending, which, in my stubbornness, I refused to do. Once I'm over this impossible sorrow, I shall have more reason to tackle a "big one."

Rick has talked—although hardly enough—about himself. The gist of it was that his passivity, his apparent lack of motivation, of letting life wash over him, stems from the loss of his brother (whom I knew) and more recently the death of his mother. I suspect that somehow his mourning got stalled. So I lent him my "How to Survive...," *and asked that he send it on to you. By the way, I also bought him a copy of* "The Road..." *as a gift that he has already begun reading.*

My love always,
Dan

Four days later Dan replied to Jessica's note.

My dear Jessica,
Thanks for your beautiful note. Everything about you is beautiful so that when I think of you I could cry.

Much is happening in my solitude. At last a major breakthrough: I learned to make friends with that child within. I'm reliving the feelings I had experienced during my three-month hospital sojourn in isolation due to scarlet fever when I was four. Now, of course, I have many more resources to draw on, so that when I emerge from this passage (it's duration is indeterminate) I shall see the world quite differently from the first time.

As you know, these were feelings of fear and anger and loneliness that led to a renunciation of the world, of having love, of women. But, at the same time, the hospital experience provided me an arena for becoming self-reliant and acquiring street smarts; thus my success in the world despite my fear.

Although I have feared death, what I fear most, it turns out, is life and being loved.

I see now, dearest Jessie, that I am largely responsible for the disintegration of my marriage. My compulsive search for the truth is leading me right back to myself, to my deep past, and I can now see what damage I have left in my wake. Of course, as I said before, there are "no saints or sinners" in such situations; but it is also true that one in a pair can be more sinner than saint. When I see my culpability, I am not doing so out of guilt (which has entirely disappeared) but from crystal clear discovery.

You may be aware that I began "leaving" you just before my guilt over the divorce consumed me. It's my pattern. And I'm sure that I considered a reconciliation with my wife due to my deepening involvement with you. I had left my wife emotionally twenty years ago and formed a relationship outside the marriage that gave me the safe distance I needed in order to receive love. Am I repeating that performance with you? Perhaps you can discover through therapy how the way I am fits your needs. I see now that my love has a catch to it: it can go only one way. My giving is a cruel deception, for I can't receive. I suffer when I realize how this must hurt you.

Now that I have insight into my early distorted view, and now that I'm reliving the feelings that led to its formation, I expect to slowly change, although I don't know yet where change will lead me. I must ask myself whether my marriage can be salvaged, whether I can deal with my wife's aggressiveness, whether her resentment will abate, and whether trust can be restored. I don't question her love. Most of my answers will only be judgments, which at the moment I'm not fit to make. I'm still too frightened.

I am most concerned about you and your pain (remember I could always love and feel), and I want to prepare you for any eventuality. I know your enormous strength, but I also know your enormous optimism, your eternal hope. Why do I love only strong and admirable women?

I shall be in touch as I promised, but I still need more time to be completely alone. I'm lonely, although not unbearably so, and things are happening. I hope they are happening for you as well.

All my love,
Dan

Jessica wept after reading this letter. Was he offering her hope, or was he preparing her for the worst? Two days later she called him. They met in a restaurant, and over dinner they talked about their uncertain future. At one point he said to her, "Remember, there are millions of people out there, and among them are at least several with whom we can be compatible. You and I are not the only ones for each other." It seemed symbolic that when they parted in the parking lot, they drove away in separate cars, in opposite directions. Still, she persisted in a desperate appeal, by writing him a long, rambling letter, a veritable outpouring, exploring and rationalizing every possibility that could bring them back together.

My dearest Dan,

I had hoped to receive a letter from you today, but perhaps we covered everything when we met and talked last night. Please forgive me for writing this if I am repeating my thoughts.

I worked at the easel all day today, and as my day progressed I felt an increasing ache that brought me nearer and nearer to tears.

I am tremendously relieved to hear that you have experienced such great relief from your breakthrough: finding self-forgiveness, self-acceptance, self-love and inner peace. I have felt so helpless knowing and feeling your torment, and realizing that its resolution rested with you alone, while I could only hold you and support you and wait. You looked so soft and mellow to me last night, as if you had entered a new plane of consciousness, and I believe you have.

I've been trying to sort through my feelings this afternoon, such sudden emotional churning after a time of calmness. Why?

Forgive me for my ramblings, but this is how my thinking goes right now. I love you as completely as I feel it is possible for a woman to love a man. I love you as I love my own life. I love you so entirely that I will give you up to another if this is what your true happiness and welfare require.

Before we met last night it was clear to me that your inner turmoil must be resolved for there to be any chance for our love and happiness to grow. While waiting, I was very sad and afraid for you, but also confident of your courage and drive, as I have already told you. Now, after our talk last night I can share your relief; it gives me great joy that you have found inner peace and hope for us.

I'm trying to get down to what is disturbing me so deeply. Perhaps I thought I could understand that you needed to give your marriage another chance since you are aware now of so much more than before. It seems logical and fair and noble.

You told me that if your wife should choose not to pursue the marriage, you could live with that. You said this so easily—almost matter-of-factly. (These are only my impressions, I know.) You voiced your fear and distrust of her at this time, as if you would be treading on very thin ice for a while until a feeling of relaxation and trust could enter the relationship again, if ever.

I feel that you have always, and still do now, trust me and can completely relax emotionally with me. I know that you do truly love me—enough to marry me—to choose to spend your precious time on this Earth with me until the day one of us dies, with no reservations or hesitation, only with confidence and trust and love. I feel the same toward you: no reservations, no hesitations, no doubts. I do choose to live out the rest of my life with you and only you. I have already told you this.

I feel that my love for you, and yours for me, is not blind love. We know each other's needs and desires, hopes and fears, strengths and weaknesses. So I do not feel that we are speaking lightly on this matter. If the "slate were clean" perhaps we would already be making plans for our future together. My problem is I feel that my future as well as yours is resting in your wife's hands, a woman whom I do not know except to feel her anger, and a woman whom you do not trust, therefore preventing your love from growing. You have never told me that you ever loved her as much as your very life itself. You even questioned your own motives for marrying her, saying that you did it to please your parents. But, I realize from what you told me that the first ten years of your marriage turned out to be loving, after all.

Dan, please forgive me if I am wrong, if I misunderstand; it is the last thing I want to do. You must know that. I can understand that thirty years of life shared with someone cannot be simply dismissed. Those years are your life; they produced your children.

Does your current enlightenment change the past? No! Do you see any possible parallel between your leaving the marriage and experiencing the tremendous loving feelings you have told me that you had felt for the first time in your life with me? Or a parallel between growing through therapy and the core realization that gives you the possibility of complete inner peace at long last? Could all these feelings be working together by forcing to a "head" the unresolved issues in your life?

Please don't let fear block the way. The future is unknown, the unknown frightening, but trust what we do know and feel for each other. Wouldn't it make sense to you that your true chance for complete happiness could very well be in sharing my complete love for you? I think what I'm getting at is that you must feel sure that you could continue to grow and thrive and realize your hopes and ambitions, joyfully accepting and basking in my love for you, and knowing the joy of giving your love to me. In our happiness with each other we would nurture a healthy and strong and lasting relationship. Do you feel truly sure of this strong possibility? Are you convinced that you could truly live comfortably if your wife chose to accept the marriage as ended now, without deep inner cravings of love and affection from her. Can you count on not feeling your heart breaking at the thought of not living out your days with her? If your choice to retry building a relationship with this woman is based on your noble sense of fairness rather than your own deep yearnings for her love to complete your own, I find it devastatingly painful to endure my separation from you. This is why I cry.

Dan, I want your heart to sing! I want great joy for you, boundless love, and from it the energy that surges forth. If I could know that this could become a reality for you and your wife, then I could pray for my own inner peace in accepting it. Somehow I have these churning feelings that, although I offer you my whole heart, the best of everything that I am, and although you now are increasingly able to realize complete joy in heart and soul, you choose to turn away. Instead, you offer in sacrifice your own life and mine to attempt a smoothing over and regrouping of a past relationship, one that never provoked in you the feelings you are experiencing now. Not until you freed yourself from the past did life truly begin.

You are so ripe for it now—and I mean NOW more than ever—that to choose to retrace your steps rather than follow a new path forward troubles me greatly. I know you want to put things right. I think you feel you owe it to your wife, and that she has a "claim" on you to finally "make her happy," to make up for her pain in her own past life. I put to you the question of the validity of this, for yourself as well as for your wife. I would usually never have spoken this strongly. But you are so very important to me, Dan, that I must be courageous enough to speak now.

If I'm wrong—in your heart you know your true feelings and those feelings you have for your wife and for me—I ask your forgiveness for being so bold and perhaps for misunderstanding you. I need to feel that you understand me. You know me so well, my love. But if I have misunderstood, perhaps I need to sort out my thoughts in letters that I don't send to you.

It is important to me to know that, if I am to suffer the loss of you in my life, it must be for the truer and deeper love you have for another. I'm afraid I would grieve forever if I thought my suffering was for less. I simply ask you to reread the Affirmations of Acceptance, and to search your heart and soul for your responses to me.

You are my heart, Dan,
Your Jessie

P.S. I am patient as long as I am understood for all that I am. These feelings, this letter, came pouring out of me. I will reread this tomorrow morning and decide whether to mail it or not. I realize this is a lot to hit you with. Together with you I can clarify my thoughts. You are spending time in solitude; I believe you are searching yourself as I am searching myself. I am encroaching on your solitude if I mail this, a break in your thoughts to my thoughts. Perhaps my own selfishness will lead me to send this to you, but I believe that my future happiness is entwined with yours, and so it is important to me that all light be shed during this crucial time. You have so often helped me in my own understanding. I pray that I can help you in yours.

More thoughts, just when I thought I would end this letter. But I have to say what's on my mind. You said that I am not the only woman who could make you happy and that you are not the only man who could make me happy. That SOUNDS good, and I'm sure it's quite true. I say to you, however, that we have sought out and found each other for reasons beyond us as well as some reasons that we have come to understand. Remember our awe at feeling that something greater was guiding us? I believe that, Dan. Do we have the courage to continue? Why arbitrarily cast ourselves apart just because eventual healing separately is possible? Wouldn't it be better to draw together and live now?

Could it be that the fear of traveling the world you told me about is but a clinging to safety? And transferring this fear to our unknown future—a new experience for both of us—is similar to fearing a trip through life itself? It is new territory with new feelings to be felt, not ones that are more known, planned, and expected which you would experience by returning to your wife, to familiar ground.

Let your courage grow, my love. I'm afraid, too, Dan. This is so great a venture that I ask you to join me in. I never could have done this before. I feel calm now. I have shared myself with you once again, and I have complete faith that as long as we continue to share ourselves with each other we will be headed in the right direction. I love you.

Their separation continued. Dan had still made no move to rejoin his wife. Jessica's letter had only exacerbated his indecisiveness. Several days after receiving her letter with its torrent of feelings and inner conflict, he responded. During this time, Jessica had become apprehensive, unsure whether what she had written would turn him away, or bring him to her. His letter follows.

My dearest Jessica,

Yesterday was a weepy one (I take after you these days), especially in the morning. You know what I mean because you said that, for no obvious reason, as you go about your tasks, you suddenly burst into tears. After your letter I needed solace, so I read the rest of "How to Survive..." *and found it helpful, including the last section on growth, which I urge you to read. Then I started* "The Prophet," *which I bought for myself. I found the sections that pertain to our experience most comforting. Not only is Gibran's truth clear, his way of expressing it helps me to know it more deeply. I asked myself what could be truer after reading his words:* "And ever has it been that love knows not its own depth until the hour of separation."

Taking a bit of my own advice to you, after seeing the hard time I was having, I called Marion, who agreed to see me at five on Friday, the end of her day. It was a disturbing and startling session. I fear telling you about it—not to raise a false hope, or to keep you in limbo, but because I have no idea what will happen since I am in a state of deep confusion. Yet, you must know the truth about what I feel; I know what it means to you.

In that session, I realized how very much I love you. Between tears I declared you my first, my deepest, my truest love. Associations to an earlier dream (in which you and I stand before the marriage altar, and you call off the ceremony) suggest that it is my real marriage of thirty years ago taking place, that I may be returning to it out of a sense of binding commitment. Of course, if this is true, I shall know soon enough after I return to my wife.

The answer will lie in whether or not I shall find pleasure in life. Gibran writes of it more beautifully than I could even dream of:

And now you ask in your heart, "How
shall we distinguish that which is good in
pleasure from that which is not good."

Go to your fields and your gardens, and
you shall learn that it is the pleasure of
the bee to gather honey of the flower.

But it is also the pleasure of the flower
to yield its honey to the bee. For to the bee
a flower is a fountain of life. And to the
flower a bee is a messenger of love.

And to both, bee and flower, the giving
and the receiving of pleasure is a need and
an ecstasy.

Here I am. We, you and I, have had such pleasure together, the pleasure of true love, and I shall miss it, and I wonder, now having tasted it, whether I can remain deprived. It is part of being alive. Will I die within, not having the pleasure of being fully alive? Without having what you have given me. As Gibran writes:

You have given me my deeper thirsting after life.

I hope you'll forgive me for using Gibran's words instead of my own to say what I feel. But they are so much better, more powerful, than any I can put together. What could better describe how I love you?

And your heart-beats were in my heart,
And your breath was upon my face, and
I knew you...,

So you see why I say you are beautiful and I can't put you out of my mind. Gibran says goodbye, yet doesn't, and it is what I say too:

It was but yesterday we met in a dream.

You have sung to me in my aloneness,
and I of your longings have built a tower
in the sky.

So my Jessie, could there be words more perfect to salve our broken hearts?

My deepest love,
Dan

Months before, Dan had given a copy of *The Prophet* to Jessica with this inscription:
"To Jessica,
For loving and teaching me how to receive love and beauty.
Your loving Dan."

Upon learning of Dan's sadness, and his extreme love for her, Jessica immediately felt relieved.

Dan, my love, my heart,
I cannot believe I'm writing to you again for, in addition to what I have sent you, I've written long pages to you unable to bear stopping, only to fold them quietly together and bind them with yours to me. All the words, all the feelings, never to be

read or felt again. For two days and nights I fought thinking of your parting as a death, a finality. My mind turned over and over with thoughts and memories, so fresh, so alive, so sweet. Together we could be the best of all we are, two wholes uniting. Our energy together is boundless.

You would never have known this, my sweet love, but you've broken the silence. I never thought, regardless of the pain, that you would, and I promised myself that I would hold back as well. The quotations you've sent me from "The Prophet" are the very ones I've dwelt upon in my own painful isolation. These words come so close to my heart, I cried to think I had taken the book from you. I agonized over buying a copy and sending it to you so that you would not be without it.

I'm so pleased and relieved that you've gotten your own copy now. Gibran's words are true; they are of our hearts and souls.

Dan, I question whether I should continue this letter, but during our brief complete life together we never held anything in our hearts back from each other. Why start now?

Part of the finality of death—no, no, no, I must not think this way. You no longer need me to give at all. I am also dead to you as you must remain to me. Yet, after the two days of feeling the agony of your "death," I can no longer accept it. I simply cannot let it go. I know deep in my soul that it is not settled. The day may come soon enough for death and then there will be no escape, but this time the "death" is self-imposed.

Dan, since our recent agreement on a three month separation—this came sweeping in so fast, too fast for me—I need to think about it a bit longer. I cannot condemn all hope to futility. Forgive me my weakness, my love. I had felt that in order for me to survive, I must silently keep to our three month commitment. I made a pact with myself that each time I had a hopeful thought of you, I would also play the devil's advocate.

Meanwhile, time away from you would pass, and I would continue my life. I am being gentle with myself about this. I require this gentleness and I will allow myself to have it.

The mourning process will be slowed, but not completely halted. I will miss you slowly and hold my heart from leaping at the very thought of you. This way, too, if the day will come that you walk to me again, my deep feelings of love for you will not have been snuffed out or scarred over. In my heart I must hold out this chance even though you were never to know it.

I know you need time. Your happiness for the rest of your life depends on this, as does mine. Time with your wife will tell. Search your heart and soul, as I do mine. I am aware of my own power and strength, my very being and my creative force. I sit here now for you; you must know that I hold myself for you to accept and love and cherish, or to abandon.

Only you can find your own truth. It is for me to step back and give space and wait. I pray daily for grace, for you to think clearly, to have strength and to find peace. I pray for myself, too. My only thought is that it is the deep tragedies of life that are to be mourned, while the hope of true love, boundless spiritual growth, inner peace, and the joy of life itself are to be grasped and clung to. It remains for you to decide which is the path to each, and to gather the strength to travel along it.

Please know, my love, that I'm happy that you wrote, that you share yourself with me, still. You do what you must, and I shall gently live my days. Never forget my love for you.

As Always,
Your Jessie

P.S. One favor please. I know you are thinking of leaving therapy, but please stay with your therapist a while longer. Please. I love you.

Jessica wrote again, but she decided not to mail the letter. It was written more for herself. Hadn't the future already been cast? Here is what she wrote:

Dearest Dan,

I have answered your letter and yet I keep reading it over and over. I feel your emotions, your love, your caring. It's as if you wish to wrap your love around me for the rest of our lives. To know that you return my feelings so deeply, that you accept my love and it becomes the lasting circle of giving and receiving, fills my heart and soul and moves me to love you ever more. There is no limit to my love. Such a miracle.

Gibran's words are beautiful and eloquent and universal for those who will listen, but Dan, my dearest, there are no words that I would rather hear or read than yours. You have the ability with your words to move my heart, to thrill me, to make me roll with laughter, to enable me to feel devastation, frustration, great sadness, great joy, and wonder at the world and at you, my love. We are all unique and you, Dan, are my special one, my most tender one, my dearest Dan.

After five days, Jessica had heard nothing more from Dan. She was bewildered by his silence. Although they had agreed to part for three months, until now he had kept writing. Were her letters back to him the reason he had stopped? Was this the death knell of his love? She was finding his indecision intolerable. Not knowing his thoughts was too painful for Jessica to bear. So she sent him the following note.

Dear Dan,
I need to ask this of you.

Please don't contact me in any way until June 12th, the date we agreed upon. No matter what happens, don't call, don't write, don't come by. I need this time for myself—alone.

Promise me, please.

Jessie

During their separation, despite his torn feelings, Dan had decided to return to his wife to see whether he could live with her again. Then the very next day, before Dan could have received Jessica's note, his letter arrived.

My dearest, dearest Jessica,

I am writing this letter not knowing if I can send it, whether I can muster the resolve to release these words from the trembling cage of my heart.

I am certain of only two necessities: one is that I must make a decision to clear the way for the pain of healing, and the other is that I know that my decision will hurt someone. No matter what I do, what decision I make, someone I love will suffer and I shall suffer with them. It is a no-win deal.

Besides all the deep psychological reasons that have led you and me to our present agony, there is a strand of conscious intent running through my actions. It all began when I received the first glimmer of personal culpability in the failure of my marriage. As my self-discovery grew, I became horrified at myself and at what I had done to those whom I love and depend on me. Still, I insisted, mysteriously, on finding the whole truth about myself no matter how ugly or painful. While my opinion of myself is rather shaky these days, the one thing that keeps me proud is that I'm unflagging in following "the road less traveled."

But I am not proud of what I have brought us to.

You offer me the rapture of love and life, the excitement of fresh springtime, the shining future. I know you no longer call yourself "young," but to me, wrinkled, aging, in the autumn of my time, you are youth. I can never recapture what I used to be twenty-five years ago, but you would be a surrogate through whom I could bask in reflected brilliance. My life is no longer sunlight, but because of you it could be moonlight, so beautiful in its own way.

By deciding not to be with you, this is what I must forfeit and forget. It is so painful, the loss so great, that at the very hint of my sacrifice I begin to weep. But I must give you up, I must. And I must tell you why and hope you will listen.

I have to live with myself, retain—or is it regain?—my self-respect. While my love for my wife lacks the fervor and passion of my love for you, it is nevertheless deep and sweet. And for the sake of that love, and myself, I must return to the time when I left her and try to rebuild our lives on a firmer base. I no longer see her through the eyes of my past neuroticism; I no longer see her as my enemy. I no longer see her as a threat to my emotional safety, but instead as a willing and loving partner. She offers me autumn, nothing as brilliant as you offer, but as a soft glow, and with this I can be content.

Wanting the best for you, knowing I can't take part in helping you have it, I have never been sadder. There was a time when I dreamed of giving you many years of happy days and hours. I pray—and you know I'm not given to such things—I pray that you will find such happiness. And I pray that somehow, someday, perhaps in another world, who knows, we can consummate our incredible love.

It has been exquisite. I shall remember what we had always. I love you and weep.

Dan

P.S. We have suffered through one parting. I don't know whether we can bear another. Though I don't think it would be easier for me, if a final meeting is easier for you, I'm willing.

This was Dan's last letter of love to his precious Jessie. He had no reason to write her again. As Jessica lowered the letter down to her lap, her hands trembling, she began to weep, and throughout the day she wept. She did not take him up on his offer to meet once more. That would only prolong the pain.

Jessica could not have known that, on returning to his wife, Dan had been miserable and had to leave her, this time for good. He had been with her hardly a month. His heart had gone out to her because she tried only to please him, seeming to do everything right. But in the middle of the night he found himself leaving their bed to spend the rest of the night on the living room couch, pining for Jessica. It is such a tragedy, he thought, that he had met and loved someone else, destroying any chance of rescuing thirty years of marriage to a woman he never stopped caring for but no longer loved in the way he had once, and in the way he now loved another woman.

He also realized that, although his wife no longer exhibited the anger she had expressed towards him in the past, he couldn't be sure that it wouldn't return. After all, he had endured it for many years without relief, remaining in the marriage for the sake of their two children, who were now adults. He also recognized his own culpability, and wondered whether he could make amends sufficiently for her to forgive his transgressions, especially since she knew he had fallen in love with Jessica.

Weeks before the agreed upon months of separation from Jessica were over, he came to understand that he would be false to himself and to his wife were he to remain with her. In an epiphany, he suddenly understood that each of them was equally responsible for the breakup. As a result, he felt a marvelous relief, a sense of freedom from the enormous weight of his guilt. In fact, he felt joy, and the need to share it with the woman he loved.

Not knowing how she would respond, he phoned Jessica. "I'm yours, my love," he declared, "and I want to be only with you."

She began to sob.

"Are you there?" he inquired.

"Yes, yes, I'm here," she said.

"May I come over?" he asked.

"Come, please come," she said in an excited, tremulous voice.

"I'll be right there," he fairly shouted.

Dan and Jessica's life together turned out just as he had presaged. At their wedding, which was attended by a few close friends and Jessica's mother, they read aloud together a passage from *The Prophet*.

Love one another, but make not a bond
of love:
Let it rather be a moving sea between
the shores of your souls.
Fill each other's cup but drink not from
one cup.

Give one another of your bread but eat
not from the same loaf.
Sing and dance together and be joyous,
but let each one of you be alone,
Even as the strings of the lute are alone
though they quiver with the same music.

Give your hearts, but not into each
other's keeping.
For only the hand of Life can contain
your hearts.
And stand together yet not too near
together:
For the pillars of the temple stand apart,
And the oak tree and the cypress grow
not in each other's shadow.

For all the joy their wedding gave them, there was
one sad note. Their friend Rick, who was supposed to
accompany Jessica down the aisle and hand her over to
the groom, died suddenly of a heart attack a few days
before the wedding. Life both gives and takes away.

Dan and Jessica's love grew through the years,
calmer perhaps, but deeper. Besides discovering more
about their natures, observing the changes due to their
mutual love, they also discovered each other's worlds.
He introduced her to a wide range of opera, literature,
and classical music, while she brought him to museums
to show him the great art of the past and present that
he had known nothing about. She exposed him to the
rock music of her era, and the great songs of protest
and pain and joy.

They occasionally sailed together in the catboat, although, cautious by nature, Jessica would go out only on calm days. As they'd sail close to the shore, Jessica would photograph the fishermen working on the docks, and then use these subjects in her paintings. But when sailing alone, Dan, having been an entrepreneur and a risk taker, loved to go out when the sea was wild. Reefing the sail, he'd bring the boat so close to the wind that it would heel just short of the water overflowing the gunwales.

As Dan had predicted, Jessica's art developed. Having freed herself from old inhibitions, she had found the solution to making her paintings come alive. She took to painting in oils using vivid colors, making her work sparkle, revealing her inner joy. She has produced hundreds of landscapes and portraits and has had a successful one woman show. Most of her works have been sold and appear in private homes and business offices around the world.

As for Dan, he went on to write novels, essays, plays and scores of short stories. Several of his essays on his business experience have been published in newspapers and magazines. In his old age, he has seen his plays staged. Although many of his books have faded into obscurity, the plays are his legacy, he says, although they may disappear with him. But who knows? He has long been reconciled to the unknowable.

From time to time, Dan and Jessie ponder the fearful day when Dan's death will cause their parting. As Gibran might put it, together they have built a magnificent tower in the sky, beautiful to behold, which eventually will reside only in one's memory.

A HOUSE IS MORE THAN A HOUSE

My wife and I were familiar with the popular admonition against building one's own house. Of our friends who had built their own homes, none would wish to repeat the experience, and some were mortified at the thought. We knew well the story of Mr. Blanding's fabled dream house spawned in a comic nightmare. Did we dare think then that our experience would be special, that it would be unlike the typical misery encountered by most men since the Neanderthal found moisture seeping through the walls of his cave?

The decision to build came as a gradual dawning. At the very outset, when it suddenly seemed that our old house was inadequate, it never occurred to us that we might build. There were plenty of good old houses around—spacious, well built, located in attractive neighborhoods and reasonably priced. So we looked, we looked for a year. There were several houses that we would have liked to buy. They fitted the image of the house my wife held in her dreams. It was a modest dream, so she thought, and I was inclined to agree with her. It took the form of a Garrison Colonial style that she associated with snug warmth, the rolling New England landscape, and the wisdom of our forefathers.

One happy day, we found the right house in the right place for nearly the right price. It was so right that we resolved to compromise our budget a bit. We meandered through it once, twice, three times. We took drives by it. Was anything more perfect?

"Well, it could be made perfect," my wife said.

Now what precisely did she mean? I pondered this offhand statement for a moment and concluded that it held dangerous implications.

"Of course," she said, "the wall between the pantry and the kitchen will have to be torn down. And the bathrooms should be retiled."

"And what else, my dear?" I asked.

"All the rooms need repapering. I don't like the floor tile in the kitchen. The sun porch should be closed in to become your den, and we should have a family room. There is no family room, you know."

"Yes, I know," I said.

"Well, we could build off the kitchen. I know just how it can be done," she said.

"Stop," I shouted. "Stop!"

And she did. And we did. A pause in our search prevailed by unspoken mutual consent.

Rumblings of interest began again a few months after our impasse. Had she ever thought of a ready built new house, I inquired. They didn't look solid enough, she replied. They defamed the tradition of the land and of history. They appeared barren and uninteresting. They didn't have personality. To me, these were incomprehensible impressions. However, she agreed to look at more such houses to prove her point.

There was not much land available for development in our city, and what existed was prohibitive in price. We decided to investigate the outlying towns. To my city-bred wife this was a venture into the wilderness. But I could envision the approaching realization of a secret wish. It was a wish to see the stars shine brightly at night, to hear the wind rustling through the trees, to smell the damp earth, and to plant in it. It was a poetic boy's wish that lingered into my adulthood. Perhaps it goes back to the beginning of man.

We found an attractive development and met the builder. He invited us to his home to discuss plans and costs. He escorted us into a room that served as his office, and sat behind a drawing board as we sat on each side of him staring at the blank sheet of paper. He was a most cooperative man.

We described what sort of house we had in mind while he drew rough schemes, struggling to translate our wishes. Something was wrong: his conception lacked proportion and style. In our opinion, the layout of rooms was disordered, and it repeated a theme that we had noted in other homes he had built. His plan contained such specific weaknesses as a pass-through room, insufficient front entry space, a prosaic staircase, and a cramped dining room.

The session was frustrating to all of us. After hours of repositioning walls and altering dimensions the builder presented a plan that approached the simplicity and practicality we sought. In appreciation for his labor and patience, and in sympathy, we granted him our reluctant approval and went on to discuss cost.

The price, not to our surprise, was beyond our budget. And as he offered less costly alternatives, we hardened our resolve not to consider them. We knew what we wanted in the clarity of my wife's dream, and, by golly, we were going to build what we wanted, or not at all. Then gradually, without compromise, the price came down until it reached close to our severe budget figure. It happened subtly. Where did the savings come from, we wondered. Soon we realized that the builder would have to sacrifice the quality of materials, and labor too, in order to accommodate us.

Thus we were not sold. We had lost confidence in this too cooperative man. Perhaps, we pondered, we were never destined to build a house. Perhaps, by the time we found what we wanted, our five-year-old girl and two-year-old boy would be in college, and we would be ready for a city apartment. Furthermore, we concluded, we really couldn't afford the house of my wife's dreams, if such a house could ever exist. We did not voice those discouraging thoughts at first. But they culminated in a strange and pathetic statement. My wife said, "I don't want another house. The one we have is good enough."

It is difficult to truly know another person, and each of us is full of surprises. A house is a personal thing; it is the mirror of an individual's and a couple's attitude towards life. The thought of a fine, solid, graceful home, uppermost in her desire, stood to be an unrealizable fulfillment of her dream; it was meant to be an unreachable goal. The attainment would be undeserved. And I suppose it is for such gentle and childlike delusions that one loves another. That house would now be built if I had to do it with my own bare hands.

Of course, I didn't have to. There was a small sign at an intersection that we had passed many times. It read simply "New Homes." We drove into a street that curved broadly through wooded lots. On some of them houses were being built, and every house was unique. At the end of the street, muddy bulldozer paths went off in several directions, indicating that more streets were planned. One house in particular startled us. It was not the kind of house we would have wanted for ourselves. But it was set on a knoll in such a way that it appeared to have always been there. It could have grown there with the trees around it. The house was a simple work of art, possessing balance and proportion.

Its front door was open. Due to the hammering from within, our knock was not heard. We walked inside uninvited, entering an atmosphere that we had not sensed in other new houses. The artistry, so evident on the outside, had been carried throughout the interior. I rubbed my hand along the white trim around the windows and doors. It felt silky and smooth. The brickwork around the fireplace was perfection. The windows were large and solid, and located in sensible places to allow for furniture placement. Complete care had been taken with details; excellence was apparent everywhere.

A carpenter in overalls walked into the room. He was a youthful appearing, heavily built man with an easy smile. We asked to meet the builder.

"I'm the builder," he introduced himself.

"Could we see more of the house?"

"Certainly can. Follow me."

He conducted a tour that was more a lesson in the skill of construction than a sales pitch. This man was proud of the house. One would suspect that it was his own, which was true only in the sense that he had put part of himself into it. Indeed, we had met an individual from the long ago past.

After this inspiring encounter we knew our direction. Only such a man as this could build the house we wanted. Everything we had seen before was, by contrast, a poor imitation of what a house should be. My wife was right about the new houses we had seen, but now she conceded defeat. We had suddenly become enlightened and enthusiastic. We also knew that such quality of materials and workmanship could not come without considerable cost. It was clear to us before we asked the question that we could not afford this excellent builder.

Could a way be found? I met with the builder, whom I shall call Gus, a few weeks later and explained our problem. We needed a fairly large house, at least four bedrooms. We wanted him to build it, but our budget, we recognized, was too limited. Did he have any suggestions? Regarding cost, he agreed that his price was high, but this was necessary in order not to compromise his art, and therefore his reputation. However, he asked if we could compromise our requirements temporarily. Compromise then became one of our favorite techniques for achieving what might otherwise have been impossible.

We also chose to use the save-and-wait method. Gus set a minimum figure for the type and size house we desired. That minimum was our maximum, and we would have been uncomfortable without a margin for contingencies. We would wait six more months or even a year if necessary.

"Good," said Gus, "Let's get together in six months and review the situation."

A year later, after construction had begun, I had asked Gus whether he had considered earlier that he might lose us as prospects.

"Not at all," he replied. My eyebrows rose. He went on. "You talked to my old customers, my references, didn't you?"

"Yes," I nodded.

"Didn't they sell you?"

"We were sold before that, Gus."

He laughed. "Well, I knew they'd clinch the deal. You had to be mine."

We laughed together and I didn't feel the least bit taken.

Six months later, in January, we were ready to open serious discussion on our project. The muddy paths had been widened into frozen dirt streets. One short street ended in a turning circle that promised to keep out through traffic. On one side of the circle a house was under construction. Here, in subzero weather, I found Gus and his carpenters working on a Saturday afternoon.

We walked over the available lots. The snow was deep and a hard crust had formed on the surface. Breaking through the crust occasionally, we had to pull each other out. We kept on, undeterred by this difficulty. The lots were thick with trees and the waxy green leaves of mountain laurel. One particular lot near the turning circle was topographically ideal for our Garrison design. (The Garrison style has a second floor overhanging slightly the first floor on the front of the house.)

I pointed at the natural ravine about fifty feet in from the road.

"Not a problem," Gus said. "We can easily divert any water that flows through it. We'll set the foundation here," as if the doing was as easy as the proposing. "Let's measure it out."

We paced the area and pushed fallen branches into the snow to represent the corners of the house. We could then see clearly where it would stand, and how it would fit on the land. With the house in this spot, a grove of giant hemlocks, each tree greater in girth than the circumference of our joined arms, and taller than all surrounding trees, would be spared—except for two. So we moved the house ten feet toward the street so that those two hemlocks would also be spared. In the rear of this setting grew a clump of towering birches, each of them large enough around to sheath an Indian canoe. This slice of land, almost an acre, now seeming hostile and primeval, was clearly eligible to become our private paradise.

On viewing this wilderness, my city-bred wife and two civilized children were not easily infected with my joy. Instead, they mutely accepted what they saw as a matter of faith in Daddy's judgment. A miraculous transformation would take place here, I assured them. This wilderness would be tamed to become a broad lawn spotted with shady groves. A stately house would rise here, snug and sheltering against the forest. One day other houses would rise, and my wife would have neighbors to gossip with and the children would have playmates. Thus, civilization will have implanted itself. How dramatic I was. I played the role of the pioneer introducing the new land to his brood.

In less than two years, my promise materialized. Our house was a success. Friendly neighbors who shared our appreciation for this land's beauty have built around us. They began with their dreams, too, and we watched as each became transformed into reality. We fully understood their satisfaction. Surely, a house is more than a house. It is what we are, and some of what we expect to be.

BETRAYED

As I entered the spacious foyer of the old stone building I heard only the echo of my footsteps on the polished marble floor, and a faint melody floating through the air from a distant room. My friend Curt had said, "She's there every afternoon. Just follow the music."

I started climbing the wide staircase toward the melody, then hesitated. "Damn fool," I thought to myself. "Don't get involved. Leave. She's spinning a web to lure me in." I turned, fled down the stairs, crossed the gleaming floor to the door, but stopped as a crescendo of high piano notes caught my ear. Surrendering, I swung around and headed back up the staircase. How could I resist seeing the source of such beautiful music? Whoever could play like this was worth the risk.

The risk? What risk? I followed the sound into a cavernous room with high windows through which shimmering sunlight shone on an enormous oriental carpet. In a corner beside the far window I saw a young woman bent over the piano keys; her face was enveloped by chestnut hair that tumbled down to her shoulders. The air seemed flooded with music that came from her soul. I sank into a low chair against a wall, away from her sight, listened and watched. Finally, she turned toward me, met my eyes and smiled, and continued playing. I was transfixed. My infatuation was overwhelming. I had fallen in love. Crazy, stupid, ridiculous, but I was as helpless as if she had woven a spell.

She continued playing for the next half hour until a middle aged, grey haired man entered the room. She stopped as he approached, and rose from the piano bench to greet him.

"Excellent," he said. "You're playing it exactly as I taught you."

Ah, he's her teacher. He reached his arm around her waist, clasped her to him and kissed her on the lips. She clung to him, not wanting the kiss to end. Releasing her, he gently closed the keyboard and said, "Stay with me tonight." Hand in hand they left the room. I heard their footsteps crossing the marble floor below, then silence. Suddenly, I felt more alone than I had ever been.

MY WIFE, THE BRAILLIST

When I first heard the expression "stir crazy" applied to a housewife, I was startled. It implied that her home is her prison and her daily tasks are futile.

"Are you stir crazy?" I asked my wife one day while she was washing the dishes. The din of the squealing kids reverberated throughout the kitchen.

"Am I what?" she shouted.

"Stir crazy, stir crazy," I repeated.

"For heaven's sake, yes!" she screamed.

Suddenly I understood, and concluded that I had heard the call for action.

After the kids had been coaxed back into their beds, like bees into a jar, for the third time that evening, an unnatural hush prevailed throughout the house. My wife dragged her ironing board into the living room near the television set and proceeded to set it up.

"Take a break," I said. "Sit down and let's talk."

My magnanimity must have sounded so uncharacteristic that she took my advice and plopped into my favorite chair, which was not exactly the arrangement I had in mind. So I sat uncomfortably on the sofa.

"So you're stir crazy," I said.

She nodded in agreement. "I think you ought to do something about it," I went on.

She pondered my suggestion, noteworthy for its generality, for a moment, then she said, "I know just what to do."

I knew the moment I made my suggestion that whatever she had in mind would automatically be suspect. Then it came.

"You stay home and take care of everything while I go out into the wide world and have fun like you."

That statement triggered what, for the sake of propriety, I shall call an impolite discussion. After the heat generated during this battle of the sexes subsided, rationality returned. We got down to the core of the problem.

"My life is monotonous, and I'm bored," she said.

"But you're doing what every housewife is doing and has done ever since the dawn of humanity," I said. "Did you expect it to be different? Housewives are better off than they ever were. Look at all the work-saving gadgets you've got. You have your own car. You have a comfortable and spacious home. You've got woman suffrage."

"Not once," she said with threatening emphasis, "did you mention anything having to do with spirit."

"Well," I stated, "one does what one does out of love for one's family, no?"

"Of course, I do it all out of love for my family, but I don't love what I'm doing."

"Why?" I asked, groping to discover the crux of the issue.

"Because I feel useless. I feel unchallenged, uncreative."

"Are you asking for…I mean do you have in mind another…"

"Another baby? Not necessarily," she said.

Relieved and suddenly inspired, I said, "I think what you need is a hobby."

She laughed. "What kind of hobby?"

"A useful, challenging, creative hobby," I suggested unspecifically.

"Brilliant! Just what I need," she said with a derisive smile.

"Art, painting…lots of women love painting. I think you ought to take up painting."

From this conversation began an astonishing change in her life. It eradicated her boredom, and consumed practically every waking hour of her day—every day. She took up oil painting at first, and then making silver jewelry, followed by refinishing furniture, followed by knitting sweaters. Such activities became her main focus while her steady job of being a mother and housewife became extracurricular.

In each endeavor, she began with enthusiasm as she engaged her creative instincts. And in each instance her enthusiasm soon waned. She would lapse into a "lost" phase during which she confined herself to performing her regular household duties. Occasionally a good book would come to her attention, which meant that the rest of the family would be on its own. While the book took precedence, beds remained unmade, meals were unimaginative, and complaints went unheard. Once she completed the book, she would return to the fold and rediscover us, and we would become a whole family again. We felt lucky that her outside interests were transitory, otherwise the children and I would have led lives of wretched incompleteness.

Currently, my wife is in a new and unique phase that has severely upset our family balance and mutual fulfillment. We fear that this phase may not be a phase at all, but rather something permanent. It has been going on for the past ten months, with no end in sight. Indeed, we can observe only her mounting dedication at each step of her progress. Her success breeds on itself. What is it, you may ask, that has absorbed her so that we, her first line of responsibility, have taken a secondary role? It is Braille—learning how to write, transcribe and read by touch.

At seven o'clock on Tuesday nights, week after week, regardless of the weather, she rushes off to her Braille class. From her reports we learned that another approximately one hundred people were doing the same thing. She returns from class after two hours either depressed or elated, depending on how many mistakes she had made on her homework assignment. On other than Tuesday nights, she bathes the children, hustles them into bed, rushes through washing the dishes, then settles down to an evening of brailling at the kitchen table.

During the early stages of this routine, the potential consequences of her dedication to brailling had not been clear. After dinner and the kids had been tucked into bed, I had gone about my pattern of reading the evening newspaper, writing my sales reports, and watching television. When I had felt the need to say something, I'd go into the kitchen where she was sitting and say it, and she'd listen and comment. That is, she used to comment. While under the spell of doing Braille she does not hear anything specific, and her comment is usually, "Wait until I finish the next line." The next line, I discovered, would take several minutes, perhaps a half an hour or more. By then I had forgotten what I had said. She would probably have found it irrelevant anyway.

I figured it was time I learned something about the root of her absorption, so I inquired, "Describe Braille. Tell me what it's about."

I quickly recognized what a challenge it was to her. But more importantly, I realized what enormous good it contributed to those who were unable to see. So I assumed the task of washing the supper dishes, bathing the children, and reading them a story before putting them to bed. Actually, her life change, which resulted in finding a higher purpose than just taking care of us, caused my own life to change as well. Apparently, without realizing it, I must have needed a change as much as she, because I've never been happier. My new role has brought me closer to my family, and has given me a deeper appreciation of how important my wife and children are to my sense of well being and I to theirs.

THE RINGING TELEPHONE

A telephone ringing late in the night is terrifying. At an unaccustomed hour, one's first thoughts are of an emergency or deep tragedy. Had Barbara, Dave's wife, received such a call? Was this how she had heard what had happened? I never asked her.

A ringing telephone brought the tragedy to me. I was at the gas station. There is an outdoor bell that rings loudly so the attendants can hear it. Ed, the owner, interrupted his conversation with me to answer it. Almost immediately he rushed out of the station office and said excitedly, "It's for you."

Not accustomed to receiving calls at the station, I picked up the receiver with apprehension. My wife, who was sobbing on the other end, said, "Dave is dead." Incredulous, I responded, "What?" She repeated her tearful statement.

"I'll come right home," I said. All the while the situation seemed unreal. When I see my wife, I thought, she will tell me that the telephone lied.

As I entered through the kitchen doorway, my wife ran to me, and clinging to me said over and over, "Dave is dead," as if to convince herself that it was true. To her,

261

too, Dave's death was unreal. Emotional shock serves a useful purpose: As human reason is assaulted, it allows our minds to deny reality. We initially reject what we most dread.

Dave's death was impossible, it was senseless. It did not accord with the normal order of living and dying. He died by accident, by an irreversible convergence of events, a sequence of 'ifs.' In his early thirties, Dave's life had been cut short. How do you make sense from the senseless? You don't. You can only accept the fact of chaos in the world.

Human lives are cut short countless times each year. We read about them every day, but they rarely touch us. They happen on highways far from us; they happen in war and in terrorist acts; they happen to strangers. What is senseless about the death of a star in our universe? Nothing. Death is senseless only in our private universe of love and friendship.

A ringing telephone brought the tragedy to Dave's friends, and even his customers who, to a person, had grown fond of him. I don't know who made the telephone ring for Dave's wife. Perhaps it was Father Mullins, the logical person to have informed her.

All responded to the awful news with an incredulous "What?" All wanted to know "how" he died to verify what was impossible to believe. Of course "why he died" is what we really mean, but "how" is sufficient for the time being.

Here is the "how": That evening, Dave and Barbara had attended a social gathering at the home of Father Mullins. As the evening wore on, Dave said he was not feeling well, and he and Barbara departed. He drove her the few miles to their home, then drove the baby sitter to hers. The pavement was wet; the air moist. On the return trip he went off the highway and collided head-on into a large tree. He hadn't drunk much; there was no obvious explanation of why the accident occurred. Had he become weary? Had he dozed at the wheel? Had his vehicle simply skidded off the wet leaf-covered pavement? We'll never know, but does it matter now? It mattered only when it happened. And as time passes, all that will endure are our memories of our good friend, Dave.

MISTER LAZARR

My science teacher is the smartest man I know, even smarter than my Pa, I think. He explains things so well that I'm interested in everything he says. I like talking to him, especially asking him questions. He makes me feel as smart as he is, which, of course, I'm not and never will be.

Yesterday, when he was talking to me after class, the principal came into the room.

He patted me on the shoulder and said to Mister Lazarr, "Ah, your star pupil." Mr. Lazarr looked at me proudly.

The principal asked me, "Are you going to become a scientist like your teacher, my boy?"

"Yessir!" I said.

"Good," the principal said. "We need scientists, lots of them so we can beat the Russians. Would you like to be a rocket scientist?"

"No sir," I said, "I'd like to be an astronomer."

"An astronomer?" the principal said. "That won't help us beat the Russians."

Well, I was very embarrassed because I knew that he didn't like what I told him.

During the conversation Mister Lazarr kept looking down at the floor, and seemed angry. I figured that maybe he didn't like what I said either, which made me feel *really* embarrassed. Anyway, I want to be an astronomer and I'm going to be one.

Then Mister Lazarr raised his head and said to the principal, "A student doesn't become a scientist because he or she thinks we should beat the Russians, sir."

"I guess you're right," said the principal. "They don't know yet what's happening in the world."

"Whether they do or not," said Mister Lazarr, "students aspire to be scientists for the same reason adults do; they simply want to learn about the universe. They need no other motivation."

I didn't understand all the words that Mister Lazarr used, but I thought I understood what he meant. I could see that the principal understood, too, because his face turned as red as the apple I'd eaten at recess. He left the room very, very quickly. I don't think Mister Lazarr and the principal like each other very much, and I decided that I don't like the principal very much, either.

JACK'S CONTINUING EDUCATION

J.J., the president of Century Lampshades, would say to Jack, "Do this, do that…and I mean now." Jack would then ask "Why?" "Why?" J.J. would repeat in a voice approaching a scream, "None of your goddamn business why. Just do it. You insolent S.O.B."

Then suddenly he'd burst out laughing. He would put his arms over Jack's shoulders and say, "Jack, I'm president of this company, and I think it would be a good idea for you to do it. What do you say?"

Jack would then do it.

It was easy to understand how J.J. was the best salesman in the lampshade business. Moderating his emotions, he could be charming, and in doing so make you feel grateful for his good will. J.J. had a lot of faith in Jack, who, only in his mid-twenties, was like a son. J.J. valued his loyalty, although he was aware of his liberal ideas and would sometimes joke, "Maybe we got a Commie in our midst, but the kid's good at what he does, and he's come up with more cost saving ideas than the rest of my crew put together."

J.J. told the company's plant superintendant, "Give Jack whatever he wants, and don't argue with him. He knows what's good for the company and that's good for me."

One morning during a period of seasonal layoffs, J.J. came into Jack's silk shade department to stir him up. "What in hell do you think this is? Playtime?" he shouted at Jack so everyone could hear. Most of the eighty or so workers, mostly women, stiffened in their positions. Some slipped into the ladies room. Jack ignored J.J.'s question. Then J.J. walked over to one of the women, who had stopped in the midst of assembling a lampshade at her place.

"Do you think this is playtime?" he demanded of the woman.

"No sir," she replied in a fearful voice.

"Well then get back to work or get out," J.J. said loudly for the benefit of everyone.

The woman returned to gluing trim around the top edge of the shade. But she was trembling under J.J.'s watchful gaze, and her glue applicator slipped. A sticky white line streaked down the silk fabric, damaging it irretrievably.

"Is this the kind of work you do?" J.J. demanded. "No wonder I don't make any money in this department."

In fact, the silk shade department was the most profitable in the company.

"Jack," J.J. shouted. "Come over here, pronto. Just look at what this girl has done."

The woman was now shuddering in fear, and some of the other women began crying. Jack went over and stood beside her.

"I want you to fire her," J.J. demanded, pointing to the woman cringing before him.

"Why?" Jack asked calmly.

"Why? Just look at what she's done. Don't ask me why."

"She's a good worker, J.J. It was an accident."

"She's a lousy worker. I want her fired now. I mean now. Do you hear me? Now."

"Let's go to your office, J.J."

"To hell with my office. You do what I say or you go with her." With these words J.J. walked out of the room as swiftly as he had entered. Some women began to scream to relieve the tension, others wept quietly. Those in the ladies room returned calmly.

Jack, white with anger, sat down at his desk. He knew that there was no use discussing the matter further with J.J. In similar instances, there had been no reversing his decisions. Jack realized that the dictums were a result of J.J.'s calculated need to exert power. Some said it was part of his nature. Others said perhaps his wife didn't cooperate with him. The company psychologist speculated that his father must have beaten him often. Why a psychologist in the company? J.J. liked to have at least one PhD on his staff.

Jack considered Elsie, the woman whom J.J. wanted him to fire, one of his best workers. Furthermore, she had enough seniority to spare her from being laid off during slow periods.

Jack asked Elsie to sit by his desk so they could talk quietly and privately.

"I have no choice, Elsie. I have to fire you."

"That's all right, Jack," she said as tears filled her eyes.

"If I don't do it, I'll have to go with you."

"I understand," she said, now openly weeping.

Jack's heart was breaking. "Look, go to the union. You have good reason."

"Thank you," she said as she got up from the chair. She walked slowly to her position on the line and began collecting her tools. Then she sat at her place and buried her head in her arms while, overwhelmed with misery, her body heaved with sobs. Jack knew that Elsie was supporting her three young children on her salary. She had been proud of the seniority she had earned, and the security it gave her. She had thought that her quietness, reliability, and dexterity were her insurance.

The next morning Jack gave his notice. He'd leave in two weeks. As soon as J.J. heard of it, he called Jack into his office.

"Why?" J.J. asked.

"Why?" Jack responded. "You figure it out."

"You mean the firing incident? It's over. Forget it. You've got a great future with me, Jack, a great future."

"J.J. I've got a better one without you."

"You're an insolent S.O.B."

"For once you're right J.J., I learned it from you."

Jack stood up, turned and walked out of J.J.'s office feeling as if his feet had grown wings. To hell with giving notice.

You may wonder what happened to Jack. Well, he went on to write this story and many more.

THE ARGUMENT

Tonight after supper my Ma and Pa had an argument. Ma said, "Pa, how'd you like to do the dishes tonight?"

When she said it, Pa was sitting in his chair reading the newspaper. I couldn't see his face, but I know he heard Ma and he said, "Your job's doing the household chores, my job's bringing in the money."

Ma's eyes got teary, but she went to the sink and began doing the dishes. I followed her into the kitchen. While she washed the dishes, I asked her, "Ma, why wouldn't Pa do the dishes for you tonight?"

"Because he's tired from working all day, son," she said.

Then I went back into the living room and asked, "Pa, why didn't Ma want to do the dishes tonight?"

He lowered the paper and thought a minute. "Because, son, I guess she's tired from working around the house all day."

"And *she* said that *you* were tired from working all day."

He put the paper down. "Is that so?" Pa said, and he got up and went into the kitchen. I waited a few minutes, then I went into the kitchen too. Ma was drying the dishes and Pa was washing them.

That wasn't much of an argument, was it? It's just that I hate to see Ma cry.

THE CARETAKERS

"Who lived here before us?" my little son asked as he gazed out the bay window of our brand new house into the dense woods surrounding it. Judging from the size of the trees, the woods were old, as old as it takes a stand of hemlocks to grow eighty feet tall, and white river birches to fill the girth of a man's encircling arms. The beeches, oaks and ash trees, their barks covered with lichen and their exposed roots with moss, appear as ancient as if they have been there since the last ice age. This suburban acre of ours, subdivided out of a vast forest on the slope of a worn New England hill, is part of an old land with a history that few give thought to these days.

Joining my son's gaze, I casually replied, "Nobody lived here before us."

But even as I answered I knew that this was incorrect. I was guilty of omission. I knew that I had seen signs of an earlier, forgotten human era. But I hadn't wondered about them, even those on our specific acre in the woods, not until that moment when I blurted, "I'm wrong about that. The Indians lived here before us."

My son was delighted. "Oh boy, oh boy!" he said.

My curiosity stirred, I too was delighted.

The history books say that the Nipmuc Indian tribe roamed this region, hunted these acres, and fished the nearby lakes. One can tell from the names of the streets and locations—Tatnuck, Wachusett, Quinapoxet—that Indians had populated this very land. The name of our street is Squantum; our wooded acre lies on the side of Asnebumskit hill. The neighborhood is called Indian Hill. A local lake is named Quinsigamond. So well beaten are some of the footpaths that meander through the forest, that a century or more of disuse has not obscured them, unless, of course, the deer have claimed them and keep them fresh. Other footpaths plunge through the growth, then fade into a confusion of saplings. Were these the settlers' paths, or were they the paths of Indian hunters before the Pilgrims landed?

Lore, passed down to our generation, has it that not only did Indians wander through, they dwelled on the very spot where our prim lawn grows. Still, no sign of their habitation or way of life lingers, no arrowheads or artifacts of any sort. They probably had been raked out by the settlers who came after them, or picked up by surveyors and engineers and hunters.

One needn't walk far among the thickets of fern and patches of mountain laurel before coming across the remnant of a tumbled down stone wall, once three to four feet high, but now hidden here and there under hundreds of seasons of humus. Running in straight lines, usually meeting at ninety degree angles, the walls wander for a mile or so then disappear into swaths of scattered moss-covered rocks. They are the relics of settlers whose dogged exertions cleared the land, and with its stones had built walls around their fields. This slope, once stripped of its trees, and having become a patch-work of denuded enclosures, had been grazing land or crop land. Much of the returning forest is relatively young, perhaps no more than two hundred years old, although parts of it probably survived the settlers' axe.

Wandering deeper into the woods, down into the damp dells around the swamps, one feels that these places have always been as they are now, untouched be-cause they were deemed useless. Only deer tracks are visible across the muddy ground, springy with tufts of moss. So the woods around us have not always been so. After the virgin land had been cleared, our present-day trees formed second or third-growth forests. Over the next two centuries, many settlers moved west to culti-vate a richer, less harsh land, while the descendants of those who stayed eventually left to work in the cities with the onset of the Industrial Revolution. By the end of the nineteenth century, the forests had nearly obliterated all signs of the past except for the footpaths and stone walls. Since then it has lain undisturbed and forgotten until this year, when we built our new house and my son asked his question.

SETTLING MATTERS

The rumble of the garage door closing sounded across the garden. Kneeling on tanned legs in the grass beside the flower bed, Anne plunged her trowel into the moist earth. It was late Friday afternoon. The sun loitered behind the maples in fresh leaf, casting dappled shadows. Insects swooped in frenzied patterns through the slanting rays. The lawn exhaled a musty dampness into the gentle air.

Anne's husband, Roy, a tall man showing signs of a middle-age paunch and a roundness to his once lean face, stepped into the garden from the garage. His tie hung loose from his unbuttoned white collar. A dark colored suit jacket was slung over his shoulder.

"I see you got rid of the kids."

Anne nestled a bulb into the bottom of the hole she had just scooped. She stood up as she dragged her slender forearm across her glistening brow.

"It wasn't easy. But you were so insistent when you called. They know it's the evening Max comes."

Bending from her waist, she spread earth over the bulb. The Begonia bulbs were now planted among the dying tulips. Gardening for the day was done.

"I don't want any interruptions tonight." Roy sauntered to his wife's side, gazed down at the newly turned earth, and kissed her.

She pulled away. "You don't want them here any night, Roy."

Her words startled him, for Anne was usually patient, rarely complained, and had never been given to innuendo.

"Can't you talk business at work? After all, you see Max all day. He comes here to relax." She headed for the patio on the opposite side of the garden.

"Tonight's different," he called after her. "I've made a decision. I'm settling matters for good."

Turning, fixing her eyes on his, she said, "You know what's best, Roy, but be gentle. He's old and alone."

He tossed his head back. "Ha, he's solid as a mountain, a volcano spewing righteousness."

"But he's still your father. And a good man."

Nodding, bowing his head, he mumbled, "That's true."

As she entered the house to prepare supper the screen door slammed behind her. Roy wrenched off his tie and flung his jacket onto the arm of a wooden garden chair. There he sat, unseeing, immersed in thought. Behind him his shingled house, low, snug on the land, stretched across the width of the yard. It faced a quiet, curbed street on which the houses were spaced far apart.

A shiny Cadillac slid into their asphalt driveway. Before opening its door, Max removed his hat revealing a turmoil of thick grey hair. His portly body barely cleared the steering wheel. He groaned as he edged himself up off the seat. Yet, bearing two packages, he walked to the house with springy steps.

"Anne," he called upon opening the screen door. She called back, and as he entered the kitchen she bussed his cheek. "Where are the kids?"

"Down the street, Max, playing with some friends."

"Don't they know I come tonight? I have some surprises for them."

"You give them too much," Anne said, her face flushing.

"They're my joy. You wouldn't deprive me of that?"

"Roy's in the garden." She was anxious to get on with the supper preparations, anxious also to avoid further explanation of the children's absence.

"How is he?" Max whispered.

"Now, Max, you see him more than I do."

"Well, we've had a little disagreement." The old man winked through a grin. "You've got a stubborn man there. Trouble is I've spoiled him."

"He's in the garden, Max."

The old man walked over to the patio, pulled up another wooden chair, and sat down beside Roy. "You've got a nice spot here. I've got to hand it to ya."

"Anne's made it beautiful. I only pay for it," Roy responded gazing at the flowers. They sat in silence for a while, just listening to the hum of the bees. "Look, Max, I think we ought to settle things once and for all."

"Well, I agree. You can take over the business once I'm gone, and the way I'm feelin' these days it won't be long."

Roy had heard it before. "Don't give me that, you'll last forever. I'm asking you to step aside...NOW."

"You're asking me to lie down and die," Max said, his voice trembling. "Your mother's gone. The business is all I've got left. What am I supposed to do, sit on my porch and twiddle my thumbs all day?"

"You've got us."

"Weekends. They're your family, but sometimes I wonder whether you know it."

Roy flinched, rose from his chair and stood facing his father. "Max, I'm quitting."

"You don't mean that, son." Max's eyes grew watery. "I've always intended that the business be yours. Not your brother's. Just yours."

"But it's not mine."

"It will be, godammit. What's your hurry?"

"Hurry? Hurry? I've been with you a fucking five years. You call that being in a hurry? I've accepted a job."

"You have?"

"I have."

"Where?"

"Consolidated."

Max sat motionless for a few minutes, stunned. "They're a godamned competitor. What are you trying to do?"

Anne came to the door and shouted through the screen "Supper's ready."

"It's what I know best, where I'm most valuable. They're paying me double what I get from you. And I'm running the show."

Roy headed for the door, but Max made no attempt to follow. Instead, he strode to his car, opened the door and maneuvered his bulky body behind the wheel. As he turned on the ignition, he slumped against the steering wheel, activating the horn. Roy dashed for the car, while Anne, hearing the horn blaring, yanked open the screen door and rushed out. Upon reaching the car, Roy lifted his father's head from the wheel and felt the artery in his neck for a pulse.

"He's gone," Roy said, falling to his knees moaning. "He's gone, I killed him, I killed him."

CHILDREN SHOULD BE NEITHER
SEEN NOR HEARD

The cab stopped in front of our little house and discharged a tall, robust man. From the living room window I watched him glide up our walk like a ballet master giving a lesson. He wore a beret and carried a brown paper bag. I turned to my four year old daughter, Ruthie, who was watching him with me.

"Tell your mother that Professor Landell's here."

"He's here, Mommy!" she shouted, annoying me because I hadn't intended her to shout.

"Now you be a good girl and don't bother Professor Landell," I heard my wife, Shirley, warn. "And when the big hand reaches straight up, you must go right to bed without a whimper. Is that understood?"

"Yes, Mommy," my daughter murmured.

Shirley's admonition to Ruthie that evening was more emphatic than usual. My wife and daughter had never met George Landell, but my wife knew that he abhorred children.

"Children should be neither seen nor heard until they are at least thirty." I had told my wife. "That's what Professor Landell says."

"Then I know in advance I won't like him," my wife had replied.

"But you will," I assured her, "because he's brilliant."

Her eyes widened with alarm. Upon looking back at her college days, she had often wondered how she ever got through. She often felt intimidated by her arrogant, self-confident professors.

"But he hates being brilliant," I quickly added. "He carries it with pain." I paused, recalling seeing George, then my English Lit professor, frequenting the seedy bars near the university. "In fact," I said, "he tries hard to lower himself to everybody else's level. No man ever wanted to be liked more than George Landell."

She remained skeptical. "Well, he's your friend," she said, implying that he could never be hers.

I searched for other ways to explain George, whom I hadn't seen since before our wedding day five years earlier. "He admires practical, down-to-earth people because…" I saw a smile of relief creep across my wife's slender face. "Because even tying his own shoelaces confuses him." Shirley nodded, pleased, suspecting that it might be possible that she could become fond of our visitor after all.

When the front doorbell rang, Ruthie dashed to admit Professor Landell. Staring down in seeming disbelief at the tiny figure dressed in her pink nightgown, he didn't budge from the open door.

"Urchin," he demanded, "where are your parents?"

"My name is Ruthie. I live on 6 Wesbroo Terrace, Cranston, Rody Isle, and I go to nursery school."

George leaned toward her as his round face reddened. "Westbrook, not Wesbroo. Let me hear you say it."

"Westbrooookkk"

"And only an idiot would mispronounce the state she was born in."

By the time I reached the door, George had switched the paper bag he was carrying to his other arm as if it had become heavy during his delayed entrance.

"Come in George," I said, "it's cold out there."

Accusing my daughter with a stiff arm and finger pointed at her, he protested, "Only after this impediment is cleared from my path shall I come in."

"Go to your mother," I ordered Ruthie. But Shirley was already on her way to the door to greet our visitor.

"So nice to meet you, Professor Landell. My husband has told me so much about you; I feel I already know you."

She reached to shake George's hand, but he took it and kissed it in the French manner. "And your husband has told me so much about YOU, that I feel we are old friends." Shirley blushed.

"Mommy, he kissed your hand." Ruthie then reached out her hand toward George. "Will you kiss mine too?"

He hesitated, taken aback, undecided. Then after a pause he took Ruthie's hand and kissed it.

"Thank you, George," said Ruthie.

"His name is Professor Landell, Ruthie," I said.

"You may call me George, urchin."

"And you may call me Ruthie."

George looked up at me. "You have an uncommonly precocious child here," he said. "How do you put up with it?"

"The clock hand is straight up," my wife said to Ruthie. "It's time for bed." She took Ruthie by the hand.

"Would you like some wine, George," I inquired.

"Don't you have anything more potent?" he said.

"Well, I have some vodka and…"

"What about the bottle of Calvert's Reserve in this bag?"

"By all means," I said as I took it from him.

"Make it neat, please."

Ruthie was still in the room. "But I want a story. Will you read me a story, George?" she begged, releasing her hand from Shirley's.

After he removed his coat, which I took to hang up, Ruthie tugged on his sleeve. "Will you, George, will you, please?"

"You are imposing on Professor Landell, Ruthie," said my wife.

"Not at all," said George. "If the urchin wants a story, I'll tell her one. Then she can retire—out of sight."

I led Ruthie and her storyteller to the living room couch, where he sat down and Ruthie climbed onto his lap. Shirley returned to the kitchen and I sat in my easy chair watching the proceedings. George seemed baffled, not quite knowing how to deal with Ruthie's closeness, her trust and acceptance. She gazed up at him while he tried to compose himself.

Finally he began:

"I'll tell you a story about Pete and Glory,
And now the story's begun.
I'll tell you another,
About their mother,
And now the story is done."

Ruthie burst into laughter. "That's not a story! I want a real story!"

"It's time to go to bed," I insisted.

"All right," said George. "Do as your father says, and I'll tell you one after you're settled in."

"Where did you get such a clever child?" George asked. "You weren't the best of students, if you recall. Obviously her mother's genes are the dominant ones."

Ruthie climbed down from George's lap, and as she led him to her bedroom, he said, "Have the whisky poured by the time I return. No doubt, I'll need it."

After twenty minutes had elapsed, I went to Ruthie's bedroom to retrieve George. He was seated at the foot of her bed just finishing up his story. Ruthie then placed her hands together and began to pray.

"Now I lay me down to sleep,
I pray the lord my soul to keep,
If I should die before I wake,
I pray the lord my soul to take.
God bless Mommy, God bless Daddy
and God bless George."

At this, George bent down and kissed her on the cheek. "And God bless you, my child," he whispered. He stood up, wiping his eyes as he turned, startled to find me there.

"So, do you have my drink poured?"

"Of course, George." We walked back into the living room to retrieve his drink and found that Shirley had poured a glass of wine for me and herself. Raising our glasses, we drank to friendship. Before downing the remainder in his glass George added, "To the beautiful innocence of children." After a delicious dinner, and much scintillating conversation, George got ready to depart. As he put on his coat and beret, he said, "Thank you for a lovely evening. And thank Ruthie for a lesson I shall never forget." He strutted down the sidewalk to a waiting cab as I hollered, "Don't you want the Calverts?"

"Keep it," he shouted, "for my next visit with Ruthie." As he opened the door to the cab, he shouted so I could hear, "Sir, take me to my lonely apartment where I may bask in tonight's memories."

The cab took off with a blast of exhaust. It was a night that I, too, would remember. George left our home a different man from the one who had arrived, a man whom I had hardly known, and a man whom I suspect he had hardly known.

6228443R0

Made in the USA
Charleston, SC
29 September 2010